THE JANE AUSTEN MURDERS

An absolutely gripping cozy mystery novel

JEAN G. GOODHIND

A Honey Driver Murder Mystery Book 4

Originally published as
Killing Jane Austen

JOFFE BOOKS

Revised edition 2022
Joffe Books, London
www.joffebooks.com

First world edition published by Severn House
Publishers Ltd in Great Britain and the USA
as *Killing Jane Austen* in 2014

This book is a work of fiction. Names, characters, businesses, organizations, places and events are either the product of the author's imagination or are used fictitiously. Any resemblance to actual persons, living or dead, events or locales is entirely coincidental. The spelling used is British English except where fidelity to the author's rendering of accent or dialect supersedes this.

Cover art by Dee Dee Book Covers

ISBN: 978-1-80405-376-8

CHAPTER ONE

'Well? Are you coming or what?' Steve was trying to play nonchalant, but Honey wasn't fooled. He was keen for her to say yes, and what's more she was keen to say yes.

Honey Driver, hotelier, also doubled as crime liaison officer on behalf of the Bath Hotels Association which was how come she'd met Detective Inspector Steve Doherty, her opposite number: him of the laconic good looks and sexual promise.

The promise had been looking quite— well, promising. Doherty was inviting her away for a dirty weekend. At least his tantalising asides made her presume it would be dirty, seeing as he told her to leave her flannelette pyjamas behind.

'I don't wear pyjamas.'

'Good. A dab of perfume behind each ear should fit the bill,' he said.

'I can't go.' The words caught in her throat and she pouted ruefully. She hated saying no. Doherty evidently hated her saying no too. His sigh of exasperation was like a full-force gale blowing down the phone.

'Don't tell me. You've got a do on for the Bone Crushers and Horse Glue Society.'

She'd taken on a few conferences of late, varied associations with strange names that she'd never known existed. However, on this occasion it was something else entirely.

'No! No, it's nothing like that.'

She was sparkly eyed as she went on to tell him why she couldn't come.

'I'm taking part in a film. Doing a bit of acting.'

'As *what*?'

'What kind of a question is that?' she responded a trifle testily, not liking the new arch tone in his voice. 'You make it sound as though I'm going to be the rear end of a panto horse.'

'So what are you?'

'I'm not sure yet, but I'll probably be wearing a frilly bonnet and a corset.'

He beamed. 'I like the sound of that.'

'I'll be wearing it beneath a dress. Something frilly and floaty. Full length too.'

He nodded. 'I get the picture.'

Of course he did. Yet another historical production was being filmed in Bath. This time it was about the life of the most famous spinster ever to write romantic fiction: Jane Austen.

A film crew had arrived in town, and two of the production team — namely the sound technician and the guy in charge of lighting — were sharing a twin-bedded room at the Green River Hotel. They also frequented the bar a lot. That was when they'd asked Honey and a few others if they fancied being film extras.

Visions of herself as a kind of latter-day Sophia Loren had sprung immediately to mind. Yes, of course she fancied it.

So did her daughter Lindsey, who was a sucker for history whether medieval, Tudor or Victorian. Regency was fine.

Her elderly mother Gloria was similarly keen. It was the costumes that did it for her. She just adored anything floaty and feminine. And young guys in tight trousers.

Mary Jane declined, which wasn't exactly unexpected. She was their resident professor of the paranormal, and had graduated from a college catering in that one subject, which was located in California — where else? She'd since retired and moved in to the Green River permanently. When asked if she wanted to be transported to the Regency period, she'd looked puzzled. 'I see people from that era every day.' She was referring to Sir Cedric, one-time resident of the room she presently occupied. She believed him to be one of her ancestors and still visited on occasion, even though he'd died back in 1792.

Anyway, being an extra had sounded like good fun, like playing hooky from school. Sit around, get shot by nothing more dangerous than a camera and have someone cook for you. The half-cut members of the production crew assured her that she'd mostly be whiling away the time reading a book or playing Scrabble.

'Shame. You don't know what you're missing,' said Doherty referring to the weekend he'd been offering her.

He was right. They'd been trying to get it together for ages, but things kept getting in the way.

'How about next week?' she asked hopefully.

'Anything can happen between now and then. I'll probably be on duty. Sure you won't change your mind?'

She said that she wouldn't. She'd promised.

'Never mind. I can make other arrangements,' he said, adding that he would ring her again soon.

It was tempting to ask him what — or who — those other arrangements might involve. *None of your business*, she told herself, and put down the phone. Hell, but it was hard to act uninterested. Visions of what might have been stayed with her and made the blood rush to her cheeks. She felt quite hot — which was far from what she was the following morning.

In order to take advantage of the quieter off season, the film was being made in February. Filming started early. Very early.

So here they were, freezing their butts off at six in the morning.

Lindsey was beating her arms around herself in an effort to keep warm. Her temper was fraying, held in check only by heated gossip she'd been hearing from other extras.

'I hear Martyna Manderley is a right bitch,' said Lindsey. 'Not really a good choice to play Jane Austen. Did you know that Jane Austen didn't really like Bath very much?'

Honey shivered. 'Was she here in February?'

Lindsey said that she didn't know and began stamping her frozen feet.

Filming had commenced in the Circus, an architectural gem not too far from the Royal Crescent and almost as famous. The elegant houses fringing the central green where bare branches stood stark against the sky, looked dormant. The sky was unstirred by dawn and the air was cold and nipping at noses.

Honey's mother, eyesight unhindered by age, sucked in her breath each time she spotted a young man in tight britches.

Enticed by the smell of sizzling bacon, the shivering extras were hanging around the catering truck. A girl with untidy hair emerged from the costume trailer. A candy cigarette hung from the corner of her mouth. Preferable to the real thing, Honey decided. Sugar was a health hazard, but not so bad as nicotine.

Small, deep-set eyes scanned the extras. She looked as though she had X-ray vision, Honey thought. How else could she define what sizes and shapes lurked beneath the thick coats, sweaters, scarves and mufflers everyone was wearing?

'You, you and you.' She jabbed a finger in their direction.

'Me?' said Honey, pointing at her chest.

'Not you. You!' said the girl. She pointed to Honey's mother and a small figure standing next to her.

Gloria was all smiles. 'Yes, yes, yes,' she murmured, her breath puffing from her mouth like a steam kettle.

'She can see herself centre stage,' Lindsey said out of the corner of her mouth.

'You too,' snapped the girl, pointing at Lindsey.

Honey was left all alone with her stomach rumbling.

'I didn't get picked either,' said the tall, gaunt man standing beside her, sipping coffee from a paper cup. 'I had a good Christmas season. Back half of a pantomime horse. Not exactly a starring role, but at least I was on stage. That's what matters, eh?'

'No,' said Honey recalling Doherty hinting at her role in this movie. 'I wouldn't want to be the back half of anything.'

He looked down at her blankly as though he couldn't possibly understand her point of view. 'Oh!' he said and moved off, looking deflated.

'Well, I certainly gave a moving performance there,' Honey muttered, regretting it. Early mornings were not her best time. Cold mornings were even worse. At least when she got up early in the hotel she was warm.

The cold was unremitting. Like everyone else she stamped her feet and rubbed her arms.

'There is a bus provided for the extras where you can sit out of the cold until they need you,' said someone next to her.

She smiled and nodded. 'Nice to know.'

Of course she knew, but her fingers and toes could last out a little longer. She wanted to see what costumes her mother and daughter ended up with.

After ten minutes the door of the wardrobe trailer opened and out they came wearing bonnets and muslin dresses beneath their winter coats.

'I insisted on keeping my vest on,' her mother informed her. 'And I asked for a shawl.'

'And got one,' muttered Lindsey, who had obviously been refused and was now turning sapphire blue. She burrowed her head into the hood and collar of her padded coat like a tortoise settling down for hibernation. 'Muslin lets the draught in,' she grumbled.

'Muslin comes from India,' Honey remarked in a knowledgeable manner. 'It's hot there.'

Lindsey grunted something indistinguishable.

'So whose arm did you twist in the wardrobe department,' Honey asked her mother.

No answer was forthcoming. Gloria Cross peered past her daughter. 'Is that Martyna Manderley over there?'

They all looked in the direction indicated. Martyna Manderley was such a huge star. Honey's mother was a keen reader of the likes of *Hello!* magazine. *OK!* too given half the chance.

A striking young woman was holding up her pale-mauve skirt while someone from wardrobe adjusted her leg warmers.

'She's a bit tall for Jane Austen,' said Lindsey, always a stickler for historical accuracy.

'She's very pretty,' said Gloria. 'And slim. Did you know that she got paid a million pounds for her *Hello!* magazine spread?'

'Nobody's worth that,' sniffed Honey.

'You're biased,' said her mother. 'And jealous.'

'Why would I be?' Honey said indignantly.

'Because she's got good looks, money and style.'

'Ah, but does she have a brain?' Honey asked.

Lindsey shrugged. 'Look at it this way, she only has to look pretty for a living. Anyway, someone must think she's worth it.'

'Hmm,' muttered Honey. 'To the tune of one million at least!'

More extras were pointed at and told to advance.

Honey watched. It was quite fascinating to see people enter the trailer in jeans and jumpers and come out wearing poke bonnets and floaty dresses. Competition as to who had the best costume was rife.

'Mine's pure silk. I'm supposed to be a young woman about town.'

'I'm supposed to be a child's governess.'

'I'm supposed to be a costermonger — whatever that is,' said a short man with a bulbous nose and a patch over one eye.

Resigned to the fact that she might be sitting on the sidelines, Honey snuggled more deeply into her fleece-lined jacket.

What did she care if she didn't get to wear a floaty, fairy-thin outfit? It was February for goodness' sake!

Sizzling and smoke suddenly filled the air. A flock of noses turned yet again in the direction of the catering truck.

'Breakfast,' Honey said suddenly.

'Smudger,' said Lindsey before she was herded off with the others in costume.

The comment was a reminder to get their chef out of bed. The Green River Hotel had guests who'd want their breakfast. Just because she was away playing dress-up didn't mean they could be neglected.

'Right.'

Retrieving her phone from her toasty pocket reminded her of how cold it was here and how warm it was back at the Green River.

Now come along. Where's the consummate professional in you? First things first. She had to get Smudger, her head chef, out of bed. They had guests at the hotel who would be expecting bacon, sausages and all the trimmings. They weren't likely to get it unless Smudger got cracking eggs and frying rashers pretty pronto.

To his credit, Smudger had promised to sleep with his phone pressed against his ear. 'I won't let you down, boss.'

'You're not out drinking tonight?'

'No. I'm having a night in. There's a football match on telly. Nottingham versus Derby. Needle match.'

Honey tried not to think of the cans of lager likely to be consumed. He wouldn't let her down. Or else . . .

She sidled over to a clear spot between the area for the extras and the hallowed ground where the director was speaking to the leading lady. While busy fumbling with her phone, she didn't realise that her small action had caused a problem — not until she heard a shrill voice split the morning air.

'Get her out of here!'

Honey looked up to see a figure in gossamer lilac pointing at her.

She carried on regardless.

'Breakfast!' She shouted it as loud as she dared and got a muffled 'OK' in response.

'Are you up?'

'Just getting up.'

He sounded very groggy.

'Take one foot out from beneath the bedclothes. Right? Now put it on to the floor.'

She heard him groan. 'Christ!'

'What's the matter?'

'This floor's cold.'

Her task complete, Honey ended the call, assured that Smudger had one foot on the floor. Where the right foot led, the left foot would follow.

Martyna Manderley, she of the million-pound photographs, flounced over with her skirts held high. She was wearing black leggings as well as leg warmers beneath her muslin dress.

Honey eyed the polished talon pointing like a dagger at her heart. She wasn't about to take this lying down.

'Sorry. I must be on the wrong set. I'm supposed to be in a Jane Austen flick, not one featuring Dracula's daughter.'

Martyna did not see the funny side of it.

'Give me that phone!'

Honey hid it behind her back. 'No. It's mine.'

A middle-aged man wearing a velvet beret and a Barbour jacket waddled into the fray. He had a three-foot-long ponytail and a trio of earrings in his right ear. He held out his hand. 'I'm sorry, but we do not permit the use of mobile phones on set.'

'Excuse me, but it's my phone, and if I wish to make a call I most certainly will do so. I don't recall this being a condition of—'

A snarling Martyna Manderley wagged a lace-mittened finger. 'Making a call, my arse! You were taking a photograph for some shitty little tabloid, you sneaky bitch.'

Honey tutted disapprovingly. 'Now, how are you going to get into character with any conviction using language like that? The divine Jane would surely disapprove.'

Martyna's beautiful face froze into a chilly mask. 'Get her off this set or I quit!'

The director squirmed. 'Now, don't be unreasonable, Martyna darling . . .'

'You need to cool down,' said Honey. 'How about you take off all that underwear you're wearing? Did you know that chicks back then didn't wear any underwear? No knickers, anyway. My daughter told me. She's into that kind of thing — history, that is. Not knickers. That's more my thing. In fact, I have a pair once worn by Queen Victoria—'

The star of film and *OK!* magazine exploded. 'Get her off this bloody set!'

The director's face went from surprise to resignation in two swift moves.

Honey felt for the man and made the effort to explain.

'Just for the record, I was phoning my chef to get him out of bed so that the guests at my hotel get their breakfast.' She spotted the sound technician, bleary-eyed thanks to the fact that he'd been in the Green River bar until gone midnight. 'Derek will vouch for that. He's staying at my hotel.'

The director looked at him. Like many others on the production team, Derek Byrne had hung back, unwilling to speak to the big man unless spoken to.

'It's true,' said Derek, just a bit reluctantly. 'I heard Mrs Driver ask him to cover for breakfast. She said she'd ring him from the set because he'd be dead to the world on account of the booze he'd sunk last night.'

The explanation seemed to satisfy the director though his eyes shifted to their big star, Martyna, unsure whether peace would prevail. He was equally unsure of Honey's reaction. Peace was all the man wanted — and a film at the end of it.

He sighed. 'I see. But we do require you turn it off while on set.'

Martyna Manderley remained red-faced and far from calm. The corkscrew curls peeping out from her bonnet sprang up and down like miniature bed springs.

'Well, it's not fucking OK with me!'

Film crew and extras fell to silence, their attention drawn to the raucous voice and bad language.

Martyna Manderley reminded Honey of all the worst guests she'd ever had stay at the Green River Hotel. She was having none of it.

'Miss Manderley, you are stuck-up and too rude to mention!'

'Why, you . . . !' Martyna attempted to strike out. The guy with the ponytail leaped between them.

'Now, now, Martyna. Calm down, calm down. You know getting angry makes it difficult to get into character.'

'Absolutely,' said Honey, determined to have the last word. 'Jane Austen was a professional busybody, not a professional tart!'

Martyna screamed and lunged. It took a whole host of minions to encircle her, mouthing platitudes of how wonderful she was and how she must think of her public.

Honey felt a dig in her ribs. Derek was grinning, his moustache spreading like a ginger caterpillar across a face made ruddier by the early-morning nip.

'I enjoyed that.'

'So did I,' said Honey. 'Is she always so touchy?'

He nodded and whispered, 'The best kind of bitch has four legs. The worst only has two — and her name's Martyna Manderley.'

The superstar's colourful language soared anew.

'Fuck off, all of you. I'm going for a lie down.'

The director scuttled along behind her, doing his best to soothe the ruffled feathers. 'Martyna, darling . . .'

'You heard. I'll be in my trailer! And I'm not coming out until *that* woman is gone!'

Silently those gathered and within hearing distance watched her march off, her skirts bundled above her knees.

The director returned looking sheepish. 'Look, I've got enough on my plate without this. How about you just get lost for the time being? Hide yourself among the other extras?'

Feeling sorry for him, Honey nodded. 'I can do that.'

He went off, still looking harassed. She wondered if the reason he had long grey hair was because he couldn't find time to visit the hairdresser.

Her eyes stayed with him as he crossed the road to the house they'd hired for the shoot. However, it was a sharp morning and her senses too were on high alert. Her ears were tuned to what was happening around her. Her neighbour whispered something that sounded like 'drop dead'. 'Hear, hear,' muttered someone else.

'I take it she's not that popular,' Honey said to Derek.

'About as popular as a boil on the bum,' he said. Then, with a grin, he whispered, 'And we all know what's best for a boil on the bum. They're best lanced — with something very sharp.'

CHAPTER TWO

Martyna Manderley had the wide, square shoulders of a supermodel and too big an ego for a woman of twenty-five. Fame had made her rich. It had also made her arrogant. That's what invincibility and a contract with a world-famous cosmetic firm does for a girl.

Courtney, the make-up girl, was trying her best. But it was early morning and Martyna Manderley was at her worst.

'Christ! I look like a bloody ghost,' Martyna snapped, glaring goggle-eyed at her reflection. 'I want more eye definition! And more blusher!'

Dear little Courtney, five-foot-two, a little plump around the middle, was a pussycat. Her naturally rosy cheeks turned scarlet.

'They didn't wear eyeliner back then.'

'I don't care what they bloody did back then. This is now!' Her tone was anything but ladylike.

'But I've been told—'

'I don't give a shit what that dickhead of a director told you. I want eyeliner! I want blusher!'

'But I don't—'

'Give it here!'

Martyna snatched eyeliner from the make-up bag hanging from Courtney's waist.

'Are you going to cry?' she asked gleefully as she snaked the pencil along her lower eyelid. Her glittering eyes stayed fixed on the unfortunate girl as she scrolled from outer lid to inner, one eye after the other.

'You stupid little bitch. Go on. Cry. And if you do I'll tell Boris you're incompetent and order him to sack you.'

Being a bully came naturally to Martyna, and she relished the feeling of power over others. A little more goading and . . .

A blast of cold air came in with Scheherazade Parker-Henson.

'Sorry I'm late.' There was nothing humble about the senior make-up artist, and she certainly wasn't afraid of the overindulged superstar.

Looking straight at Martyna, her jaw tightened.

'No eyeliner,' she snapped, snatching the pencil from Martyna's classically long fingers. 'We can't have Jane Austen looking like a bloody goth, can we?'

Martyna turned petulant. 'Then hire a fully qualified make-up artist, not some ignorant little junior just out of comprehensive school!'

Scheherazade Parker-Henson was one of the best make-up artists on the circuit, and big enough not to be intimidated.

'Cut the crap, Martyna. You know the score.'

'Oh, Schezzer . . .' whined Martyna. She flashed her most pleading smile.

Scheherazade had been around actors for ever. She knew very well what that smile meant — *look at me, aren't I wonderful?* Smiles could be offered like a gift or used as a shield to hide inner feelings. They were as much a part of the actor's stock in trade as crying on demand.

Clamping the star's shoulders in a vice-like grip, Scheherazade spun her to face the mirror. 'Like I said to you. Cut the crap. And don't call me Schezzer. Only my friends call me that.'

The actress in Martyna took over totally. 'Aren't I one of your friends, Schezzer?'

Scheherazade glanced dismissively at the long finger tracing a line up her arm. Her expression soured.

'No.' She shrugged her off. 'If I wanted a friend like you, I'd buy a pet. A snake perhaps, or a tarantula.'

Martyna's face clouded. 'How dare you speak to me like that! I could get you sacked. You know that, don't you?'

Beneath the bonnet, Martyna's own hair had been strained back into a top knot, ready for more false drop curls to be added. Scheherazade's strong fingers grabbed the top knot and tugged Martyna's head back. Using a wet wipe, she not too gently swiped and rubbed at the eyeliner.

'Go ahead. And I could return the favour — fivefold — couldn't I?'

The make-up artist's eyes met Martyna's via the mirror.

Uneasy with the air of menace and not privy to what was going on, Courtney backed towards the door. Her scrabbling fingers found the door handle. Once outside, she lay panting against the trailer, fumbling in her pocket for the inhaler she knew was there.

'You OK?'

Derek, the sound technician, eyed her with genuine concern.

She nodded at the same time as inhaling as though her life depended on it. One, two, three, four . . .

Derek patted her shoulder. 'Problems with the Wicked Witch of the West?'

She managed to nod, though her face was streaked with tears.

'Never mind. Trust Schezzer to sort her out.' His grin was infectious.

Courtney smiled hesitantly. He was right. Scheherazade Parker-Henson could handle herself. She could also handle Martyna Manderley.

'I . . . hate . . . her,' gasped Courtney between deep breaths.

‘Doesn’t everyone?’ Derek replied.

‘I thought you got on with everyone,’ said Courtney.

His grin diminished. ‘Only human beings. I don’t rate Martyna as being one of those.’

CHAPTER THREE

The phone rang. Martyna jerked her eyes open and pounced on it. 'Yes?'

'Hey!'

She instantly recognised the voice of her fiancé, Brett Coleridge. Her firm grip lessened. 'Say, sweetheart. What a surprise — a *wonderful* surprise.'

Snapping turtle had changed to purring pussy cat. Even her eyes became more catlike.

'I wanted to surprise you. I wanted you to know that I was thinking of you.'

'Brett, that is so cool. Not as good as having you here physically — if you know what I mean — but good all the same. I love your voice. I love your body, but not necessarily in that order. Speak to me. Turn me on.'

She stroked the receiver as she spoke and curled her legs beneath her. Damn her call time. It served Boris right if she was late for her scene. He should have had done with the woman and her phone, told her to get off the set. The woman had upset her. Boris had upset her.

Brett was the tonic she needed. He was more deserving of her time. Keep him panting, keep him interested. Brett was rich. He had inherited the multimillion-dollar Coleridge

Croup from his father. Gold-plated beefcake — the best kind to have.

'O . . . K . . .' He said it slowly, just like he did when he told her the rest of the stuff he said he would do to her — and with her — once they were together.

She laughed frequently and throatily as he spoke. Besides being rich, Brett Coleridge was sexually adventurous.

'I'm very sex positive,' he had said to her on the first occasion they had met. 'So forget sticking to the missionary position. I'm a guy with a fertile imagination. Hope you don't mind that.'

She had wanted to bed him there and then, but reasoned that she'd do better to keep him hanging on. A night in bed with a rich man was one thing. A wedding band and a share of his fortune was something else.

So she had purred and pouted over her glass of wine. 'Practice makes perfect, so they say. With you holding my hand, I dare say I'll cope.'

She smiled at the thought of that memory. A true actress, she'd milked the girl-next-door image for all she was worth.

She fingered the phone as she spoke to him. 'You certainly know how to turn a girl on, Brett. So when can I expect you to flick my switch?'

He made a low contented sound like a lion stretching its whole body. 'Sooner than you think, honey. Sooner than you think.'

'How's New York?'

'Throbbing.'

'Just the city?'

He laughed. 'Hey, baby . . . what do *you* think?'

'I think I could do with more than thick underwear to warm me up.'

'I won't ask how you're doing being Jane Austen. Piece of cake, huh?'

Martyna growled. 'Give me street talk any day. Will you listen to this?'

She picked up the script. 'Follies and nonsense, whims and inconsistencies, do divert me, I own, and I laugh at them whenever I can.'

'What does that mean?'

'Sweet Jane didn't like the Bath social scene that much. Called it "glaring white". I suppose we'd say that it was too in your face. Jane wasn't much for nightclubbing and dancing till dawn. In fact, I think her legs were superglued together.'

Brett's laugh was low and dirty. 'Just goes to prove that she never met the right man. I could have gone where no man ever went before.'

'Or after,' Martyna retorted.

If Brett could have seen her face, he would have loved the jealous pout and the deep frown. Brett got off on stuff like that. But he couldn't see it, and Martyna was thankful for small mercies.

They murmured 'ciao' down the phone at each other before hanging up.

Martyna lay back against the cushions, smiling. Someone had told her years ago about cosmic ordering — the will to pray for and believe that you will get what you ask for. In her case the cosmos had gone into overdrive. She'd got the looks, which helped if your talent was only average. The looks got you extra coaching if you had the money. Stir in a little luck and the right kind of backers — those with the cash and an eye for a beautiful girl — and you had the recipe for success. She'd got what she wanted and more. Being on set was like a drug; she could never get enough of the buzz it gave her.

She was like a queen bee at the centre of the hive, the workers buzzing around to do her bidding. Except for that cow Scheherazade!

A terrible shiver ran over her. There was no way she could go out in front of the camera feeling as she did.

'Right. Calm down. Close your eyes.'

She did what her shrink had told her and brought her fear out in the open.

'Everyone has secrets.' She repeated it three times just as he'd told her to do.

The words were out, the fear was out, but a silent truth lurked in her mind. Some have darker secrets than others.

Shaking the thought from her head, she picked up the phone.

* * *

'Boris? I haven't had any breakfast yet.'

Gripping the phone tightly to his ear, Boris rolled his eyes. 'I'll get a tray sent over to you.'

'Don't send me that crap from the hot dog van. I don't eat crap. I want breakfast from the Royal Crescent Hotel.'

'Sweetie, we've got work to do! We're already behind schedule!'

'Get someone to fetch it for me, *sweetie*.'

She cut the line before Boris had time to point out that breakfast from the Royal Crescent was likely to be cold by the time it got to her.

On replacing the phone into his pocket, he caught Scheherazade studying his expression.

Boris flung down the script he'd been reading. 'That woman. I should have known better than to cast her as Jane Austen after the way she behaved on the last shoot I did with her. I find myself wishing that she'll trip over the hem of her dress and break a leg — literally. And now she wants breakfast — from the Royal Crescent Hotel, no less.'

'So I gather. And our divine superstar won't get off her butt and go to the catering van?'

He shook his head forlornly. 'No. She's in a cocky mood and wants waiting on. I think she's been speaking to her fiancé. She always wants everything her own way after speaking to him. I think it's got something to do with the jangle of money,' he added bitterly. 'He owns the production company — if only partially — and she owns him.'

'That shyster!'

Scheherazade Parker-Henson was scathing but damned accurate in her opinions.

'Martyna knows best,' said Boris, accompanying his bitterly spoken words with another pained rolling of his eyes.

Scheherazade patted his shoulder. 'Leave it to me. I'll sort her breakfast out. She'll never know the difference. Got a spare script? Mine's disappeared.'

'Sure.'

He handed her a spare copy, taken from the three he needed for himself and the assistant director. Two was enough.

Left alone for once, Boris rubbed at his brow. Hassle, he thought. This business is all bloody hassle. Why don't I accept that offer to lecture at UCLA? He knew the answer, of course. Going back to lecturing in California carried a death sentence. He'd never get to direct such a plum project and a big star ever again. He had to hold on.

Just to confirm it, the wardrobe woman came along and asked if he'd borrowed her camera. His stance was enough to confirm that he had not. She went off muttering something about thieves and crooks. He couldn't catch it. He didn't care. Filming was running behind schedule. Heads would roll. He hoped they wouldn't include his.

* * *

Brett Coleridge was in bed, sandwiched between a blonde and a brunette. He stretched like a satisfied tomcat; life was good. The company was good. The king-sized bed was situated in such a way that he had a panoramic view of the city skyline. Red, white, blue and green strobes pierced the sky from the highest buildings. If there were stars, they were obliterated by chequer boards of light — like an upended dominoes set with diamonds.

'Girls, I need to stretch my arms.'

He arched his back. The girl with dark hair raised her head from his right arm. The blonde did the same from his left. He stretched his arms above his head and looked at the ceiling while the girls stroked his torso all the way down to the tree line. He groaned with pleasure and closed his eyes. Life was good when you had money.

'Off again soon, Brett baby?'

Pools of velvet brown eyes looked up at him. He smiled and wound his arms back around both her and the other girl, and let out a deep satisfied sigh. 'Right on, baby. It's the only way to live. Family one place, business interests all around, and fun where you can find it. That way you're never tied down.'

The blonde scratched circles in his chest hair with wine red fingernails. 'How do I get not to be tied down?'

He tapped her nose. 'Take a tip from me. Marry a rich man. Work on your back.'

CHAPTER FOUR

The extras had been provided with a converted ex-London bus on which to eat and get relief from the cold. This was where Lindsey headed once her costume and make-up had been checked and photographed. The photographs were taken of each costume so that no day-to-day variation occurred. Continuity was God.

Shivering, the extras reclaimed their puffa jackets and nylon windcheaters. They didn't match well with Regency hemlines and poke bonnets, but what did they care as long as they were warm?

Lindsey was wearing fine mesh mittens and warming her hands around a paper cup of steaming coffee when her mother spotted her.

'I've been told that I won't be performing today,' said Honey. 'I'm not needed. Not even for a tiddly part. I think our superstar bitch might have had something to do with it.'

A smart-arse smile shone out from beneath the shadow of Lindsey's straw-brimmed bonnet. 'It looked as though you gave an Oscar-winning performance from where I was standing.'

Honey smirked. 'I wasn't entirely sure how to play it. Mary Poppins or Raging Bull.'

'Told you she's a cow.' Lindsey took a sip of coffee.

Honey grimaced. 'She's certainly got a temper.' Her face brightened. 'So what do you think? Am I ever likely to be an overnight success?'

'Not as a movie star.'

'You're right. Never mind. I'll award myself a consolation prize. A mug of hot chocolate would be nice. With two sugars. I need the energy.'

'Grandma's still out there somewhere, playing to the crowd.' Lindsey shivered. 'She must be freezing.'

'Or she's making new friends.'

'Could be.'

'Which is very worrying. My mother is a poor judge of character.'

'Though old enough to know her own mind,' Lindsey added.

Honey countered, 'And there's no fool like an old fool.'

* * *

Honey's mother was enjoying herself. She was dressed in a sprigged muslin gown trimmed with pale green lace, and a dark pink bonnet complete with a pair of ostrich feathers. She was also carrying a fan.

She'd got talking to an elderly gentleman wearing a frock coat and a pale green topper. They got on well enough for her to bring out a satin and lace corset she'd borrowed from her daughter. She had intended wearing it, but Lindsey had dissuaded her by saying it was Victorian not Regency. She'd held on to it anyway just in case. She was holding it against herself.

'Think it's a little young for me?' she asked him.

'Not at all. Sexy. Very sexy,' he said appraisingly, his eyes out on stalks.

Gloria almost swooned at that.

Honey couldn't tell at this distance whether he was serious or not, since an ostrich feather in the hat of another woman had flicked a contact lens out of her eye. She could listen though.

'My daughter gave it to me. I'm going to try it on properly when I get home.'

Honey narrowed her eyes. Never mind what her mother looked like, she was flashing the corset! How big a come-on was that?

Honey waved. The wave was supposed to mean 'give me back my property'. Her mother waved back, but dismissively, as though she just couldn't spare the time right now.

Grinding her teeth and rolling her eyes, Honey headed for a grouping of chairs situated on the other side of the rope that encircled the extras' 'recruiting' area. Just a few extras were left sitting there in their period costumes waiting to be called. They looked forlorn, like limp flowers waiting to be thrown in the bin.

One of them was a scruffy man — a very scruffy man. Make-up and wardrobe had made him that way.

His costume consisted of dowdy, dirty-looking trousers, misshapen brown boots and a battered top hat. On closer inspection she could see his jacket wasn't just one jacket, it was two. The top jacket was sleeveless, the sleeves apparently ripped from their seams. His arms were covered by the sleeves of another jacket which he wore beneath that.

She flashed him a polite smile. Her smile froze as she regarded his dirty face. Could it be who she thought it was? No! Surely not.

Recognising her before she recognised him, he became fidgety and turned slightly away.

She stared harder. Surely she knew that aquiline nose, that regal bearing . . .

'Casper?' Her jaw dropped. 'Casper! It is you!'

Casper St John Gervais, chair of Bath Hotels Association, was well known as a snappy dresser. But not today.

'Not a word,' he growled through clenched teeth.

She barely hid a smirk as she asked him who he was supposed to be. Not a Regency dandy, obviously.

‘A crossing sweeper!’

‘What’s that when it’s at home? Never mind, I’ll ask Lindsey. She’ll know.’

Casper bristled and hissed like a disgruntled snake as he sucked in his breath.

‘I do not need your daughter to tell me what it is. It is someone who used to sweep the road — specifically after horses had passed.’

‘Oh,’ said Honey. It was hard not to laugh. She bit her bottom lip. Casper! The dandy of all dandies, dressed up as a bloke employed to sweep up horse manure. ‘I’ve no doubt the roses were always good back then. They grow well after being spread with horse manure!’ Her laughter bubbled to the surface. ‘Sorry.’

Casper’s scowl deepened beneath the thick make-up.

‘I saw myself as a Regency dandy — silk britches, creamy white cravat and a handsome frock coat in a subtle shade of lemon. Call themselves casting directors? They do not know the meaning of the word!’ His anger and humiliation curled around every word he uttered.

Honey wiped the tears from her eyes, sniffed then coughed. She mustn’t laugh any more. She mustn’t! It was February and the Green River Hotel was half empty. Casper referred guests to her — part of the deal of Honey’s posting as liaison officer between the Hotels Association and the police.

‘At least it’s a relatively warm outfit compared to what the women are wearing — and the men for that matter,’ she said as reassuringly as she could.

‘Small recompense,’ Casper responded bitterly. It was pretty obvious that he was in no mood to be cheered up.

‘I hope I get something warm to wear,’ she said, even though she knew full well that she wasn’t required today. ‘I must admit I’m not looking forward to this. I thought I would, but those dresses are only made of muslin or silk. Perhaps I’d be better in a summer production.’

Someone from the costume department was making the rounds again, gathering up those already decked in Regency finery.

'Extras in costume over here, please.'

Casper got up. Snail-like he followed the flock, his eyes shooting daggers in the direction of the woman from wardrobe.

Honey remained with the wallflowers. Should she go or should she stay?

'We may not be picked,' said a woman who'd suddenly sat down next to her. The woman sounded severely disappointed.

'Never mind. It's too cold for wearing muslin and baring bosoms anyway.'

'This scene is supposed to be spring,' said the woman. 'It's all right to flaunt your bosoms in spring.'

'That's true. It's a different matter in February.'

'Shame though. I think I'd look good in sprigged muslin and a straw bonnet.'

Honey was not so turned on at the vision. Instead she thought of Smudger the chef in the — by now — very warm kitchen back at the Green River Hotel. Cooking breakfast was hard work, but it beat freezing your arse off pretending to be something you weren't.

Warm thoughts caused her eyes to stray and her feet to wander. She found herself eyeing the brightly lit house immediately next to the area in which they would be filming. The house had been hired specifically to cater for the real actors and the senior production staff.

The thin muslin that brought out the coward in her. Her mind was made up. Stardom could wait. Being warm could not. She headed for the house across the road.

Two director's assistants dressed in jogging bottoms and thickly padded coats fell in on either side of her.

'Should be better than the script,' said one of them. Honey smirked as though she knew what he meant.

'Blood on the carpet,' said the other warmly clad individual.

Obviously they were expecting conflict on set. No surprise there then.

'As long as it's warm blood and a warm carpet,' returned Honey, turning her collar up against the cold.

They nodded at her as though she'd said something very profound.

She followed them into one of the spacious rooms. The Georgian ceilings were bordered in astonishing plasterwork. The windows stretched from ceiling to floor and, once daylight was streaming through them, were guaranteed to flood the room with light.

Only the marble fireplace and the pure silk curtains remained of the normal décor and furnishings. Gone was the usual assortment of antique furniture — every stick had been put in storage during filming. In its place were plastic preformed chairs with metal legs.

Honey paused by the door. Being a hotelier, she recognised the familiar layout. Chairs set in a circle meant a lot of fat was about to be chewed. She guessed that some kind of production meeting was about to take place. She stood in the doorway. She had no business staying — but she did.

Squeezing through a gap between the rows, she found an empty chair set slightly apart from the rest and occupied by a wad of paper. She picked it up and gave it a quick glance. Script. *The Life of Jane Austen.*

Scripts didn't need seats. She sat down on the chair. The script sat on her lap.

Boris Morris, the director who had told her off for using her phone, took a seat next to her.

Boris was in his late forties and his hair was waving goodbye to his head. His forehead was high, naked and looked as though it were regularly polished with a good helping of beeswax. Beneath the Barbour jacket, he wore a flowery shirt, blue corduroy trousers and a patchwork waistcoat. He seemed to look directly at her. Was he questioning her right to be here? Due to the contact lens situation, she couldn't be sure.

Head down, girl, she thought to herself and pretended to study the script.

She turned the first few pages and frowned. They were sticky. Whatever the director was saying went over her head. Fingerprints — her fingerprints — dotted the pages. She turned one more page. It appeared to be smeared with something dark and red.

Someone tapped Honey on the shoulder. 'Excuse me.'

She looked up into a hard face set around a broken nose. His cap badge said *Ace Security*.

His eyes met hers briefly before dropping to her hands.

She managed a light laugh. 'Please,' she said. 'Tell me it's only . . .'

She was about to say it was probably only ketchup or fake blood — though she couldn't for the life of her remember whether Jane Austen had ever encountered murder, fictional or otherwise. She certainly wouldn't have come across ketchup. In which case . . .

The double doors crashed open and all heads turned to see a young woman with dark curly hair. Her face was deathly pale above a purple pashmina. Her eyes were glazed with horror, her voice hysterical.

'She's dead! Martyna's dead. She's been stabbed.'

The room erupted with noise.

Honey's eyes and those of the security guard returned to the script and the dotting of fingerprints.

The guard's meaty paw landed heavily on her shoulder. 'Don't move,' he said to her.

To everyone else, he shouted, 'Call the police. There's been a murder.'

'I didn't do it,' said Honey, her hand and bloodstained fingers held high in front of her astonished eyes.

'They all say that,' said the man. 'I've seen the movies.'

CHAPTER FIVE

The medical examiner was doing his thing and the Scene of Crime boys were loitering around the catering truck waiting for him to finish. Hot coffee and bacon sarnies were scattering like falling confetti.

There were moans and groans as DI Doherty pushed in front of everybody.

'As senior officer at the scene, I'm first in the queue,' he said. The aroma of fried bacon was enough to make anybody pull rank.

Armed with coffee and a bacon sandwich, Doherty was collared by a security guard. The guard was hopping impatiently from foot to foot, bubbling with excitement.

'A woman did it. My colleague apprehended 'er immediately and told 'er to stay put.'

'Where is she?' asked Doherty. It wouldn't be the first time that someone had carried out a citizen's arrest and forgotten to keep an eye on their suspect.

'We've got 'er over in the 'ouse there.' The security guard stabbed a blunt finger in the direction of the house across the road.

Chewing crusty bread and crispy bacon, Doherty urged him to go on. 'You saw her do it?'

'No. But her fingers are covered in blood.' He wiggled his own fingers as if to emphasise the point.

Doherty chewed as he walked. It was supposed to be his day off, but he'd been called out of bed.

The guard preceded him by a few paces across the road to the house. Things were looking good. They'd apprehended a woman with blood on her hands. With a bit of luck this case could be wrapped up quickly. What a turn-up that would be. First time ever, in fact, unless you counted the time when he'd encountered two Irish brickies knocking each other senseless on a building site. One died. The other did it. Simple.

If it hadn't been for the crusty roll and coffee he was carrying, he would have rubbed his hands together.

'She's in 'ere,' said the guard. 'My mate caught 'er with blood on 'er 'ands.' He licked his lips as he said it. Excited, maybe, at the sight of blood.

'I see,' said Doherty, thinking it must be a flood of blood for both security guards to keep on about it.

The 'mate' nodded and got up from the chair that he'd set in front of a pair of double doors.

Doherty shoved another hunk of food into his mouth and took another slurp of coffee before asking, 'Bit of a hard case, is she?'

'Not so much aggressive as sharp-tongued. Had a set-to with Miss Manderley earlier on. So there's your motive. Right?'

'We'll see. Let's get on with it.'

* * *

Honey had settled herself in a leather armchair, her feet resting on a matching stool. She was wearing plastic bags on her hands and making waves.

'Crap coffee. Can you get me a fresh one? Better still, see if there's any more of that hot chocolate . . . Hi, Steve! Here to solve the case or land a supporting role?'

She couldn't help sounding glad to see him. Martyna Manderley had died at a very propitious moment. Doherty had had to put his weekend on hold. She guessed he wasn't too pleased.

Doherty groaned and rolled his eyes. 'OK, lads,' he said to the two guards who had followed him in. 'I think I can handle this.'

Honey leaned out of the chair; one arm outstretched. 'I would really appreciate you guys getting me a fresh cup of coffee — better still, hot chocolate, please,' she added, wiggling the cup until one of them took it from her.

Once the door was closed, Doherty pulled up a chair, a stormy expression on his face.

'See what you've done? If you'd have come away with me, you wouldn't be a suspect in a murder case.'

She wiggled her fingertips inside their plastic covers. 'Look. All I did was pick up a bloodstained manuscript.'

'Explain.'

She did. She explained about the misunderstanding over the mobile phone. 'That woman was paranoid and greedy with it. She hates the thought of anyone making money out of her fame. I'm not surprised someone bumped her off — but it wasn't me.'

The corners of his eyes wrinkled mischievously when he grinned. 'You didn't lose your temper?'

'I never lose my temper.'

She went on to tell him about being cold and getting involved in the meeting.

'The script was left lying on a chair — honest. I picked it up. It felt sticky and when I looked down . . .'

'You saw it wasn't jam.'

She ignored that. 'The first I knew that Martyna Manderley had been killed was when that woman came crashing into the room and screamed it out for everyone to hear.'

'They've bagged the script.'

'They've bagged me too. When do these come off?' The plastic bags crackled as she wiggled her fingers.

Doherty stroked his chin thoughtfully.

She saw the remains of the bacon butty in his fist. 'I'm starving. Can I have a bite?'

He jerked his chin at her bagged hands. 'Could prove difficult.'

She heard her stomach rumble. So did Doherty.

'Abstinence is good for your figure,' he said, wolfing down the last piece.

Honey shot him a warning look. 'This is cruel.'

A knock sounded at the door. Detective Sergeant Ali Fleming, the station's latest addition, poked his head round the door. 'Sorry to interrupt, governor, but it's just to say that Mrs Driver's alibi checks out.' His face beamed broadly as he turned to Honey. 'She's free to go, if that's alright with you, governor.'

Honey beamed. 'With or without the mittens?'

The sergeant left without giving Honey an answer.

Doherty grimaced. The crime had turned serious. He had no prime suspect.

Holding his gaze, Honey slowly stripped off the bags as though they were elbow-length evening gloves.

'Let's put this little episode behind us, shall we? Let's get down to the nitty-gritty. How was she killed, where and when, and who are the suspects?'

He eyed her warily. 'You want to get involved in this?'

'You need me. I was here when it happened. I was on the scene before you were.'

He sighed. 'You're right. I need to know everything that happened.'

'So do I. Before Casper comes in here demanding we arrest someone.'

Steve ran his hand through his hair and shook his head. 'If he'd like to suggest who we should arrest, it will make my job a lot easier.'

'I think he favours the wardrobe mistress.'

Doherty raised his eyebrows. 'You mean she's got the strongest motive?'

'No. He just doesn't like the costume she gave him.'

CHAPTER SIX

Casper St John Gervais, chair of the Bath Hotels Association, waylaid them on their way to the scene of the crime. He pulled Honey to one side.

'I don't think I need to tell you how important it is that this is wrapped up post-haste. Do you realise how often movies are made in Bath? Do you realise how much money they bring in?'

Of course she did. Tons. The novels of Jane Austen were filmed and re-filmed ad infinitum, plus other classic historical novels and bawdy romps like *Tom Jones*, *Moll Flanders*, and *Fanny Hill.* If anyone wanted genuine eighteenth-century surroundings, they came to Bath. It was like living on a giant film set.

Casper went on to emphasise that Hollywood production companies would be wary of decamping to a place where their leading lady might get bumped off.

Honey sighed. 'Perhaps it wasn't her they were pissed off with. Perhaps they were sick to the back teeth with Jane Austen. In which case, I sympathise.'

Casper's limpid blue eyes widened as though they'd become full to the brim with water. 'Don't be facetious, Honey! I don't believe you dislike Jane Austen.'

'It's true. Too slow. Too insipid.'

Casper gasped. Instant speechlessness.

Doherty dragged her away. 'Naughty girl! So cruel!' he tutted, but grinned as he did so.

'I was being honest.'

'So you don't like *Pride and Prejudice*?'

'My mother does. It's the britches. They're very tight. Women like tight britches. It brings out the animal in them.'

'Hmm. I might get myself a pair.'

'Well, that will brighten my mother's day.'

* * *

Martyna Manderley was the only star in the film with her own trailer. Everyone else had a dressing room in the big house, and the extras had their ex-London bus to pile onto.

Doherty had been handed an envelope containing photographs of the victim. Coming to a halt outside the trailer, he took the opportunity to look at them, though only briefly.

'Grim?' asked Honey.

'They won't make the centrefold of *Hello!* magazine, that's for sure.'

Slipping them back into the envelope, they entered the trailer. A family of eight could live comfortably inside, and the fittings were luxurious. The upholstery was a soft shade of spearmint. The carpet was white. The whole interior had been customised, and the bathroom boasted a full-size bath, gold-plated taps and a separate shower cubicle. An automatic atomiser perfumed the air at frequent intervals. It was currently sitting on the floor next to a fan heater and beneath a six-foot-long dressing table complete with make-up lights. A wall-mounted mirror ran the full length of the ledge. Tubs, jars and bottles of perfume sat in a sea of blood.

Doherty took a photograph from the brown envelope and passed it to her. It showed Martyna Manderley slumped over her dressing table.

'Stabbed with a hatpin.'

'Ouch!' said Honey. 'We need to find out who left that script on the chair.'

He nodded. 'Quite right. Questions have to be asked. I'll start with you. Who did you see in the immediate area?'

Honey knitted her eyebrows and tried to picture the scene. She recalled empty chairs to one side of her with a gap in between. A few people had been seated in the row in front of her and a few people standing up behind had been getting organised to sit down. Who else? What else?

'Whose fingerprints were on the script — besides mine, that is?'

'We won't get the results for a few days, but I can make a guess. Those of Martyna Manderley, of course. There's bound to be plenty. Scripts get passed around and checked, alterations are made, and Martyna also had a prompt who read the script while she recited her lines. The prompt sat at the side sometimes.'

'How do you know all this?'

The boyish grin. 'I used to know an actress.'

'I bet you did. Have we — sorry — your lot questioned the prompt?'

'My DS has. He's very keen. As you saw earlier,' he said, a lopsided grin sending a twinkle to his eyes. 'She was popping a couple of throat lozenges at the time. Martyna had been getting her to read the script out loud. She was seen taking the lozenges with a cup of hot coffee while cuddled up to one of the director's assistants. She didn't like Martyna, but she said she didn't kill her. Apparently, Martyna shouted a lot.'

'As I've already said, she began the day by shouting at me.'

'All because you were on the phone.'

'Getting Smudger out of bed. He was supposed to be cooking breakfast this morning.'

Doherty picked up a copy of *Hello!* and flicked to the feature on Martyna Manderley and her fiancé, Brett Coleridge, multimillionaire, and man about town.

Will They Be Mr and Mrs Perfect? ran the headline.

'Well, they won't get the chance to find out,' said Honey.

Doherty didn't appear to be listening. He was thinking out loud.

'Why was the script left there? Why take a bloodstained script anyway?'

'Dropping it in a hurry — found by someone else and left there . . . or maybe even planted to incriminate somebody else.'

'That's a little far-fetched, but hell, what else do I have?' said Doherty.

They continued to sniff around. Literally, in Doherty's case.

He wrinkled his nose. 'Smells strong in here.'

'That thing,' said Honey, pointing to the air-freshening atomiser which had fallen onto its side beneath the fitted dressing table. A portable fan heater sat next to it. 'It's supposed to keep the air perfumed. Though it's a strange place to put it, down there next to the fan heater.'

'Smelly feet?' Doherty suggested.

Honey did a few poses in front of the mirror. Jean Harlow. Marilyn Monroe.

'Movie stars don't have smelly feet,' she reliably informed him while fixing her hair. 'They have sponsors providing them with every luxury item you can think of to make them look, sound and smell ravishing — including foot powder.'

Thrusting her hands in her pockets so she wouldn't be tempted to touch anything, Honey wandered from one area of the trailer to another. Everything was as tidy as could be expected considering a murder had just taken place. There were no books. No magazines except for the one they had looked at. And no script.

She pointed the fact out to Doherty. 'There should be one.'

'I suppose so.'

'In which case why take it?'

Doherty shrugged. 'We're setting up an incident room over the road. Someone must have seen the murderer going into her trailer. No one leaves this site until I'm satisfied with everything.'

'Does that include extras?'

'Of course it does.'

'Including members of my family?'

Doherty froze and appeared to be holding his breath. 'Your mother's here as an extra?'

''Fraid so. She's an incurable romantic. You should know that by now. She's got herself a muslin gown and a straw bonnet.'

'And there I was thinking that you and I could star in our own skin flick.'

'Not in this weather, we can't.'

'We should have gone away.'

'Let's get this put to bed first,' Honey retorted.

Doherty seemed to remember where he was and turned serious. 'I've got work to do. I'll catch up with you later — if you're free. I'd invite you to my place, but I don't know when I'll be there. Do you mind if I call round?'

She didn't hesitate. 'Whenever you like.'

The smell of fried bacon drifted anew and was now joined by the unmistakable, mouth-watering aroma of cottage pie. Cooked mince in a thick gravy with onions, carrots and a topping of fluffy mashed potato. The catering truck was doing a roaring trade. Honey's stomach rumbled. Her eyes stayed fixed on the truck.

She looked over at the lovely Regency house they'd just come out of. The Circus was aptly named, as famous as the Royal Crescent and an architectural gem. Designed by John Wood, the elder, it comprised three sets of eleven houses formed a circle overlooking a green island.

Honey turned her head a full 180 degrees to the trailer. The house and the trailer were opposite each other. Directly in front of her, halfway between the two, was the catering truck. She double-checked. There was no doubt about it. The big old truck dispensing hot food and drink was slap bang in the middle of the site and had the best view possible of Martyna Manderley's trailer. The guy running it had to have seen something.

Doherty noticed it too. 'That truck seems a good place to start.'

Perhaps he would have taken the opportunity to head in that direction, but his phone rang and someone from Forensics also begged his attention.

Honey took the opportunity.

CHAPTER SEVEN

The cast, including the extras, had been ordered not to change out of their costumes. They stood in groups, sipping from paper cups. One would-be actor was standing slightly aloof. Honey headed straight for him.

'Casper!' She spoke breezily. 'How are you feeling?'

He was wearing a strained, long-suffering expression; his jaw was tightly clenched.

'This is a totally unpalatable situation,' he said, and followed it with a pursing of lips, already blue with cold. 'Look at this dreadful outfit!'

Honey buried her hands into her coat pockets and her mirth into her throat. Casper was still wearing the costume of a man who sweeps up horse droppings for a living.

'Shouldn't be too long now.'

'I should hope not,' he snapped impatiently.

'The police must do their job. We really can't have the city's reputation besmirched like this. The culprit must be caught — and quickly.'

She had used a similar line to the one Casper himself often used when a serious crime had been committed. It was usually him prodding her to get a move on. She tried to massage his severely dented ego.

His large head receded into the high coat collar. His jaw set like cement. A young woman from costume came to take a photograph.

'The show must go on,' she said brightly. 'We do have an understudy until such time we get a "name" replacement.'

Casper played Mr Curmudgeonly to her Miss Bright Shiny Day.

'Why?'

The woman managed to retain her cheery smile. 'Filming is going ahead as planned, despite the present difficulties.'

'It's a murder, not a difficulty,' Casper pointed out.

Ms Bright Shiny Day went on undeterred. 'We need to record the exact details of you and your costume, so we get it right for the next time.'

Casper pulled himself up to his full height. His voice rolled like thunder. 'There will be *no* next time!'

Nose in the air, chin hard set and jutting forward, he stalked off across the road.

The young woman stared after him, her camera hanging slack in her hands.

Honey shrugged. She'd always known Casper loved theatricals. He saw himself as a leading man, or at least as someone cultured. The only cultivating done by men who swept up horse shit for a living was the growing of roses and rhubarb!

'Cup of coffee, miss?'

The voice came from above. The counter of the catering truck protruded out at chin level. Honey looked up. She couldn't see the face attached to the voice, just a pair of black hairy arms leading up to broad shoulders. Apart from a white-spotted red handkerchief around his neck, the rest of him was hidden by height and shadow. If she tilted her head back she could just about see his shiny red chin and cheeks. She presumed they were the result of the steam forever rising in front of his face. She stood on tiptoes so she could see him better.

'Yes, please,' she responded, and watched as he changed aprons.

He saw her looking. 'Got to keep up appearances. Won't let anything get in the way of my standards.'

'I assume your standards are very high?' she asked.

He leaned forward. 'Extremely so! The stars of stage and screen have congratulated me on my Welsh rarebit. That famous Dame What's-her-name said that my flapjacks were the best she'd ever tasted. And Kevin Costner praised my Thai curry beefburgers up to high heaven, he did. Yes, indeed! If you want good grub on a film set, dial up Dick Richards. See?'

He pointed to the red lettering above the open serving hatch. 'Richard Richards. Caterer to the stars!' As he leaned outwards, she saw his full features — dark bushy eyebrows and big bouncy black hair streaked with grey. 'Call me Dick!'

'Nice to meet you . . . Dick. My name's Honey. Honey Driver.'

'Ah, yes. As in honeypot. Made by bees. Honey does you good. I use melted honey with a touch of maple syrup poured over my breakfast pancakes.'

This honey thing was going on a bit. 'My real name's Hannah, but Honey's more familiar.'

He didn't seem to hear. 'My bacon is best Wiltshire. Did you notice that?'

Honey said that she'd only had toast and butter. On seeing his crestfallen expression, she felt obliged to comment that the bread was the freshest she'd ever tasted.

'I've catered to the best — some of the greatest stars of screen, stage and television. They all praise my cooking. I'm the king of the catering wagon. That's what they say.'

Flourishing the fresh apron like a matador's cape, 'King' Richard tied the strings and threw the dirty one into a dark corner before turning to the coffee machine.

Honey found herself wondering if the biggest drama queen on set was here in the food truck. *A little flattery might not go amiss*, thought Honey.

'You must be as good as you say you are. I've heard no complaints from anyone.'

'And why should you?' he demanded indignantly.

Not quite the right thing to say, she realised. Not flattering enough.

He thwacked her cup of coffee onto the counter and glared at her fiercely. 'Who did you hear complaining? Tell me. Tell me right now!'

'I didn't hear any complaints. Only praise. Honestly.'

His eyes were dark brown and yet coldly piercing. Brown was usually warm, like velvet. His were like frozen mud.

'I understand the understudy will be taking over until the part is reassigned.'

'Ah! There'll be a good few after the part. My money is on Penelope Petrie.'

'You've met her?'

The broad beam resumed.

'I 'ave indeed. Loves my cottage pie, she does. Mind you, she can eat stuff like that till the cows come home. Never puts on an ounce.

'Wish I could eat stodge and not put on a pound.'

'Stodge?' The frozen-mud look came back with a vengeance. Time to back-pedal — and fast.

'What I mean to say is that traditional food really fills you up on a cold day.'

The affable expression half returned. Honey judged it best to keep off the subject of food. Dick Richards was a bit touchy on that score.

'I'm glad I'm only an amateur,' she said in humble fashion. She wasn't au fait with the world of film production, but she'd heard plenty of gossip about deadly Hollywood rivalries — too many actors and too few parts.

He grunted something about wannabes not pulling their weight. She made no response to that. It wasn't why she was here.

'You're in a good spot here,' she said, getting back to the job in hand. She peered in the direction of the house across the road, then turned and looked more significantly at the trailer. Yes. She was right. The truck marked the halfway stage between the two.

A man wearing a muffler was finalising the tying of tape around the trailer. Honey recognised him as Detective Sergeant Ali Fleming. The voice of Dick Richards boomed down at her.

'If you're asking did I see anything — well, yes! Of course I did. I'm thinking about coming forward to give a statement.'

'Then you're talking to the right person for that. I should have introduced myself properly,' said Honey, sensing she had an opening here. 'I liaise with the police on behalf of the Bath Hotels Association. Would you mind telling me what you saw?'

He pulled in his chin and eyed her warily. 'Well . . . I am a bit busy. Just 'cause there's been a murder don't mean to say I can shut down, you know.'

'It doesn't have to be here,' she blurted. 'We could meet somewhere. Perhaps I could buy you lunch.'

Richards eyed her speculatively. 'Where?'

'Somewhere nice! Somewhere that would suit your palate. I wouldn't take you to any old place, not an experienced chef like you.'

She'd cottoned on that Dick Richards was full of his own self-importance. He was dying to tell someone all he knew. And she was here to hear it — she could beat Steve Doherty to solving the crime!

'Not that I saw anyone going in there who shouldn't be going in. The make-up girls, the second director's assistant, the sound technician, the wardrobe mistress and the continuity girl. Everyone you'd expect to see.' He leaned over his drop-down counter. 'Could be any one of 'em. They've all got an axe to grind if you know what I mean.'

Dick Richards looming over her like that made her feel like a frightened gerbil confronted with a ten-foot grizzly.

'Your evidence could be crucial,' she said, trying desperately to regain her courage.

'You'd think the police would notice that!'

Dick Richards was smarting that he hadn't been the first to be picked out to give evidence. Martyna Manderley clearly wasn't the only prima donna on the set!

He rested a beefy forearm on the counter flap, and the warped wood groaned in protest.

'I'm glad to see somebody's on the ball. Tell you what I'll do,' he said, glancing around him melodramatically. 'I'll write down everyone I remember going in there, plus —*plus*,' he repeated with a heightened degree of self-importance, 'I'll jot down some notes regarding their relationship with Martyna, and their probable motive. How does that sound? We'll meet for coffee. How's that for you?'

'Great. Include those who went in but didn't have an axe to grind, will you?'

He pulled a so-so kind of face. 'Not sure about that. I mean no one was that friendly with Martyna. She didn't want them to be. Thought she was a cut above the crowd if you know what I mean. Bit below them now, ain't she? Or she will be — once she's in the ground.'

His comment was so matter of fact it made her blood turn cold. He obviously hadn't liked Martyna, but then, she countered, it seemed that neither had anybody else.

CHAPTER EIGHT

At home a day later, gone ten at night, Honey was doing some floor exercises in an effort to iron out her disappointments — as well as her stomach. To start with, Steve Doherty had not yet kept his promise to drop round. Under the circumstances it wasn't that surprising. However, Steve being a dutiful officer of the law did nothing to placate her own selfish reasons for wanting him to herself.

Ab crunch after ab crunch! Her wobbly bits were aching and so was her mind. She thought about Steve. Where would they be a year from now? They were making progress, but slowly.

As for her wobbly bits, where would *they* be this time next year? Consigned to history? Hoping was one thing. Achieving was another. She liked food, and at this time of year it was hard to resist.

Thinking of food inevitably led to thoughts of Dick Richards.

He had a strange way with words. He was fine when he was talking about food — his food, of course, prepared by *his* skilful hands. Perhaps it was something to do with all that steam and grease he inhaled, thought Honey as she struggled to do her thirty-ninth ab crunch.

The fortieth was even harder; her abdominals were refusing to be pushed any further and, quite frankly, she didn't blame them.

She lay flat for a moment to get her breath back, staring at the ceiling. Christ, she thought. Imagine doing five hours of this torture per day. That's what movie stars did — or at least that's what the likes of *Hello!* and *OK!* reported. How the hell did they have time for anything else?

Her phone played 'Ding Dong! The Witch is Dead' — just a little snippet she particularly liked from *The Wizard of Oz*. Her phone was lying on the floor beside her.

'Hi,' she answered.

'Hi.'

It was Steve. As she looked upwards, she was surprised to see a butterfly — no doubt brought out of its chrysalis by the warmth rising from the radiator.

'Sorry I didn't get round to see you. I'll try again tonight.'

'I might be busy.'

'Are you?'

He didn't sound adequately perturbed.

'Would it worry you?'

'I'd be disappointed, but I know what a busy lady you are. If I don't make it, can you give me a thought before you drop off to sleep?'

'While I'm in bed?'

'Why not? Dream a little. Fantasise in fact.'

'I'll do my best. Shall I stick to romantic or indulge in the erotic?'

'Go with the flow and keep everything warm.'

The butterfly was still fluttering around after he'd disconnected. The heat rising from the radiators that lined the walls had fooled it into thinking it was May instead of February. Poor thing. Just out of its chrysalis and about to get its butt frozen off.

She raised an arm and waved at it. 'Hey, little guy. You don't want to go out there. Trust me.'

The butterfly paid no attention of course.

She let her arm fall back above her head. Yesterday had been cold. Anyone with any sense would have stayed indoors, snuggled up before a roaring fire.

Once her muscles had stopped complaining, she rolled over onto her stomach and up on to her knees. You were supposed to take things slowly after exercise — something to do with the blood pooling in your arteries.

She was still dwelling on blood when she got into the shower — the blood on the script. She shuddered at the thought of it and didn't warm up until she was dressed and looking fit to be seen.

While delving around in her walk-in closet, she thought about the Victorian corset her mother had borrowed. The item was as beautiful as it was fragile. She didn't like lending it. Give it another two days. After that she'd remind her mother to bring it back.

At least it wouldn't be wasted. Most of her collection was now kept in a military chest in her closet, and that was where the corset would return — once it had done its work on the guy her mother had in mind.

She pondered that. Was that what had happened with the bloodstained script? Did it have to be returned somewhere? Had there been an argument over the size of the part and/or the amount of dialogue? She'd heard that big stars sometimes cut up rough over scripts. Depending on their profile, they could have their own way with most things. Had Martyna Manderley belittled a scriptwriter to breaking point? Had the murderer got angry, lashed out with the hatpin, tried to mop things up, then panicked and dashed out of the trailer, still grasping the script? Or was he cooler than that? She called a halt to this train of thought. Why was she thinking the murderer was a man? There were bound to be rivalries between women, bound to be blood on the carpet — even on the script.

Doherty phoned back and suggested lunch at a little café called Blanc et Noir. She heard the disappointment in his voice when she told him she had a prearranged date.

'Who with?'

'That's hardly your business.'

Initially she hadn't been planning to tell him that her lunch date was Dick Richards. It didn't hurt to throw a little jealousy around. Her conscience pricked her.

'Dick Richards, the caterer, wants me to meet him for coffee. He's miffed that you didn't question him. He's a little self-important.'

'If he wants to talk with you, that's OK by me. I'll be round later to hear what he had to say.'

'Very masterful, but—'

Doherty put the phone down on her before she could finish her sentence.

* * *

The café where she had arranged to meet Dick Richards was a favourite of hers. It had the right ambience, the right food, and was situated in a cobbled courtyard not far from Bath Abbey. On summer days it was pleasant to sit outside at a green metal table covered with a green checked tablecloth. At this time of year, you had to dash inside before twelve o'clock if you wanted to stay warm.

Snap-happy tourists, though thinner on the ground in February than in high summer, hugged the pavements, forcing her to sidestep on to the road. She thanked her lucky stars that the office and shop workers hadn't spilled out just yet. A seat inside the café was not yet out of the question. She marched crisply on.

The case for the prosecution looked straightforward. Martyna Manderley had a less-than-perfect working relationship with the production team.

Her musings on murder were suddenly disturbed by a clipboard. A small, elderly woman dressed head to toe in lavender muslin was shoving it in the general direction of her nostrils.

'I beg your forgiveness for interrupting your sojourn on this chilly but bright morning. I put before you a petition to halt the filming of historical drama in Bath. This particularly applies to dramas based on the work and the life of Jane Austen. Those of us imbued with a great liking, nay, a great love for Jane Austen and her novels have decided to take a stand and point out to those who would think otherwise, that this is *not* Disneyland!'

'Ah! You read a lot of Jane Austen, I take it?'

'Indeed I do, my dear friend. Jane Austen's pen created the greatest romantic novels ever written. No one has surpassed her insight, her gift for emotion. Indeed, no one has equalled her grasp of the genre.'

'You dislike films being made about Jane Austen?'

'*Especially* Jane Austen.'

She stressed the 'especially', stretching the word out like a piece of tight elastic.

Honey stated the obvious. 'She's dead, you know?'

The woman raised one eyebrow and fixed her with slate grey eyes.

'I know very well that England's most wonderful literary genius is dead. Dear Jane has been dead for years. But not forgotten!' she exclaimed, raising a warning finger three centimetres from the tip of Honey's nose.

'I meant the actress who was playing her.'

The woman's deep-set eyes seemed suddenly in danger of exploding from their sockets. 'One would not wish to be cruel with one's words, but some of dear Jane's devoted followers view the departure of Miss Manderley from the role as something akin to divine justice.'

Honey gulped. Muggers and murderers were dangerous enough, but a Jane Austen devotee with petitioning intent might prove unpredictable.

Honey did a quick sidestep — not quick enough.

'Sign!'

Clipboard and pen were thrust against her chest.

She eyed both with fearful eyes. Sign? Should she? She decided she would. She told herself that nobody was likely to take any notice of it. The whole thing would probably end up on a bonfire in some city councillor's backyard.

Filming, like tourism, brought money to the city; people saw films and noticed the background, which in turn fuelled more tourism. A simple equation.

'There was only one redeeming feature to the whole production; the quality of the food they served on the film set was of sufficient merit,' the woman said suddenly.

Frowning, Honey gave her back the clipboard. 'Who told you that?'

'I partook of a number of quite delicious dishes while waiting around to be called.'

'You went on set?'

'I was taken on as a consultant on the life and times of dear Jane. I also took advantage of a little extra income by enrolling as an extra. That, my dear, is how much I wished to keep an eye on what was going on. Someone must protect the great heritage Jane Austen left us. It fell on my shoulders to be her defender and defend her I did!'

Honey's eyes flicked from the woman to her clipboard and back again. 'And now you're doing this?'

The woman's eyes glittered. 'I was ordered off the set. The *big* star decided that my constant remarks regarding historical detail were injurious to artistic expression.'

Honey thought about it. Could this woman be a killer or was gathering names her only stab at revenge. She decided she wasn't capable of murder and made to carry on to the café.

'I understand she got stabbed with her own hatpin,' the woman called after her.

Honey stopped and turned round. 'That's right.'

'If they'd listened to my greater wisdom, she might not have been stabbed. Women didn't wear hatpins back then. Wrong period. Wrong kind of bonnets.'

CHAPTER NINE

Dick Richards came in on the dot of eleven. The café boasted an old-fashioned brass bell above its dark green door. It jangled as he pushed the door open.

His narrowed gaze swept over the green wooden chairs and the round tables topped with green-and-white gingham.

She waved.

He acknowledged her with a curt nod then continued to look around him, his keen eyes taking in the décor, the table placements and the three chalkboard menus hanging on the wall. The middle chalkboard was the biggest and listed the main courses. The ones on either side were smaller — one listed starters and the other desserts.

She asked him if any filming was going on. He said it was not. The extras had been told to go home so his services were not required. His tone was gruff, a deep growl embedded in his vocal chords.

He perused the menu on the chalk boards before sitting down.

'No steak and kidney pie,' he said loudly. 'You can always tell a good chef by the quality of his pastry. Did you know that?'

Indeed she did. Smudger was full of the same crap. Chefs had big egos.

'No,' she lied, smiling at the same time as she thought things through. First things first. Do not alienate this man. Chefs were touchy types and had access to very sharp knives. 'Did you bring your list?'

'I did,' he said gruffly, adjusting his position as he pushed a meaty paw into his right-hand pocket.

Honey felt her heart pounding as he pulled out a multi-coloured notebook with a pink pencil attached to the spiral spine. *Takes all sorts*, she supposed.

Her stomach rumbled. If she was going to do this with a clear head, she needed food.

'So what do you fancy to eat?' she asked brightly.

He sniffily perused the menu. 'I wouldn't get away with muck like this,' he said loudly. He said it just as a waiter walked past carrying a plated baguette steaming with garlic butter and king prawns.

The smell was hypnotic.

'I think I'll have the prawns,' said Honey.

He grunted something incomprehensible before continuing with his denigration of the menu. 'Venison sausages with sweet red onions. Bought in, no doubt.'

'I don't think so . . .'

'Cornish crab with pea soup. Huh! Tinned! And if it's not tinned, it won't be a patch on mine. Catherine Zeta Jones loved my soup, she did. Asked me for the recipe, in fact.'

'I take it she had a mind to cook it for Michael when she got home?'

'Exactly!'

'So!' she said, before he reached the desserts. 'We've got time for a chat. What do you have? Who do you think are the front runners?' She looked pointedly at the notebook.

Her lips smiled in an unhurried, interested manner. Only her hands might have given her true feelings away — if Dick had cared to look — which he didn't. Neither did he hear the rhythmic tapping on the table. Dick was too wrapped up in Dick.

After carefully shaking out the gingham napkin, he tucked it into his shirt collar. Once that was done, he picked up the notebook using his thumb to reach the right page. He cleared his throat as though he were Pavarotti making ready prior to a performance.

'Scheherazade Parker-Henson.'

Honey ran her eyes down the menu. 'Is that a foreign dish?'

'Senior make-up artist. I saw her go in.'

'Ah! It's a wonder she didn't murder her parents for giving her a name like that. No matter though.' Honey got out her own notebook. 'At about what time?'

'Six forty-five.'

'You're sure about that?'

'Positive. That's the time I put the flapjacks and black pudding in the oven. I cook them separately to the sausages and bacon, which I cook in the oven first then transfer to the griddle. That's how I get the sausages so juicy,' he said. 'The secret to cooking a good sausage is to give it a good pricking first.'

Honey cleared her throat. 'So I understand. Now, this Scheherazade — bit of a mouthful that name.'

'Double-barrelled always means upper class, Mrs Driver.'

'Call me Honey.'

'Honey. Honey,' he repeated. She could tell he liked her name. That was something.

She primed her ears as she scribbled. Dick was in full flow.

'Very upmarket family. Landed gentry. Acres of land and a stately home in Shropshire. You get good produce from Shropshire, you know. If you want good *and* fresh, Shropshire's the place to get it. Especially asparagus. They grow very nice asparagus.'

'Horsey type?'

'You could say that.'

Their meals came. Honey tucked in. Dick eyed the bowl of lime-green creaminess disdainfully before picking up his spoon.

'Hmm. I needed this,' said Honey, munching.

Dick called the waiter over.

'*Garçon*, I am going to give you and this establishment the benefit of my experience of superior cuisine.'

Honey could tell the waiter wanted to tell Dick to bugger off. She'd felt the same with some of her more awkward customers on many occasions.

Dick was in full flow.

'Many famous people have praised my culinary skills. I've catered to the best — Sydney Sidon, the quiz show host. He likes a sausage sandwich with relish on the side.' Dick wagged a warning finger. 'Wait there while I taste this.'

Honey watched as Dick, with a flourish of his meaty hand, lowered the spoon into the soup. A green spoonful came out with a flake of crabmeat in the middle.

'Not bad on the eyes,' said Dick. 'People eat with their eyes,' he informed Honey.

'Really?' As if she didn't know.

She could have added that smell mattered too, but she didn't wish to be drawn into this conversation. She was here to talk about suspects and motives and how many people Dick had seen enter Martyna's trailer.

Dick pursed his lips and made small sucking sounds. He looked up at the ceiling as he did so, then swallowed and gave his verdict.

'Passable,' he said with an air of majesty. 'Give my compliments to the chef, and if ever he's scratching his head for an idea, refer him to me. I've cooked for Costner, you know. And Michael Caine. He likes a good roast.'

The waiter looked relieved to go.

'Now this Scheherazade,' said Honey. 'What motive would she have for killing Martyna?'

'Simple,' he said, wiping his mouth. 'Martyna used to bully young Courtney something rotten. Schezzer used to pull her up about it —Courtney's her assistant.' He grinned suddenly. 'Scheherazade's a bit of a mouthful. She's Schezzer to her friends.'

Judging by the way he said it, Dick counted himself as one of them. Honey flicked the crumbs he'd sprayed off her notebook.

'So there was bad blood between them?'

'Martyna was good at creating bad blood,' he said, setting down his spoon and making a face directed at the pea and ham soup. 'That's enough for me. I don't want to offend anybody, but I do have very high standards.'

'How long was she in Martyna's trailer?'

'About ten minutes max.'

Honey stayed the pen. 'That's enough time to stab someone.'

Dick's attention had already gone back to the chalkboard. 'Their desserts look a bit unadventurous for my taste,' he said. 'I do a mean meringue, you know. My baked Alaska is to die for.'

'Let's hope not,' said Honey. She badly wanted to ask him who else had entered Martyna's trailer, but it was hard to get the subject matter away from food.

'What was that?'

Here he was again, referring to her comment with regard to his desserts.

'Your baked Alaska. Wouldn't want anyone to die on account of it.' She laughed. 'It was a joke.'

His face remained deadpan.

'I don't think it's funny!'

He started to get to his feet.

'Dick, it was only a joke. Look. Don't go. I need your input. Of all the people on that set, you're the best placed to study who went into Martyna's trailer and who came out.'

'Not today.'

'I'll give you my phone number. Phone me when you're ready to talk again.'

He seemed to be thinking about it as he tucked his notebook and pen back into his pocket.

'Humph!' he said at last.

She pressed her phone number on him and beamed.

'Any time, any place, anywhere. I've always got my phone with me.'

Eventually the hard lines of his face relaxed and drooped as befitting his age.

'On one condition.'

'Which is?'

'Next time you take me to a more epicurean establishment than this one.'

CHAPTER TEN

Honey was propped up on the reception desk with one hand cupping her chin and her elbow resting on the desk. Doherty came in with a blast of cold air. He drew off the black scarf he was wearing around his neck. His look was sardonically sexy.

'Don't you ever shave?'

There was a familiar grating sound as he rubbed at his stubble with chunky fingers. He grinned. 'Wrong time of year for shaving. It's too cold. In fact, I'm considering growing a beard.'

'You're not!'

'Don't you like beards?'

'You're not here to talk about beards. You're here to take me out. Am I right?'

He grinned. 'Nothing could stop me.'

'Hey, Honey!'

Honey sighed. She was definitely up for a night out. However . . .

Mary Jane flounced down the stairs and into reception looking like an advert for old Scotch whisky. Doherty's jaw dropped at the sight of her.

'She's just got back from a trip to Edinburgh,' Honey whispered by way of explanation.

'Some tartan, Mary Jane,' Doherty exclaimed with over-the-top enthusiasm.

Mary Jane's face lit up. 'Why, thank you, officer. It's an antique, you know. The guy I bought it from reckoned it was worn at the Battle of Bannockburn.'

Doherty's nostrils closed to tight slits.

The heavy tartan skirt Mary Jane was wearing reeked of camphor. It had probably been in mothballs for years, though perhaps not as far back as the Battle of Bannockburn. Even the best Harris tweed didn't last that long.

Honey wanted to breathe again, and the best way to do that was to assist Mary Jane so she would go away.

'Can I help you, Mary Jane?'

'I'm sure you can, dear. Sir Cedric suggested I get out and about a bit more. I've been snuggling up to the radiator, and my chilblains are suffering on account of it. He suggests I get onto that film set, despite my reservations. I don't mind just a small part. I don't want to be a star or anything. What do you think?'

Mary Jane's bright expression was fighting a losing battle against a lifetime's accumulation of wrinkles, though her eyes still twinkled.

'I think filming's at a standstill at present,' Honey declared. 'Did you not hear that the leading lady's been murdered?'

Mary Jane waved one long arm dismissively. 'Sure, but Hollywood stops for nobody. *Entertainment News* says they've got a new star and they'll be requiring more extras. I thought I'd put my name down real fast.'

Mary Jane addressed Doherty. 'Derek, the guy who does the stuff with microphones, said they could use somebody like me. I'm tall, but I'm skinny.'

So Derek was the culprit!

Honey had been out earlier. She'd gone round to her mother's to get her antique corset back, but Gloria had a very good reason for wanting to hold on to it.

'I need to borrow it, Hannah my darling,' she'd said. 'There's this cute little guy at the Conservative Club with a lot of potential, but he's in need of something to fan his flames a little — if you know what I mean.'

Honey knew all right. Anyway, a little romance on her mother's account meant she wouldn't be attempting to fix her daughter up with a potential second husband.

'I hear being skinny is an advantage,' said Doherty. He threw Honey a sidelong grin. 'The camera adds ten pounds, so I'm told.'

'That's what I heard too,' said Mary Jane, nodding like an overexcited donkey.

Honey rolled her eyes. 'I don't suppose Sir Cedric wants to be an extra too?' She was being facetious, but Mary Jane took it very seriously.

'I haven't asked him,' she said. 'Anyway, I doubt the camera would catch him.'

This was all very true. Everyone knew that ghosts were camera shy. Only Mary Jane ever saw Cedric.

Doherty was wearing a deep frown. It was fetching and made Honey want to reach out and smooth it away.

'They're quick off the mark,' muttered Doherty. 'Martyna Manderley's barely settled into her ice-cold cubicle at the mortuary and they're already carrying on without her.'

'The show must go on,' said Mary Jane. She looked at Honey. 'I've got a call for tomorrow at six. How about you?'

'Sure,' said Honey, thinking a little more prying might be in order. 'I'm up for that. Fix it with Derek for me, will you?'

Mary Jane said that she would and was gone. The smell of mothballs went with her.

Both Honey and Doherty took deep breaths.

'What is she like?' Honey asked.

'Come on. Get your coat. Let's go breathe in the smoke from the sizzle platters and sniff some fine wines at the Zodiac.'

'Hmmm. Heaven,' said Honey. 'Beats camphor hands down.'

'Is that what it was?'

'Don't tell me that you thought it was perfume?'

He gave a casual toss of his head. 'Well, you know how these old girls are — lavender, camphor, syrup of figs.'

She looked at him and laughed out loud. 'Syrup of figs?'

'They all go in for that kind of thing,' he responded defensively.

* * *

The Zodiac was busy, though not as busy as it would be closer to midnight when late-working hoteliers, publicans and guest house proprietors flooded in to brood and brag about the relative advantages of *their* businesses as opposed to the competition. Or they just came and got drunk.

Clint — real name Rodney — Eastwood was on the door. The Zodiac was having another of its theme nights. Tonight it was the Wild West. Clint was suitably dressed and there was something of the Clint Eastwood about him.

'Nice outfit,' said Doherty.

Clint grinned and did a twirl with the pretend firearm he had tucked into his belt.

He beamed proudly. Despite his appearance, Clint wasn't a bad lad deep down. On the surface he was a bit hit and miss, and not entirely honest, but he was good at washing dishes. Honey employed him when needed, that is when she couldn't get anyone else and Clint needed the money.

'Here,' said Clint, beaming proudly. 'I've only got a few of these to give out.'

He pinned a tin star on to Doherty's chest.

'Seeing as you're a sheriff — in a manner of speaking.'

He made some excuse about why Honey couldn't have one.

'Very authentic costume, Clint, but I don't think the Man with No Name — Eastwood as is — had a neck tattoo.'

CHAPTER ELEVEN

Miss Lavender Cleveley carefully unfolded the piece of paper she had secreted in her handbag. Phone numbers she needed to remember were mostly listed in a small notebook kept primarily for that purpose, such as the doctor, the dentist and those few relatives who had not yet been scythed into eternity by the Grim Reaper.

This phone number was different. She didn't want anyone knowing that she had it. She had no intention of being tripped up like a hopeless character in a TV cop show.

Her mouth moved silently as she read the number. Once she was sure she'd got it right, she picked up the phone and dialled.

She heard it ring four times before it was picked up.

What sounded like a female voice answered.

'Is he there?' asked Miss Cleveley.

The woman hesitated.

She probably thinks I'm one of his women, Miss Cleveley mused. Hardly that, she thought, chuckling to herself.

It was easy to imagine what the woman was thinking and what kind of expression she wore. A slight frown, a pout coming to painted lips — they were all the same.

'I'll get him,' said the faceless person on the other end.

The phone went quiet.

Lavender Cleveley pursed her thin lips as she waited. Her chill eyes, which had been a brighter blue when she'd been younger, now narrowed as she contemplated what she would say.

'Hello! Who is this?'

'Mr Coleridge?'

'Yes,' he said gruffly. 'What do you want?'

She wouldn't tell him who she was, but she would certainly tell him what she wanted.

'What you do and what you did are quite despicable. But I'll have my revenge. You just see if I don't.'

'What are you talking about?' His tone of voice had altered, imperceptibly to most ears, but Miss Cleveley knew voices. She'd trained voices in her time, whole choirs in fact. Oh, yes, indeed! Mr Coleridge had been thrown off balance.

She put the phone down. He'd check the number, but of course it wouldn't mean anything. Thank God not all the red telephone boxes had been swept away with the coming of the mobile phone.

An elderly gentleman waiting outside heaved the door open for her.

'Built these old things to last,' he said jovially, tipping his flat cap to her as he stood aside to let her pass.

'A bit like me,' she said in a fluttery manner, suddenly feeling as though she could walk on air.

The old man laughed and entered the phone box.

Miss Lavender Cleveley waltzed on home, singing quietly as she went.

* * *

Unnerved, but determined not to show it, Brett Coleridge went back to his friends. He was having a party, a men-only type of party. There were just four of them attending.

He needed a drink. The caller had rattled him and blighted the evening.

'Everything all right, old boy?'

The question came from an ex-RAF chap called Nigel. He was thin, sandy-haired and about six feet tall. He'd been trying on a pair of stiletto shoes. They were delightfully pretty: a combination of petrol blue and vivid snake green. The material shimmered and changed colour in the light.

Nigel didn't see the warning look and wasn't really one for sensing a change in atmosphere.

'Just look at these little beauties,' he said, pointing his right toe. The skirt he was wearing had a slit up the side. He held it so that more of his leg showed. He was wearing fifteen-denier tights.

Brett hated tights. He stared at the leg, and at the dress that so beautifully matched the shoes.

The shoes were a size ten and handmade. They had to be. Few women wore a size ten. Nigel was only pretending to be a woman. They all were.

Brett's eyes turned steely cold. His stomach hurt. He felt sick. He wanted to destroy these men and in so doing destroy the part of himself that made him do these things.

'You disgust me,' he growled.

Nigel still hadn't got it. 'Brett, darling—'

A fist smashed into his face. The big man toppled and fell.

Brett laid into him with both feet, kicking his stomach, his ribs, and specifically aiming for his crotch. Nigel was wise enough to cover his private parts, and that wasn't all.

'Brett! Not my face!'

One hand on his privates, the other on his face.

By the time the others had pulled him off, Nigel was in a pretty bad way.

'He needs an ambulance.'

Of course he did. But none of them wanted to call one. None of them wanted to be exposed.

Brett came to his senses. 'We've got to get rid of him.'

'Dressed like that?'

The man who asked was himself dressed in a red dress with white polka dots. His face was round and red.

'That's for him to explain, not us,' said Brett. 'Take care of number one. That's my motto.'

CHAPTER TWELVE

The extras were kept hanging around as crowd scenes and other scenes that didn't feature Jane Austen were being shot.

Honey watched the comings and goings. Nothing of note was happening, as in nobody was getting killed. People — the extras, that is — were just hanging around.

The guy sitting next to her was dressed up as some kind of workman. He told her that his name was Bernard and that he did this kind of work in between doing up old properties for renting.

'I used to work near the Bank of England in the City of London. I was an actuary.'

'A bit like a stockbroker?'

He shook his head. 'No. It's to do with banking and insurance. I assessed the probabilities and possibilities of underwritten bonds, insurance coverage et cetera — on a massive scale, of course. But I wanted a change. I enjoy getting my hands dirty with the houses but need something completely different on occasion. I like to meet people. Besides, the food's good.'

Food had been mentioned. Honey's stomach rumbled. Nobody should diet in February.

With a piled-up paper plate in one hand and steaming coffee in the other, they headed for the extras' London bus.

Downstairs was fully taken. Accompanied by Bernard, she went upstairs and found some free seats with a Formica-topped table at the front.

'Nice view,' said Honey after setting down her goodies.

Bernard agreed. 'Yes, you can see all the way to the other side of the green.'

But Honey was more interested in Martyna Manderley's trailer. Things were happening around it.

A low-loader truck had brought in a new trailer for Martyna's replacement. A crew of brawny men were attempting to manoeuvre the new one into place.

Her companion's attention had already shifted to his plate. Bernard rubbed his hands together then attacked his steak and kidney pudding.

'Very nice! Very nice indeed. Golden crust, prime steak and thick gravy.'

Honey did the same. Not completely guiltless about veering away from a diet, she'd chosen risotto. The food was good. The plastic fork was small and flexible. Small portions only; anything else fell off the end.

Tired of chasing her food around the plate, she watched as the new trailer was hoisted into place. The old one was still bound around with Scene of Crime tape like an enormous birthday present.

Bernard shook his head. 'I bet the insurance company are getting jittery about this film.'

'Hmmm,' agreed Honey. 'I suppose they have to cover the costs of lost production.'

'More than that. Production to final stages is insured. It's been known for insurance companies to pay out millions if something happens to stop production, you know — like the star getting injured or suing for wrongful dismissal. But it isn't always a bona fide injury or death. Sometimes it's a case of the production company deciding the film's a turkey and contriving to get a fat payout.'

'They're covered for most eventualities?'

'Absolutely.'

'Like a top-rate superstar being rubbed out?'

'No doubt they were insured against that actuality for a very reasonable fee. I mean, it's very unlikely for a star to die during production — unless they're terribly old, of course.'

'So the premium was small, but the payout was large?'

'You bet it was!'

Despite the fact that Bernard was less than dazzling as a lunchtime companion, what he said gave rise to some very disturbing thoughts. Potential accidents were all around, just waiting to happen. Murder too, though not so frequently.

She eyed her sorry forkful of risotto and wondered how dangerous it was. What was the chance of it sticking in her throat and choking her? What was the chance of her falling down the stairs when she ventured to take her paper plate and plastic fork to the bin?

At the sound of shouted orders, her gaze moved back to the action outside.

The trailer was being hauled upwards. So far it was only a few feet. 'How about being crushed to death on set? Would the insurance cover that?'

'Simple, straightforward public liability. Your family would be paid out in the event of your death.'

'That's very reassuring. My daughter would probably buy herself a museum, and my mother would very likely move into one.'

No matter how hard she concentrated on what Bernard was saying — and it was pretty sensible stuff — the scene outside the window was getting scary. The crane had hauled the trailer up to roof height. It was swaying and turning on the end of the wire.

Bernard noticed her attention had strayed. 'I expect you're wondering if it's going to fall on us. In the light of what I've told you, you are now considering the possibilities.' He fed and chewed as he spoke. He was a noisy eater.

Honey kept her attention fixed on the trailer.

'It had occurred to me.'

Bernard paused between finishing his steak and kidney pudding and starting on the heaped bowl of trifle he'd fetched himself.

'It looks to be a pretty precarious operation. Quite worrying, in fact.'

'It is?' This was not what she wanted to hear. This was a guy who *knew* about possibilities and probabilities. She forced her mind to return to questions regarding the case. 'I can't believe that anyone would murder purely for money. I must be naive. Would a production company get that desperate?'

'Depends on the fiscal health of Banana Productions Ltd,' Bernard explained between mouthfuls.

Honey frowned. 'Banana Productions?'

'Just a little joke. Banana as in Banana Republic. Can't say I think very much of their operation.'

Honey was losing her appetite. Bernard was coming out with some pretty unpalatable stuff. The trailer wasn't helping. It hung in the air, throwing a long, dark shadow across the ground. A sudden gust of wind sent it spinning slightly. The men on the ground looked upwards, shoving their bright yellow hard hats further back on their heads. They looked nervous. Someone shouted something.

'I guess I don't fancy trifle,' said Honey, already getting to her feet.

'Umm . . .' Bernard seemed loath to leave his dessert.

The shadow of the trailer fell over them.

The men in hard hats cried out a warning. The trailer swayed some more. The bus was plunged into darkness. A vibration rattled through it as the side of the trailer scraped along the roof of the bus.

Honey headed for the stairs. Bernard was right behind her. They could make it — couldn't they?

She punched the button that operated the automatic door. Sluggishly, it opened the first few inches. She tugged it the rest of the way, surprised at her own strength. Electric motor versus woman in jeopardy was no contest.

They jumped off the bus, and the trailer crashed to the ground.

Everyone stared open-mouthed — except for the guys in the hard hats. They christened the trailer's earthbound arrival with a few well-chosen words, none of which were likely to be included in a family-orientated film.

Bernard stated the obvious. 'I don't think anyone's hurt. It just landed heavily.'

'So I noticed. Heavily enough to rock Martyna's trailer.'

Having been delivered a glancing blow, the trailer rolled on its axles before settling sedately.

Suddenly the door of the trailer banged open. The crime scene tape was ripped as a figure swathed in warm woollies bolted out and hurtled down the steps.

'Who the hell's that? Nobody should be in that trailer.'

Bernard shrugged.

'There should be a policeman on duty. Where is he?' she murmured.

'Perhaps nature called?' Bernard offered, in what she could only describe as a boringly affable voice.

'Steve Doherty will kill him!'

Honey looked down and realised that in the panic, she'd brought her plate and the remains of her risotto with her.

'Hold that!'

She banged the plate hard against Bernard's gut. Risotto and plastic cutlery flew everywhere, and she was off in hot pursuit.

There was no sign of the figure.

Think positively, she told herself as she ran. *If you were going to escape this little lot, you'd head for one of the three roads dissecting the ranks of houses.*

But which one?

There were few people around. After feeding their faces for free at the catering truck, a large number of extras and crew had decamped to the Salamander, a small pub with a big atmosphere.

Everybody she asked said the same: No, they hadn't seen anyone running past, they'd been watching the trailer drop. *Did you see that? Did you?*

'I'm not built for this,' Honey muttered to herself as she ran. 'And I'm not wearing a sports bra!'

Boobs jiggling up and down, breath laboured, she loped along at something less than a gallop but more than a trot. Not quite a canter either. A lollop?

She collided head on with Boris Morris. She didn't need anyone to tell her how he felt; he had pissed off written all over his face. Though at this moment in time he was trying to make the best of it. No doubt this was due to the company he was in. She was blonde, slender and had bumps in all the right places — not too many bumps and not too big.

Palms fixed on boobs, Honey slid to a breathless halt. 'Did you see someone run past here?'

As she waited for his answer, she leaned sideways so she could see round him. Whoever had come out of the trailer couldn't have got that far.

'I don't know. I might have. It happens all the time — people breaking in to pinch mementoes of Martyna. Autograph hunters and such like. Look, can we move on from here?'

Boris Morris sounded irritable, as though the murder of Martyna Manderley was done and dusted and he didn't want to be reminded of it.

Honey turned to his companion. 'Did you see anything, miss?'

'I believe I saw somebody running in that direction.'

'Male or female?'

The woman shrugged. 'No idea.'

Honey thanked her. That was when she recognised Penelope Petrie, the movie star.

'Welcome to the set, Miss Petrie.'

'Thank you. I'm glad to be here.'

As she headed in the direction suggested, Honey pondered on why Penelope Petrie had been chosen for the role of Jane Austen. Her accent was far from being plummy English — more Atlanta, Georgia.

She asked a few more people about the well-wrapped-up figure she'd seen emerging from the fatal trailer.

'Did you see anyone?'

Nobody had. No matter how much she asked them to think very carefully, their eyes had a faraway look, mostly fixed on the director's second assistant, who was gathering people for the next scene.

The curly-haired young woman was wearing a multi-striped muffler. 'We need three people over there, and three over there.' She pointed to a parking meter and a rubbish bin fixed to a lamp post. Both needed screening from the camera.

All the world's a stage and everyone wants to be on it. 'Even if it's only to hide a rubbish bin,' Honey muttered to herself.

The policeman who should have been on guard outside the trailer emerged from the on-site lavatory services.

Honey didn't spare the tongue lashing. 'Steve Doherty is going to make mincemeat out of you!'

He paled. 'I had to pee.'

'Why didn't you call for someone to relieve you before you relieved yourself?'

'It's only a trailer.'

'Well, somebody popped in while you popped out, very likely nicking a memento of the great star's life and trampling over the evidence in the process. Forensics are going to be really pleased.'

His face drained of colour. 'Christ!'

Holding on to his cap, he dashed off.

Honey didn't have the heart to tell him that his flies were undone, but then again, he deserved to have his nether regions frozen.

She called Doherty on her mobile phone and explained what had happened.

'Did you see who it was?'

'No.'

That was the trouble with February. Everyone was in disguise. The weather dictated it that way.

CHAPTER THIRTEEN

Someone staying at the Green River Hotel had dropped a mobile phone in room sixteen. If they'd dropped it somewhere in the bedroom, retrieving it would not have presented a problem. Ditto if they'd dropped it in the bathroom — even in the bath. No. They'd dropped it down the lavatory and the flush had been pulled. Said phone had jammed in the U-bend and the water was backing up.

The culprit was a pint-sized three-year-old named Joel. His parents called him their pride and joy. Biting hard on a conciliatory smile, Honey was mentally calling him something else.

In response to Honey's phone call, the plumber promised to come as soon as possible, but was not at all sure when that would be.

In the meantime, he suggested somebody try and fish it out with a wire coat hanger. 'Someone with long fingers,' he added.

Honey felt the finger of fate point in her direction. *The buck stops here*, she thought to herself.

In the absence of other volunteers, she got the coat hanger and the rubber gloves, but it meant she was late meeting Doherty as arranged the night before.

Breath steaming in the cold air, she raced along to the Petite Chasseur coffee shop, situated down a narrow lane just off Quiet Street. The cobbles were slippery with condensation. Slate grey figures moved around in the mist. Given a vivid imagination, it would be easy to believe that some of them were ghosts.

Honey tried not to believe in ghosts. It wasn't easy with Mary Jane around, insisting that the spirit of her dead ancestor haunted the Green River Hotel.

She set her thoughts aside and pushed the door open to the welcoming smell of freshly percolated coffee.

Doherty was already there. As she settled on a spindly bentwood chair, he smiled his crooked smile, only one side of his mouth lifting. He made a clicking sound with his tongue.

'Of all the joints, in all the world . . .'

The clingy smell of rubber gloves tickled Honey's nostrils. 'Not now, Steve. I've spent the morning with my hand down a lavatory.'

He wrinkled his nose. 'Too much information for a guy trying to be Prince Charming.'

'Sorry. I can only think rubber gloves and not glass slippers.'

'The day can only improve.'

She pulled a face. 'I'm not sure about that. I've got a WI event this evening.'

His eyebrows almost went into orbit. 'You?'

'I'm not a member or anything. Though the Women's Institute is a very worthy organisation. Their profile went into orbit after they posed naked for that charity calendar, and their home-made jam and Victoria sponges are said to be out of this world. However, I'm not tempted to join their happy band. I don't make jam like they do, but I do have to go back to the Green River and stuff a few vol-au-vents this afternoon.'

He nodded with sarcastic sympathy. 'Stuffing is a task close to my own heart.'

She didn't respond to the sexual innuendo. It just wasn't in her this morning.

He got the message. 'I've ordered cappuccinos.'

Over two cups of creamy froth, she began telling him about what Boring Bernard had told her. She'd only recently added the prefix to Bernard's name.

'Money is always a prime motive,' said Doherty.

Secondly, they went over the question of why anyone would break into the empty trailer.

'Who the hell was it?'

Honey licked the foam from her lips. 'It could have been Frosty the Snowman for all I know. He or she was certainly wrapped up against the cold.'

'There was nothing missing. We checked.'

Honey frowned. 'There had to be some reason.'

The lazy way Doherty shrugged his shoulders captured Honey's attention. He had a mean look about him when he shrugged — hints of Philip Marlowe. For a moment she forgot the lavatory and the rubber gloves.

'What about height?' he asked, lounging back in his chair as she tried to remember. It was difficult to concentrate when he looked at her like that. There was no alternative but to imagine she was having a cold shower. It worked.

'Tall. Quite tall. It could have been a man.'

'Or a very tall woman.'

'Scheherazade Parker-Henson is quite tall.'

'She needs to be with a name like that.'

'So's Derek Byrne, the sound technician. So's Boris Morris, and Graham who operates the clapperboard, and—'

'Sounds like you're making a shopping list.'

'Works for me.'

Doherty rubbed at his eyes with finger and thumb. 'I'm sorry. All work and no play make Steve a dull boy.' He abruptly stopped rubbing his eyes and looked deeply into hers. 'Fancy coming out to play tonight?'

She shook her head.

He put up his hand, palm facing her. 'Don't tell me. You've got the Women's Institute coming to dine and they all want stuffed vol-au-vents.' He looked both amused and disappointed.

'No . . .' she said slowly, smiling with her eyes. 'I'll do my best to make room for you. But I can't promise. Anyway, there's something else.' She leaned across the table, savouring the smell of his aftershave. 'And if you're a good boy I'll tell you something really exciting.'

He too leaned closer. 'Yeah?'

'Women didn't wear hatpins in their bonnets in the late eighteenth century.'

Doherty looked at her blankly. Then the penny dropped. 'So the pin didn't necessarily come from her bonnet. Maybe the perpetrator was wearing it.'

'Possibly. Oh, and Dick Richards saw the senior make-up artist go into Martyna's trailer shortly before she was found. I think he knows more, but he's being awkward. He likes to think that he's important enough to bestow rather than give information.'

Doherty frowned. 'He told you quite a bit, though we did note this earlier. He must have known that, so why did he tell you the same stuff?'

She thought about it. 'One reason could be that he wanted to implicate that person. On the other hand, he likes other people buying him lunch. I also praised his cooking. He especially likes that.'

'Sad sack.'

'Me or him?'

'Him, of course.'

Honey scooped the chocolate from the frothy coffee and scraped it on to the side of the cup. The flaky bits were barely a mouthful, but still a load of calories she could do without.

Doherty scooped a finger into the chocolate chips she'd discarded and sucked them into his mouth. 'Normally, the first port of call would be her fiancé — but he was in mid-air over the Atlantic, so I've been told.'

'That would have made life easier.'

'Darn right it would. So what motives do we have?'

Honey frowned. 'Professional jealousy?'

Doherty thought about it. The playful cop mask hardened when he turned serious about the job. 'Suspects galore. Fifty per cent were honest about not liking her and fifty per cent tried to hide the fact.'

'Any favourites?'

He made a sound between a *mew* and an *umm*. 'About six.' He began counting them off on his fingers. 'Two make-up artists, the understudy, the wardrobe mistress, the sound technician and the director. I would have included the scriptwriter, but he's never on set — or not much of the time. I discounted the seventh suspect, the person who found the script, on the grounds that she'd never met the deceased before the day of the murder.'

Honey gave him a wry look. 'Though we did have a set-to,' she pointed out. Reaching across the table, she dabbed a paper napkin at the foam on Doherty's upper lip. She'd already made a statement about the argument over her using the mobile phone. 'What a bitch. I think I might have murdered her if I'd been working alongside her for long enough. She accused me of taking a photo to sell to the tabloids. Can you credit it?'

'Would you have done such a lucrative, underhand thing?'

She grinned and made an up-and-down motion with her eyebrows. 'How much do they pay?'

He grinned right back. 'Superstar paranoia. It's crazy that with all the money they earn, they still begrudge someone else making money without their say so.'

'She wanted to control her image.'

Doherty's frown returned. 'Let's take another look in that trailer.'

CHAPTER FOURTEEN

The generator that had supplied power to Martyna Manderley's trailer had been switched off. Inside it was cold and gloomy.

Hands on hips, Doherty stood in the centre and looked around him.

Honey hung around by the door, not liking the musty odour. The trailer was beginning to smell mouldy. The blood might have something to do with that, she thought.

'We're absolutely *certain* there's nothing missing?' she asked.

'Only the stuff Forensics have bagged up and taken in for analysis.'

Despite being icy cold, the inside of the trailer still looked quite luxurious, though bleak with nothing left on the shelves or in the wardrobes.

Once outside, the smell coming from Dick Richards's mobile catering unit was too good to ignore. They drifted in that direction just as surely as the sweet-smelling smoke drifted enticingly in theirs.

Food took the edge off the chill. Doherty ordered two coffees and two bacon baguettes.

Honey protested that a coffee would be enough. Doherty informed her that the two bacon baguettes were for him.

Dick peered down from the counter.

'What did I tell you? Is my food irresistible or not?'

Remembering he was sensitive about his cooking, Honey threw him a big smile.

'Who could resist a baguette as big as this?' she exclaimed.

Richard seemed only half satisfied with her praise. 'You're missing the point! It's not just the size of the portion, it's the quality that counts!'

'Of course,' said Honey. 'That's exactly what I was saying to the inspector here.'

'My sentiments exactly,' smirked Doherty. He was stifling his laughter with mouthfuls of baguette and bacon.

Things sizzled on the griddle above their heads, behind the drop-down flap of the mobile canteen. The waft of bacon and plump pork sausages was like a light from an onshore lighthouse.

Honey sipped her coffee enjoying the warm, pleasant feeling of it inside her.

Doherty interrupted her moment. 'I understand from the director that Martyna insisted that some of the scenes be changed. She wanted Jane to be less of an observer and feistier. And more sex scenes.'

Honey's eyebrows almost took off. 'She wasn't married! Back then respectable girls didn't shed their kit on a first date. Not even on the ninety-fifth date. They waited until they were married. Ask that little woman with the petition.'

'What little woman?'

'Surely I told you? The one who dresses in character – even when she's not being an extra. She got ordered off the set because she dared protest about historical accuracy — or rather the lack of it. It was her who made the comment about hatpins.' Honey giggled. 'She spoke as though she *were* Jane Austen. Even her clothes went some way towards playing the part. Initially she was employed on set but got the push when she kept complaining about the film being inaccurate and not adhering to facts. Apparently, she had a run in with the Wicked Witch herself.'

'Martyna?'

Honey nodded and chewed.

'Did you get her name?'

Honey swallowed and looked at him. She knew where this was going and just couldn't let it get there. 'No, I'm afraid not. But, hey, she was just a little old lady. Too old to be a murderer.'

'Age has no bearing on murder. Mind you, I doubt that our dead superstar could tell her Jane Austen from her Jayne Mansfield.'

'Both historical.'

'Both dead,' he pointed out. 'Anyway, there were plenty of fingerprints on the script, though only one person is responsible for the bloody ones, of course. They're yours and yours alone.'

Honey winced. 'Sorry. Won't do it again.'

'Even if you'd seen the blood straight away, you might have thought it was tomato sauce. Isn't that what they use in these films?'

'Not quite. But anyway, why take it in the first place? Martyna made enemies, more so than friends. Anyone could have picked it up and everyone is a suspect.'

Honey recalled the photograph Doherty had shown her of Martyna's head slumped forward. 'She must have been reading the script when her attacker struck.'

Doherty sighed. 'I think I need to talk to my six suspects again.'

Honey's phone rang. It was Lindsey.

'We've got a gas leak and we've had to switch the supply off at the mains.'

Honey exhaled a big sigh. She could always count on day-to-day life to interfere — just when she'd started to enjoy herself.

'Have you called for a gas fitter?'

'We have, but Smudger's having a fit. If the gas was on, I'm sure he'd put his head in the oven.'

'Lucky it's not, then. Anyway, I don't think the gas is poisonous, just explosive.'

'So's Smudger.'

Lindsey was most likely right. 'I take it he's going prima donna over the vol-au-vents.'

'You'd never think these little things could evoke such a hysterical response.'

'I'll get there as soon as I can.'

'Give my regards to Doherty,' said Lindsey.

Honey was taken aback. 'How did you know I was with him?'

'Your voice is always different when you're with him.'

'We're on set pursuing our inquiries,' she blurted, feeling her face get hot.

The call ended.

Steve Doherty eyed her quizzically. 'Problem?'

'We have a small gas leak, but the fitter is on his way.'

'Good. So the Green River won't be blasted into eternity?'

She didn't want to talk work. The hotel was work. Assisting on the crime front was something else. Being with Doherty was icing on the cake. 'Have you met Penelope Petrie, Martyna Manderley's replacement?'

'Not yet. Looking forward to it, though. I've seen her half-naked.'

She eyed him with one eye closed. 'In a magazine, I take it.'

'Afraid so.' He sounded genuinely disappointed.

'I got the impression from the gossip columns that she and Boris, the director, were a bit more than friends.' She eyed Doherty over the rim of her paper cup. 'So what do you think? Sex or money?'

'Let's start with money.' He winked. 'We'll look into the sex later.'

CHAPTER FIFTEEN

The good news was that the gas fitter arrived and Smudger got over his threat to stick his head in the oven.

Creating and producing high-quality meals was as important to Smudger as being celibate was to a monk. Perhaps more so. Faced with the prospect of having no gas to cook with, Smudger had become totally illogical. Once the problem was solved, he was back to his old self. This meant the vol-au-vents were baked, stuffed and ready for distribution. It also meant Honey could go out tonight.

Doherty rang to make arrangements. 'Zodiac later, Brett Coleridge first. Can you drag yourself away from the WI event? Martyna's fiancé has arrived in town and is demanding to see whoever is in charge of the case. I've drawn the short straw.'

'And you need backup?'

'I settled for you.'

He made it sound as though she was last choice. 'Thanks for the thought. So where is he?'

'He's staying in a suite at the Royal Crescent Hotel.'

Honey whistled. Five-star accommodation at the Royal Crescent Hotel didn't come cheap. Not content with a room, this guy had booked a whole suite.

* * *

The car wheels rumbled over the cobbled road at the front of the Royal Crescent. Apart from the houses constituting the hotel, the rest had been converted into apartments years ago. To rent one would cost a fortune. To buy one would cost an arm and a leg. The one original house would cost more like two arms and two legs, and maybe a head as well.

To deter traffic using the crescent as a rabbit run, bollards had been placed at the Marlborough Buildings end — to the left if you happened to be standing four-square in front of the Crescent. Anyone going in had to turn round and come back out again.

Doherty made provision for this when he parked at the far end, which allowed him to turn more easily when he needed to. His car was a low-slung and very sporty Toyota MR2. Honey's face was still juddering in time with the bumpy surface when they came to a rest. He parked facing the bollards on the grassy side of the road.

Once at a standstill, she had a moment to catch her breath and take in the sweeping curve of the buildings to her right. The greenery of the Crescent's private gardens, so rare in the centre of a modern city, swept off to her left. Beyond that was the ha-ha, a folly of a gazebo type structure pushing up against a glorious row of mature trees. The city's skyline of mansard roofs, square towers and modern buildings was slightly obscured by a distant mist.

Honey sighed. The air up here tasted different somehow. And birds sang. What was more, she could hear them because there wasn't much traffic noise.

She struggled out of the car, the door bumping against the kerb and her knees protesting that sports cars were for younger limbs.

'How fancy is this?' said Honey as they approached the plate-glass doors. 'If only I had the money . . .'

'To buy it?' asked Doherty.

'No! To stay here.'

'Ah! You wouldn't just need the right money. You'd need the right occasion.'

She looked up at him. 'You asking?'

'Absolutely.'

'You buying?'

'How much is it to stay for a night?'

She told him.

He shook his head. 'Maybe when I'm on a chief constable's salary. Better still, maybe I'll switch sides and become a criminal kingpin.'

The impeccably decorated surroundings oozed expensive taste and style. The price of a suite was enough to furnish a house.

Although Honey had never met Brett Coleridge before, his type was familiar. He had a composed, confident expression, his shoulders were held well back, and his clothes were immaculate and expensive. Everything about him gleamed as though he'd been sprayed with high-gloss varnish. His ultra-white silk shirt shone like snow reflecting sunlight, and his tie was navy blue and as silky as a dolphin's back.

He probably sleeps on pillows stuffed with money, thought Honey in a moment of whimsy. Egyptian cotton, of course. Or silk. Embroidered with gold.

Two bodyguards walked three paces behind him, faces inscrutable, chins like doorstops. Both sported headsets. Top-level security types. As though he's the president of the United States, thought Honey, not a silver-spoon son of Lithuanian descent. Lindsey had done the research. Was there nothing that daughter of hers couldn't find out given half the chance?

Brett's grandfather had changed the family name from something unpronounceable. The new name had been picked from a book of poems. Honey filled Doherty in on what she knew, and vice versa.

'Smooth dude and loaded.'

Coleridge looked it. His all-over tan screamed health and wealth. Honey presumed the tan was all over. Naked bathing on a private Pacific island sprang to mind.

Brett Coleridge didn't smile, though she guessed that if he did his teeth would flash pearly white — courtesy of porcelain enhancement. She reminded herself that he had just lost his fiancée. It was only right to offer her condolences.

'I'm sorry . . .' she began.

Coleridge cut her short, looking straight past her to Doherty. 'Are you in charge?'

Doherty nodded and began to offer his condolences. 'I am. May I first offer my—'

'I want you to catch whoever did this. No excuses. No bullshit. Clear?'

Honey saw a swift flash of anger in Doherty's eyes. But he stayed cool — very cool.

'We will do our best, sir. May I take this opportunity to offer my sincere sympathy at the loss of your fiancée . . . ?'

Coleridge seemed not to hear what Doherty said. Either that or he'd chosen to ignore it, as though sympathy was trivial — especially when it came from someone who didn't have a luxury car and matching bank account.

In an outright act of dismissal and contempt, he turned away from them. Hands in pockets, his back a blank wall, he gazed out of the window towards the city.

'And if I hear any further accusation that I may have been responsible for Martyna's death, you'll be hearing from my lawyers.' His voice was as sharp as his suit.

Doherty's jaw lurched from side to side as though he were chewing his tongue.

'I was not aware you were being accused, Mr Coleridge. Is there any reason that I should I be accusing you?'

He sounded so polite, so controlled, when visibly he was chewing on iron. She guessed that inside his head he was using the guy's pure silk tie to wring his sun-kissed neck.

'I realise that local police have limited resources. However, I will not tolerate the finger of suspicion being pointed in my direction. Is that clear?'

'It is clear, sir. I think we both agree that the sooner this matter is cleared up, the better. But why should we suspect you? As I understand it, you were in New York when Miss Manderley was killed.'

'That is correct.'

'I'm sure the airline and hotel you used will confirm this.'

Coleridge spun round. 'How dare you question my honesty! Anyway, I used my private jet.'

'Is that so?' Doherty smiled. It was only a faint smile, yet it spoke volumes. 'If your conscience is clear, then I'm sure you won't mind us checking, Mr Coleridge. Will you?'

The insinuation hit home like a wrecking ball, and the superior facade came crashing down. When he did speak, his tone had turned a full 180 degrees.

'I'm sorry for being curt. As you can imagine, I am rather cut up by all this. I've lost my fiancée. We'd planned a life together.'

Doherty didn't smile or blow a fuse. Neither did he eat humble pie.

'Of course, sir. I quite understand.'

Honey wasn't fooled. Steve had boxed clever. Coleridge had been unnerved by Doherty's promise to check his alibi.

She managed to control herself until they were outside. 'Got him!'

'You reckon?'

'He crumbled! He cracked! He wasn't in New York at all. He came here and he killed her.'

'Why?'

'Um. I don't know.'

'Great.'

'But there's bound to be a motive,' she argued.

'Of course there's a motive. But what is it? Martyna was beautiful and wealthy enough in her own right. OK, a guy could pretend to be in love with her in order to get his hands on her money. But not Coleridge. Come off it. The man could buy a whole studio of leading ladies and not make a hole in his holdings in the Caymans.'

'What about sex?'

'Honey, I just haven't got the time . . .'

'Spare the jokes,' she drawled, pretending to be immune to his humour.

Doherty grinned.

'What?' said Honey, recognising his 'I know something you don't know' expression.

'Did you see his face?'

She nodded. 'Yes.'

'So what did you see in it?'

She thought about the way his expression had changed from arrogance to agitation in one swift step. 'Tension.'

'What else?'

She thought hard and deep. Now where had she seen that guilty look before? She turned her thoughts to times past. Then it came to her. Carl! Her departed husband thought he was pretty good at cheating on her and not getting found out. He'd been seriously wrong and came close to wearing his testicles around his throat.

'Guilt,' said Honey. 'He was doing something he shouldn't have been doing in a place where he wasn't supposed to be. If Martyna had found out she would have called everything off — might also have cut something off.'

'Ouch!' He winced.

'Do you know that for sure — about the cheating, I mean?'

Smug of expression, Doherty opened the door of his car. 'Want a lift?'

She got in. This she had to hear. 'So?'

'Curiosity killed the cat.'

'Never mind the cat! Where's this cat at? Who was he cheating with? And what makes that a motive for him to kill her — rather than vice versa?'

Doherty shrugged. 'Not a clue. It was just the look on his face. By the time I get back to him, he'll be convinced that I know all the details.'

'He'll confess to everything?'

Doherty's grin was fast becoming permanent. 'We'll see, won't we?' He started the car, slid the gear stick into first and let up the clutch. 'Now, I think we need to have a word with Boris Morris.'

'Any particular reason?'

'Someone needs to tell him that old guys with bald heads and ponytails look like a horse's ass with the hair scraped off!'

CHAPTER SIXTEEN

They caught Boris Morris getting into his car. Penelope Petrie, Martyna's replacement, was sitting in the passenger seat, smothered in palomino-coloured fur. It looked real. Honey was immediately sorry for the creature who it had once belonged to.

Doherty leaned down over the open window. Honey lurked behind him.

'Mr Morris,' said Doherty with an air of authority. 'Mind if I have a quick word?'

A thin ponytail of sulphur-tinged greyness whipped round the director's narrow shoulders. Boris's face stilled for a split second. *Like an actor waiting for a prompt*, thought Honey. She clicked her biro into operation and readied her notepad.

The director's thin face was as flushed as ever — probably an age thing, broken capillaries, no doubt brought on by high blood pressure or drink, or possibly both. He looked at Doherty as though trying to remember who he was.

'Detective Inspector Doherty.' Steve reached for his warrant card.

Boris bit his bottom lip and looked decidedly shifty. 'Ah, yes. Of course. Sorry. So many things on my mind. Can we make this quick? Miss Petrie and I have an appointment at six.'

Boris Morris glanced at his gleaming Rolex. The watch was nestled on a bed of hairy arm.

Penelope Petrie got out from her side of the car, long legs first.

'Are they the police, Boris darling . . . ?'

Despite her gravely Southern drawl, if ever a woman deserved to play Jane Austen it was Penelope Petrie. She had an elfin face, large brown eyes and glossy brown hair. Long, fine fingers folded over the top of the car door. At the sight of her perfectly manicured pale-pink nails, Honey shoved hers into her pockets. The appearance of one's nails was not of prime importance in the hospitality trade, especially at the Green River. Dishwashing had a lot to do with it.

'I'm sorry,' said Doherty. 'There are just a few questions I need to ask Mr Boris . . .'

'Mr Morris,' whispered Honey.

'. . . regarding the death of Martyna Manderley.'

Penelope's smile was as pink and warm as a puppy dog's tongue.

'That's quite all right, Detective Inspector,' she said in a husky voice that sounded just an itsy bit contrived. 'You have an important job to do. Please take as much time as you wish.'

Satisfied that this had nothing to do with her, she got back into the car and shut the door. The aura of her presence, plus the lingering pong of French perfume, was left hanging in the air. Only with great willpower did Doherty manage to keep his jaw from falling onto his chest.

'Mr Boris . . .'

'Morris,' Honey prompted him again, giving him a nudge.

'Mr Morris. Just checking on a little technicality. Does the production company gain anything of a financial nature if their leading lady falls by the wayside?'

Boris shook his head. 'Not my department. You'd have to ask the producer. He'd know the details.'

'Can you give me the name of the producer?'

'Certainly. Kevin Bond is the man to speak to. He's what you might call the front-of-house man, the administrator for those putting up the money behind the scenes.'

Honey's eyes narrowed. She'd heard about businessmen and bankers getting together on film projects. 'Am I right in thinking that shareholders are taken on board for individual projects?'

He nodded. 'Yes. That's right.'

Doherty picked up on where this was going. 'So if any of those backers found themselves in difficulty — say through other less prosperous ventures — a little insurance money would hit the spot.'

Boris was outraged. 'You're saying that the company might have killed Martyna for the insurance money? That's a terrible thing to say!'

Looking resigned, though not satisfied, Doherty stepped back from the car. The couple drove off.

'What are you thinking?' Doherty asked.

Honey pursed her lips as she watched Boris's BMW glide out of the Circus. 'I'm placing my money on a sure-fire winner.'

'Didn't think you were a betting man — woman.'

'Only on sure-fire certs. What's the betting that Brett Coleridge is one of the backers of this film?'

Doherty sucked in his breath and shook his head. 'I'm not taking your bet. It's bound to be evens.' Folding his arms he squinted thoughtfully. 'I wonder whether our Mr Coleridge is still wealthy enough to keep a yacht in the Caribbean, or . . .'

Honey raised a questioning eyebrow. 'Or has he downgraded to a rowing boat on the Avon?'

* * *

Penelope Petrie pulled down the mirror above her seat and checked her make-up.

They were heading for dinner at a highly recommended restaurant.

With long, soft fingers, she tested the area around her eyes and felt an instant surge of satisfaction. Her plastic surgeon had done an excellent job. She looked far younger than her forty-five years.

'Well,' she said, still eyeing her peaches-and-cream complexion. 'In my opinion it's just good riddance to bad rubbish — and I don't mean that fine-looking policeman, Boris darling.'

'I know you didn't.' Boris patted her hand assuredly, though anyone could tell from his face that he was unnerved by the questioning. 'All's well that ends well. You've got the part that you thoroughly deserve.'

Sighing with satisfaction, Penelope sat back in her seat and thanked her lucky stars that at some time in the past she'd gone against her better judgement and spent the night in a hotel bed with Boris Morris. It paid to have contacts. Never mind all this stepping into dead men's shoes nonsense. Martyna had got her just deserts.

She smiled, noticing his hands tightly gripping the wheel. Everyone gave something of the truth away with their actions. It wouldn't hurt to have a little fun at his expense, she thought, and almost laughed out loud. Penelope Petrie, born Betty May Cartwright, was good at winding people up.

'Darling, you remember Martyna said I would only get this part over her dead body? Well — you didn't take her at her word, did you? You didn't do the dirty deed just for little old me, did you, darling?'

The car swerved.

'What? Of course not. No . . . How could you think . . .'

A fine sweat had broken out on his forehead.

Penelope threw her head back and laughed. 'No! Of course you wouldn't. Not Morris the Mouse. Not Boris the . . .'

'Don't you dare!'

Surprised that he was shouting at her, Penelope's pink lips remained parted. His response had been far from mouse-like, and it quite turned her on.

She began stroking his arm. 'Come along, darling. Only joking.'

Boris had a long face and sunken cheeks, though his nose was bulbous at the end as though coming out in rebellion against his gauntness. A tic fluttered beneath one eye as he clenched his jaw and sucked in his cheeks.

'It's not funny. None of this is funny,' he hissed.

CHAPTER SEVENTEEN

Room four needed a new coat of paint. The big ceiling-to-floor windows had been designed back in Georgian times to let in lots of light. The fact that the paintwork needed attention showed.

Rodney 'Clint' Eastwood had promised to do the job, but providence, in the form of a nubile twenty-year-old with pierced ears and belly button, had intervened. Honey had tried finding a willing replacement, but without any luck. Every painter and decorator for miles was fully engaged readying winter-occupied hotels for the summer season.

Armed with a ladder, mint-green emulsion for the walls, and frost white for the doors and skirting boards, Honey decamped to room four. The ceiling was first, and her least favourite part to decorate. Regency ceilings were high and had elegant plasterwork around the light fittings and along the picture rail. No joke when you hated heights. But needs must, so up she went. Two hours and a lot of paint splashes later, an interruption occurred.

'Mother, I've got a Miss Cleveley wanting to speak to you.'

Honey looked at Lindsey somewhat blankly.

'She said it's a private matter,' Lindsey added, and opened the door wider.

A small figure stepped into the room.

'Perchance you may remember me.'

Honey looked down from the top rung of the ladder into the upturned face the Jane Austen fanatic.

Today, the wee lady was wearing a floaty pale-mauve skirt and satin slippers. The ensemble was topped off with a knitted bonnet and matching poncho in a velvety yarn.

'I'm looking for my niece. Perdita was supposed to stay with me last night. I made a promise to her mother that I would make her feel welcome in my humble establishment. Perdita and I have always been very close. We share the same taste in literature and history. A sweet creature of whom I am very fond. The police won't help, but I hear tale that you might. I heard that you're a detective.'

Honey got down from the ladder feeling quite elated. Could it be possible that she was being presented with her first case independent of the Hotels Association or the police? It seemed her fame as an amateur detective was spreading.

'I saw your picture in the paper. I didn't realise you were a detective when I apprehended you in the street with regard to my very worthy petition. The fact was that I saw in your edifice the integrity only attributable to a woman of mature years.'

'I see,' said Honey, her smile stiffening. She made a mental note to have a word with that press photographer. Hadn't he heard of airbrushing? 'Well,' she went on. 'Let's discuss your problem over some tea, shall we?'

'Tea? No. I would rather have nothing,' said Miss Cleveley, with a wrinkling of her pert, though rather scoured, nose.

Lindsey, thankfully, had made a pretty shrewd appraisal of the situation.

'Perhaps you'd prefer hot chocolate,' she said with a smile at the aged spinster. 'Very Jane Austen.'

Miss Cleveley beamed and thanked her. Lindsey exited.

'Right,' said Honey. 'Now we're alone, would you like to fill me in on why you've come to see me?'

'Perdita!' Spidery thin fingers half covered in lace mittens delved into a tapestry-printed reticule complete with hanging tassel in a faded shade of pink. Miss Cleveley handed Honey two photographs.

'My niece, Perdita Moody!'

Honey studied the first photograph — a portrait, head only.

Perdita had a handsome rather than pretty face. Honey was drawn to the smile. It was fixed as though she were trying too hard, as if someone had told her to say 'cheese' but her mind was elsewhere.

The second photograph was of a tall, gangly woman standing in front of railings against a background of deserted beach and far-off sea. It wasn't quite a full-length figure, though. Whoever had taken it had cut her feet off. Not very professional, thought Honey, and wondered whether Miss Cleveley was responsible.

Like Miss Cleveley, she was dressed à la Jane Austen. A tangle of curls peeped from beneath a straw bonnet, ribbons tightly tied beneath her chin. The bodice of the dress strained over a broad chest from which floaty muslin draped around narrow hips.

'Does she live alone?' Honey asked.

'She has a flat in Clevedon.'

Clevedon was only some sixty miles from Bath on the west coast — a quiet place with Regency and Victorian houses overlooking the sea.

'And she hasn't gone back there?'

Miss Cleveley shook her head. 'No. I checked with her landlord. She has not been seen since the day she left to work on this film. She wants to be an actress, you see.'

Suddenly thin fingers were gripping her wrist. Miss Cleveley's eyes were glittering and looking into hers. 'I feel, dear Mrs Driver, that I was wrong in decrying these people by merely accusing them of defiling the great works of Jane Austen. I fear more sinister deeds are afoot,' she whispered.

How cold her fingers are, thought Honey. *How firm her grip.*

'Now, what sinister deeds might these be?' Honey asked while making a determined effort to dislodge the bony fingers around her wrist.

'White slavers!' Miss Cleveley exclaimed. 'Dear, innocent Perdita has been whisked off and sold into the harem of some eastern potentate. Can you imagine it? That poor girl at the mercy of a barbaric man intent on ravishing her, as yet, unsullied maidenhead.'

Honey looked into the earnest expression. There and then she decided that not only was Miss Cleveley living à la Jane Austen, but she'd read and digested a great deal too much romantic — and dare she think it — slightly erotic fiction. As for Perdita . . .

'So she didn't report to the film set.'

Miss Cleveley shook her head vehemently. 'No.'

She looked at the first splashes of paint on the bedroom wall. She wanted to say, *sorry, but it's not my job*. But knew full well that she couldn't. The look was so intense, the concern sincere. *And who knows, at her age I too might retreat into a fantasy existence*, thought Honey. *I'd have good company. Mary Jane's already there.*

She smiled and prised away the tight fingers that were now threatening her circulation.

Lindsey reappeared then with a tray of hot chocolate and biscuits and placed them on a small table by the door. 'Enjoy!' she said before making herself scarce again.

'So she hasn't returned home?' said Honey. 'Neither friends nor family have seen her?'

Miss Cleveley took a sip of hot chocolate and gave a demure nod. It was the sort of nod conjured up from reading old historical novels, especially Regency ones. 'Be assured, my dear Mrs Driver, I have made enquiries of all those I knew to be of her social circle and also her family. Need I add that her mother is beside herself with concern? My dear sister is of a most nervous disposition. She frets most desperately if ignorant of her child's whereabouts.'

As Miss Cleveley leaned forward again to impart some other pearl of information, Honey tucked her wrists behind her back.

The whites of Miss Cleveley's eyes were bloodshot and frightening.

'Beware when making your enquiries, my dear Mrs Driver. You are beyond the age of white slaving, I would think, but one can never be too sure. Men have very strange tastes, you know.'

Great! So she was now beyond the pale as far as sexual attraction was concerned, and if a guy did fancy her, it was only because he was an out-and-out weirdo.

'I will do my best to find your niece, Miss Cleveley.'

What am I saying?

There was no proof that Perdita was really missing. Perhaps the girl was a figment of Miss Cleveley's undoubtedly rich imagination.

The small, frail woman drained the last of her chocolate and slipped a few biscuits into her reticule, a fancy beaded and embroidered affair with a silver clasp, before taking her leave.

'For the pigeons,' she said with a winning smile.

'Of course,' Honey smiled back, suspecting the biscuits would be consumed later by Miss Cleveley herself.

After insisting that Honey keep the photos, Miss Cleveley floated out of the room, a slightly comic figure in muslin and old lace.

Honey took another look at the photographs and was still doing so when Lindsey came to collect the tray.

She slumped into a chair. 'My feet are killing me.' She exhaled audibly. 'So what did the old girl want?'

'To find her niece. She thinks she may have been whisked away by white slavers. What do you think?'

Lindsey studied the photos.

'They're almost good,' she said.

Honey adjured to her. 'They are? I wasn't sure.'

'The portrait's better than the full length.'

'I thought so too. She's got no feet.'

'Or hands. Look.'

Honey looked. Perdita was standing in front of some railings, her hands hidden behind her back. And that smile again — winsome yet nervous. Like an actor about to go on stage.

Casper chose that moment to ring and remind her that he was very concerned that Martyna Manderley's murderer had not yet been caught.

'Have you any leads?' he asked imperiously. 'What about the lover?'

'You mean the fiancé.'

'Him. Did he do it? I hope he's guilty. Then we can get this whole thing wrapped up and archived.'

She kept it simple. 'Things are progressing. I've just had someone come to see me about an actress who's gone missing.'

'Oh Lord! Please do not tell me it's someone of great importance. Not a dignitary of the theatre, I hope?'

'Not famous, if that's what you mean. Her name's Perdita Moody.'

She sensed a sudden pause before he made comment.

'I cannot say that I have ever heard of her,' he pronounced dismissively. 'Prioritise, Honey! Prioritise! That is how you should approach this. The murder is the highest priority. Do bear that in mind.'

She rang off thoughtfully.

Don't be ridiculous, she thought to herself. She decided she had to be low on energy and wolfed down a few biscuits from the tray.

'What's on your mind? You look a million miles away.' Lindsey was eyeing her mother with an expression of bemused affection.

'I'm just feeling a little low on energy.'

'I think not. It's that woman. She's infected you.'

'Don't you mean affected me?'

'No. Infected. She's the sort who lives on a different planet to the rest of us. She's drowning in all things Jane

Austen. That's the world she wants to inhabit. Some people are so obsessed with history, that they want to live that person's life and in their time. Hence the bonnet and muslin. Even in winter.'

'You're right. I need to focus on what I'm supposed to be doing not looking for the lost relatives of dotty old women.'

'Unless they pay you to, of course. Did you ask her for a fee?'

Honey felt feeble beneath her daughter's searching gaze.

'I didn't think of that. I was thinking that it was a big coincidence that her niece had left the film set without telling anyone where she was going. Curious, don't you think?'

'Never mind curious. Money doesn't grow on trees — and neither do private detectives.'

'Talking of detectives, the look on Steve Doherty's face the other day reminded me of Philip Marlowe — or of one of the actors playing him. Humphrey Bogart perhaps, or Robert Mitchum.'

'Whatever made you think that, Mother? Steve Doherty's a professional cop, not a gumshoe.'

'Gumshoe?' Honey wrinkled her nose. 'What a daft term.'

'There you are. You don't want to be considered daft, do you? Graham asked what she was doing here.'

Honey blinked. 'Graham?'

'The guy who operates the clapperboard.'

'Oh. Him.'

'I told him I didn't know. He went on to tell me that he'd seen her on the set. She caused a lot of trouble there. Apparently she protested that they weren't sticking to the facts. She got quite angry about it and had to be escorted off the set by three security guards.'

'It took three to chuck out a little old lady?' Honey chortled.

Lindsey slid off the desk. 'Well, she was armed.'

Honey read Lindsey's expression. 'Don't tell me. A hatpin?'

'Correct.'

CHAPTER EIGHTEEN

'I've brought it back!'

Gloria Cross flung the satin corset onto the sofa in Honey's upside-down living room. Honey's private accommodation was in the old coach house to the rear of the hotel. The living room was upstairs and the bedrooms downstairs.

Honey regarded her mother with a hint of envy and misgiving. Gloria Cross always looked the bee's knees, not a hair out of place, make-up perfect, and dressed in something expensive with a designer label. She was also something of a romantic. The corset had been borrowed to entice a possible suitor at the Conservative Club.

'So! Did he fall for your charms, Mother?'

'Kind of. It set his pulse racing too much. The sight of me all laced up in that giddy little number, plus the pill he'd popped and that was it.'

Honey guessed the pill was Viagra and had been bought over the internet.

'So how did he perform?'

Her mother screwed up her face. Lips the colour of crushed apricots chewed to the left and the right.

'He didn't perform. He dropped dead.'

'What!'

'His heart gave out. They're burying him next Thursday.'

'Mother, I'm so sorry!'

'Oh, it's OK. A bit inconvenient, I suppose. It clashes with the literary club. I told you I've written a play, didn't I?'

'Yes, you did.' Honey wasn't sure whether she had, but she sure as hell wasn't going to admit it.

'I want my family's support at the reading of my work. I'm sure you'll enjoy it,' her mother said brightly. 'I've told Lindsey about it.' She paused to think, with her painted fingernail resting on her chin. 'I could just about attend the funeral, though not the food afterwards. That way I'd have time to prepare for my reading. I need to do a rewrite and make sure everything is in order.'

'All that hymn singing at the funeral might leave you without a voice,' Honey pointed out.

Gloria adopted an aloof expression as her eyes fell on her daughter.

'I am not reading my work! I am the writer. An actor is reading it. Someone who knows how to get the most out of a work.'

'I stand corrected.'

Her mother was already onto another subject.

'I've been called back on set tomorrow for the Jane Austen film. I have a big part to play in a crowd scene.'

'Bin or parking meter?'

'What?'

'Nothing,' said Honey. 'I was just wondering about putting the trash out in the morning and whether any of our guests have left their cars illegally parked.'

Her mother was intent on telling her exactly what the professional film makers were doing wrong, and the fact that the leading man had a boil just behind his ear, but that the make-up girls had taken care of it.

She was still talking when Honey began yawning.

'Honey, you need to nap more regularly.'

Honey's eyes snapped open. 'I need to what?'

'I'm off,' said her mother, springing to her feet in super-quick time — for a woman in her early seventies, that is. 'I made sure I had my nap this afternoon.'

'At your age you should,' said Honey, getting to her feet. If she could get her mother out, the bar closed and everyone else where they should be, she might have an early night.

Her mother stopped at the big doors that divided the hotel reception from the big world outside.

'Audrey Hepburn used to take an afternoon nap every day. She reckoned that's what kept her eyes so bright. Just like mine.'

Honey managed a few drinks with the film crew before bed. The cold air made them drink more; at least, that was their excuse.

A wee bit tipsy, she was still sober enough to ask how things were going.

Graham put his arm around her — more out of the need to stay upright than out of affection.

'I think old Boris is giving Penelope Petrie the benefit of his *expertise*.'

'I'm surprised.'

Graham tapped the side of his nose.

'Boris got her the part. It's payback time.'

Derek was standing behind him in the act of raising a whisky to his wide mouth. Judging by the deep frown, he wasn't happy with what Graham had said. Once Graham had loped his way to the gents, he slid closer.

'You don't want to take any notice of him.'

'Why do you say that?'

While awaiting an answer, she put her glass on the bar and nodded at the barman to refill it.

'Boris isn't so bad.'

She decided it was time to be outspoken. 'You mean you all depend on him for your livelihoods and no one wants to rock the boat. I get the impression that Martyna called the shots before. Now Boris does.'

She'd been casual in ordering another drink, her eyes on the barman. Now her gaze darted back to the sound technician. The directness of her look seemed to unnerve him.

Derek blustered. 'It's not exactly that . . .'

'Martyna complained about the script quite a lot from what I can gather.'

'Huh!' he said, tossing his head disdainfully. 'She was finding fault with it every which way she could. Nothing was right as far as she was concerned. She was a right bitch about it.'

'Enough of a bitch to make the scriptwriter want to kill her?'

'I would.'

'Who wrote the script?'

'Bennett, Chris Bennett.'

She eyed him over the rim of her glass. 'What sort of guy is Chris Bennett?'

'Not a clue.'

Honey was intrigued. 'So he's not present during filming?'

Derek frowned. 'No. Not as far as I know. They're not often around. Directors reckon that scriptwriters get in the way.'

'Do they now?'

'True.' He nodded gravely. 'Never saw him at the casting either. Scriptwriters do like to be around when the actors are auditioning. They like to think they've got some say . . .'

'Even though they haven't.'

'There was no one there that I didn't recognise. Perhaps this was one scriptwriter who wasn't interested in who was playing one of his parts as long as he got paid. Can't fault a man for that, can you?'

* * *

It was nearing midnight and Honey's mind was still whirring. She felt a strong need to soak in the bath, warm her bones and muse over what was going on.

She took the corset into her bedroom and laid it out on the bed while she got ready to take a bath.

Eyeing it lying there, all satin and sensuality, she decided her mother was right. It was quite exquisite. She picked it up and stroked the sleek, turquoise satin. She fingered the black lace, still crisp despite its age. The temptation was too much. She hugged it close.

'You are the slinkiest, sexiest and most sensual thing I have ever come across. And you're mine! All mine!' she murmured against the cool, soft satin.

After the warm bath she tried it on.

'Wow! Wow, wow and wow again!'

There was such a lot to be said about constrictive corsetry!

A good buy at auction some weeks before, it made an excellent addition to her quite considerable collection. She bought underwear as an investment. Some she displayed behind glare-free glass on the walls of the living room.

She eyed her reflection and almost purred. Slivers of black lace decorated the boned breast cups. Spines of black satin whalebones ran from bosom to groin. Silk cord provided the drawstrings lacing up at the back to secure a narrowed waist.

She tugged at one of its whalebone inserts and was sure half an inch, perhaps even a whole inch, vanished. Those Victorian gals certainly knew a thing or two when it came to smoothing a silhouette and trimming a waistline.

Bracing her hands on her waist, she pouted and wriggled her hips.

'Does it do things to you, Detective Inspector Steve Doherty?'

No wonder the luscious lovelies of yore had squeezed themselves into these things. Torture for the sake of fashion, but hey, was it any different to some of the modern stuff girls were wearing?

Lacy little thongs sprang to mind — underwear no bigger than a handkerchief. Thongs served no practical purpose, except to entice. No change there then.

She'd purchased the corset, plus black silk stockings and matching garters, from a house clearance sale. The proceeds were going to a deceased estate and the items she'd bought had belonged to the lately lamented — who happened to be a man named Ken, a bachelor who'd never married.

The romantic side of her preferred to think the corset and accessories had belonged to some long-lost love that he'd never quite got over. The more pragmatic was suspicious that Ken himself might have worn them, but she tried not to dwell on that.

Off came the corset and on went the flannel nightdress. That too was Victorian but meant to hide the female form rather than flaunt it.

Once attired in flannel from head to toe, the corset still enticed.

Honey couldn't resist. She wanted to feel sexy. She also wanted to keep warm. She'd wear both. Flannel nightdress against her skin, sexy corset on top of it.

* * *

The feeling that she was not alone woke her up in the wee hours of the morning.

At first she blamed a particularly lurid dream for snapping her awake. That wedge of St Agur she'd consumed for supper could be the culprit. Ditto the gherkins.

However, on second thoughts, she changed her mind. She was one of those rare people who could drag the details of dreams into the cold light of day. She tried to do exactly that, but on this occasion, it just wasn't happening.

Yet she was sure she'd heard something.

Suddenly she heard voices.

Although her heart began hammering, she lay very still, hardly daring to breathe. Low voices, as hushed as softly gasped breath, drifted in from the other side of the door. The door began to open. Light fell in from the hallway.

'Mother? Are you awake?'

Honey shot upright in bed.

'What is it?'

'We've got company. Didn't you hear me knocking?'

Honey blinked. Someone bigger and darker was standing immediately behind her daughter. Steve Doherty!

'What the hell are you doing here?'

Lindsey slid into the room. Sprawling on the Victorian nursing chair she patted her mouth to hide a yawn. 'He insisted.'

Honey dragged the bedding up over her chest in shocked-virgin style. 'This had better be good,' she said grimly.

'Get dressed. We've got a train to catch.'

'Explain.'

'Martyna's husband. He wasn't in New York staring at skyscrapers.'

'Don't tell me. He was airing his assets with members of the board.'

Doherty shook his head and grinned. 'No. Airing his member with two naked broads. But he did have a view of skyscrapers from his window — Canary Wharf as opposed to Manhattan. So that's where I'm going. London. I need to make an early start. I thought you might like to tag along. If we're quick, we should get there just before the rush hour.'

Honey peered at the space on the bedside cabinet where her mobile phone usually sat charging. It wasn't there. She vaguely remembered getting a notification in the night, grabbing the phone and throwing it to the floor.

Doherty looked down at his foot.

'Whoops.'

A jagged spider web had spread across her phone's screen.

Honey groaned and rubbed at her face. 'Can someone tell me what time it is?'

'Five o'clock,' said Lindsey.

'Five o'clock and you've destroyed my phone. Give me one good reason why I should go with you to London.' She directed a snarl at Doherty.

'To nail Brett Coleridge for his fiancée's murder?'

Doherty was looking at her as though not quite sure what he was seeing — not exactly lascivious, just surprised. She'd forgotten the corset. And the Victorian night dress beneath it. How crackers was that?

There was a dual intake of breath.

'What is she like?' Lindsey covered her face in an effort to stifle her giggles.

Doherty stared.

Honey winged it. OK, she could feel her face flushing with embarrassment, but hell, she'd brave it out. Shrugging as though it were perfectly normal to wear a sexy corset over a dowager's nightdress, she spread her arms. 'So what? I wanted to feel sexy in bed!'

'So,' said Doherty, retrieving his chin from the floor and taking a deep breath. 'How come the garment from Rent-a-Tent got in on the act?'

'Warmth!'

She stormed off to the bathroom, slamming the door behind her.

After stripping off both corset and nightdress, she stepped into the shower. The water ran fast and furious, forcing her eyes shut and cooling her head.

She got out and began feeling for a towel. The rail was empty and there were none on the shelf. How about her dressing gown? Her fingers flicked towards the bare coat hook.

She swore.

Ear to the door, she called out, 'Can someone get me a towel?'

Nobody answered. She decided Lindsey had taken Doherty to get some breakfast. Good. She could sneak out naked, get a towel from the closet and get dressed.

She cracked the door open an inch and looked out into her bedroom. Nobody around. The closet was to her left. She picked up the corset, unwilling to let it soak up steam and end up water stained. Holding the bundle of silk and lace against her chest, she tiptoed out into the hallway leaving a trail of wet footprints behind her. The closet door creaked open. The shelves were full. She took out a towel, headed for the living room and began drying herself, shivering and making 'brrr-brrr' noises.

Placing her foot on a chair, she bent over to dry her toes, and Doherty's head appeared over the back of the sofa.

'What the hell are you doing there?' she demanded.

He blinked the sleep from his eyes, sizing her up as though she was available by the pound.

'Great outfit, but maybe not right for where we're going. Don't want to frighten the bellboys!'

She bottled her annoyance and turned tail.

'Nice tail,' Doherty shouted out.

She flicked the corset around to cover her rear.

Back in her bedroom, she put on her underwear and make-up. The latter took a little longer than the former. Concealing the dark rings beneath her eyes, opened before they were ready, was her top priority.

Once her face looked as though she were still alive, she took out a smart suit from the closet. It was navy blue with a white collar and cuffs, and small gold chains looped around the buttons. She matched the outfit with plain black court shoes, Christian Dior diamanté earrings and a matching brooch. A final inspection in the full-length mirror and she was ready for anything.

She sauntered back into the living room, hand on hip, her other hand behind her back. She did a twirl. Naomi Campbell eat your heart out!

'Does this fit sir's requirements?'

He eyed her up and down, though not with quite the enthusiasm as when she'd been naked.

'Hmm. You look good, though I have to say, doll, I was more drawn to the other outfit.'

'Out!' She pointed at the door.

Doherty pretended to be startled. 'I was only saying that I liked what I saw.'

'Out!'

He laughed.

Honey brought her hidden hand round from behind her back. The corset fetched him a hefty whack around the head.

'Ouch!'

'Clear off!'

She beat him all the way to the door. Like a rabbit bolting into a burrow, he shot through it. Honey slammed it behind him.

As she turned away, it opened. Doherty's grinning face poked round. 'Loved the corset,' he said. 'It was made for women like you.'

Laces streaming behind it, the corset flew through the air, smacking the door just as Doherty slammed it behind him again.

She looked down at the corset and smiled. She would continue the facade of being angry with him for a little while, though she didn't mean it. He'd said something flattering about her body. At her age, every word of praise counted.

CHAPTER NINETEEN

It was 8.30 a.m. by the time they reached London Paddington Station. From there they got the Underground to Canary Wharf and a taxi to the hotel where Brett Coleridge had played away.

Miss Rhoda Tay, the hotel manager, was very business-like. She was also small and neat, and had catlike eyes that appraised them and hardened from the word go.

'We have a reputation to uphold and are loath to betray our guests' privacy,' she warned in a crisp and efficient manner.

They were standing in her office, which appeared to hold nothing except a desk and a single chair. A black-and-chrome design formed the walls, as though a giant chessboard had been turned on its side.

'This is a police investigation. I can get a warrant,' said Doherty.

The elegant, petite woman seemed suddenly to grow in stature. 'Are you threatening me, *Mr* Policeman?'

'Detective Inspector Doherty. No, madam. I am just following procedure.' Professional to his size-ten boots, Doherty appeared cool.

Honey was not fooled. She saw a muscle flicker in his jaw. She guessed it cheesed him off to be referred to as though he was Constable Plod from Toy Town.

Miss Tay's expression was as cold and still as that of a china doll. 'Please. Sit.'

She pressed a button. Two cubes appeared out of the chequerboard wall and upholstered panels rose from their backs to form chairs.

They didn't look particularly comfortable and had presumably been designed so that guests did not outstay their welcome.

Honey jumped into the uncomfortable silence left between Doherty and Miss Tay. She explained that she represented the Bath Hotels Association with regard to crimes committed that could affect the tourist trade.

'As someone involved in the hospitality trade, I'm sure you can understand our concern. This is a competitive field, and murder is bad for business.'

Miss Tay seemed to consider this most carefully, although no sign of a change in attitude came to her face.

'I see,' she said at last. 'So Mr Coleridge is a witness?' She addressed Doherty.

Honey jumped in again. 'The police would like to eliminate him from their inquiries. You could help do that. I'm sure Mr Coleridge, or any guest, would appreciate your help clearing his good name.'

Miss Tay blinked in her direction. 'Quite so, Mrs Driver.'

Although her mouth smiled, everything else about Miss Tay remained the same.

Now it was time for Doherty's input.

'We already know the date of his stay and the fact that he phoned the murder victim. We have that person's phone record, so we know she received a call from his mobile phone while he was here. We also know from his secretary that he was staying here that night. All we need to know now is whether he had guests while he was here.'

Miss Tay's eyes swung to each of them in turn. Her red-tipped fingers were interlocked like a tightly shut gate.

When she saw the fingers slacken and then break apart, Honey knew that Miss Tay had been won over.

'I will check with reception.'

A long, elegant finger pressed a button on a touch-dial phone.

'They will come back to me,' she said once her orders were given.

Honey shifted slightly in her seat. A thought had occurred to her. It was a long shot and she hadn't asked Doherty's permission, but, hey, Honey Driver was a free spirit who flew by the seat of her pants.

'Have you ever seen this girl?' she asked, taking out the photos of Perdita Moody and flashing them at Miss Tay.

Miss Tay looked at the headshot first then the full-length version of the missing young woman. She shook her head. 'No, I have not. I suppose you're going to ask me to enquire of my staff. I will have them take photocopies.'

Ignoring Doherty's burning gaze, Honey thanked her and added, 'Her name's Perdita Moody.

'Perdita!' She raised her finely cut eyebrows. 'What a terribly old-fashioned name. It sounds like a character from an Agatha Christie mystery.'

They were interrupted by a knock at the door. The slim young man who brought in details of Brett Coleridge's guests also took the photos to be copied and shown to the staff.

'Ah,' said Miss Tay after studying the printout lying in front of her. 'Mr Coleridge was visited by his two nieces.'

'Was he now?' said Doherty.

Honey noted the cynical tone. On their journey Doherty had informed her that Mr Coleridge had no siblings — thus no nieces or nephews. However, nothing could have prepared them for the next piece of information.

'And a woman who said she was his sister visited.' Miss Tay's pert head jerked up, her expression one of surprise.

'Perdita Moody!'

Coleridge being a cheat and a liar was no big surprise, but Honey was somewhat rattled.

Miss Tay invited them to reception, where she introduced them to the receptionist who'd been on duty that day. Leila Dewar was slim with coffee-coloured skin and dark, melting eyes.

Honey showed her the photographs.

She shrugged and winced and frowned all at the same time. 'It's difficult. We see so many people here. But I think it's the same woman. The features are definitely familiar, but the hair's different. Blonde with long reddish-brown stripes — hair extensions, I shouldn't wonder. But I'm sure it's the same face. And she was tall. That's what made her stand out. She was very tall.'

Doherty sighed. 'Let's have a cup of tea. I think we need to discuss this. Do you do tea?' he asked Miss Tay.

'Of course. I will order some for you. Please take a seat.'

She indicated the array of comfortable chairs and sofas arranged over and around the reception area. Close by was a bistro area with dining tables and chairs. They took a seat close by so they could see both the people in reception and the lunchtime diners.

Miss Tay bid them good day.

Doherty was grouchy. 'So what possessed you?'

'Miss Cleveley was on the film set for a while and so was her niece Perdita. Miss Cleveley informed me she was a budding actress. It wasn't that much of a long shot that Perdita and Brett Coleridge had met. Anyway, he looked the type to stray, regardless of promising to marry. Too smooth. Too sure of himself.'

'Have you ever thought of being an agony aunt?'

'I am already. Have you ever served in a bar? People tell you things. They pour out their hearts and you give them the benefit of your advice,' explained Honey.

'Hardly trained counselling.'

'No. It's better than that. People tell the truth when they're tipsy.'

'What about when you're tipsy?'

She tossed her head and couldn't help looking smug. 'The tippling philosopher. That's me.'

A tray consisting of crockery, a teapot and a plate of small shortbread biscuits arrived. Honey and Doherty tucked in, having had no time for breakfast, then got round to discussing their next port of call.

Besides having a yacht in Antigua, an estate in Scotland and a horse ranch in Kentucky, Brett Coleridge had a penthouse in Kensington.

'Why use a hotel when you've got a penthouse close by?' Doherty wondered aloud.

'Because his nieces were paid for by the hour?'

'Well, I don't think he was inviting them to be bridesmaids.'

Honey paused in the act of reaching for her second piece of shortbread. 'I just knew he was a rat. I've got a nose for them.'

'Quite a pretty nose.'

'And an empty stomach.'

'Me too. I'm starving.'

While she chewed and sipped, her attention drifted. An experienced hotelier, her eyes scanned the clientele milling around the reception area.

There was a dusting of country types up to the city for shopping and lunch or to see their financial advisors or lawyers. There were tourists from every corner of the world. There were also singular types more difficult to categorise — some sitting alone reading a newspaper, others pretending to, looking up each time someone came through the main doors.

'Posh place this,' said Doherty, dunking the shortbread into his tea. 'Upmarket people.'

Honey smiled.

'You'd be surprised,' she said quietly.

She let Doherty prattle on. He was talking about actors and how it must be difficult switching character.

'They must sometimes forget who they are,' he commented.

'As good old Will Shakespeare said, "All the world's a stage" — we're all actors to some extent.'

'Is that so?'

'He was right.'

Doherty grunted and dunked more shortbread.

Honey studied the comings and goings over the top of her teacup.

There were white linen tablecloths, comfortable chairs and a bevy of good-looking wait staff. The food would be good, Honey decided, and beautifully presented.

Businessmen in Gucci suits and shoes, ladies who lunch but never work and ladies who did both. One working lady in particular caught Honey's eye. To those not involved in the day-to-day running of an upmarket hotel, she appeared to be a high-powered executive type. She was wearing a crisp suit with square shoulders and looked all set for a scrum with male colleagues in some city boardroom. But there were small giveaways and Honey knew just what to look for.

Look respectable. Better still, look affluent. She did look affluent. Good costume jewellery, probably, designer clothes, the right make-up, the right colour coordination — faultless presentation. But certain things gave her away.

Her heels were too high and had ankle straps. Her skirt was too short. The legs between were covered in fishnet — but not ordinary fishnet, thick black diamonds covering the finer mesh.

Besides an Italian leather handbag in a fetching shade of coral, the young woman — Honey put her age at around twenty-seven — was battling with a number of carrier bags from Harvey Nichols, Harrods and upmarket boutiques. They shouted she had money to spend.

Doherty suddenly noticed where Honey was looking.

'Looks as though she's been doing some serious spending.'

'Looks as though she's been shopping in Knightsbridge.'

'Wherever. Looks as though she's spent a packet.'

Typical man. Doherty wasn't seeing what she was seeing. His naivety made her smile.

'No. She's not here for the shopping. She's here to sell. And our friend Mr Coleridge was here to buy.'

Doherty looked at her in disbelief. 'She looks too upmarket. What are you seeing that I'm not?'

'She's top-drawer totty and charges a top-drawer price. Stay here. I'm going to have a word with her.'

'Hey, I'm the copper . . .'

'Precisely.'

Placing a hand on his shoulder, she pressed him back down into his chair and looked tellingly into his eyes. 'I am a woman with a missing friend named Perdita Moody. Who do you think she's more likely to open up to?'

Humbled by the obvious, Doherty did as he was told.

'Order yourself some more tea and shortbread,' Honey said to him.

Armed with Perdita's photos in the bag slung over her shoulder, she made her way to the corner table.

Close up she could see the jewellery was indeed costume, but expensive. It looked vintage and as classy as her clothes. The suit was understated — no frills, no bows and no bustling cleavage. Along with the mesh tights, the shoes were a let-down, more Battersea nightclub than Biarritz bistro.

'Excuse me,' she said in a friendly manner. 'I'm a reporter for a national newspaper and I couldn't help thinking that you might be somebody famous. Am I right?'

An impeccably made-up face scrutinised her. Shaped eyebrows only achieved by professional plucking arched in surprise. 'I'm afraid you're mistaken. I'm waiting for a—'

Honey cut across. 'Let's talk. Or would you prefer I had hotel security check your identity?'

Honey sat down and pressed her advantage.

Fingers adorned with gold and diamonds reached for and then tightened over the carrier bag handles. The brown eyes looked wary.

'Are you with the police?'

'Only by the most tenuous of threads. I'm looking for a missing person. Can you look at these? You may have seen her here in this hotel.'

'I'm sure I can't help you.'

Her gaze didn't waver from Honey's face.

'I think Perdita came here to meet a client and now she's disappeared. Her family are worried about her. Wouldn't you want somebody to help your family if you went missing after meeting a client?'

For a moment the knowing eyes held her own as she made the decision whether to help or not. At last she looked at each photograph in turn.

'No,' she said, shaking her head. 'I've never seen her.'

Disappointed but not surprised, Honey considered how to play this. More than one high-class tart frequented this hotel, and like working girls in a factory or office, they all got to know each other. Experiences were shared and grievances aired around the coffee machine or in the canteen. Heaven knows where these girls did their moaning and groaning, but no doubt they did. And girls swapped lots of things — boyfriends, lipsticks. And information!

Honey kept up the sisterly pretence. 'I would much appreciate if you could take these with you and show them around. I've got spare copies. The hotel was very generous. Do you mind?'

Diamanté fingernail inserts flashed as the girl's four lengthy talons tapped thoughtfully on the table.

At last she raised her eyes to Honey's friendly smile.

'OK. But I can't promise anything.'

The woman slid the photos into one of her designer carrier bags. While in the process, Honey glimpsed something that was decidedly not available at Harrods. It resembled a cucumber but was made of rubber and definitely not intended to be used in a salad.

Seeing where Honey was looking, the woman glanced down. 'I've got a living to make. I've got two kids to think of.' She tossed her head defiantly as if inviting her to cop that for bonus-related pay. 'I'm not ashamed of how I make my living.'

'I wasn't criticising,' said Honey. 'I need your help. Besides, we'd do anything for our kids, wouldn't we? Anything also for a friend in trouble?'

The woman's features softened. They were on neutral ground, both hard-working and both mothers. They knew what counted.

She turned her head slightly so she was eyeing Honey sidelong. Honey sensed a question was coming.

'Can I ask you something? How did you know I was on the game? My clients expect class. I can't afford to make errors. I don't want to upset the management either. This is a nice hotel. I like coming here. What gave me away?'

Honey pointed. 'Your shoes. They've got ankle straps and they're too high. Your stockings are a bit of a giveaway too, but mostly it's the shoes. How about sticking to a plain pair of court shoes with a three-inch heel? Plain stockings — I presume you wear stockings, not tights?'

'Absolutely. Most of my clients feel that whoever invented tights should be strangled with them.' She slid a shapely leg out from beneath the table and looked at it. 'Do you think plain tights would be best?'

'Why not? You've got good legs. Great calves and slim ankles. Why muddy the water? Tan or black would be best. But not patterned. And a plainer shoe with a slightly lower heel.'

'You think that will convey the right impression?'

Her expression was interesting. The beautifully made-up face held a vulnerability recognised by all women — the need to meet the approval of their peers. Every girl appreciated what her best friend thought of her outfit.

Honey obliged. 'Power dresser. Businesswoman of discreet and particular taste.'

Heavens above, she thought to herself. *I'm aiding and abetting prostitution! I sound as though I know everything there is to know about the sex game. Truth is, I'm more than a bit rusty.* It occurred to her that Steve Doherty was more than willing to oil her engine. *In time*, she told herself. *All in good time.*

She gave the woman her card. 'Give me a ring if anyone knows anything.'

The woman examined the card. 'Honey Driver. You could pull a trick or two with that name,' she said with an impish smile.

'I'll stick with the bank overdraft,' said Honey. 'I prefer undressing alone in the dark. It's an age thing.'

'Shame. Take my card,' said the girl. 'Zoe Valli. That's my name. I specialise in French polishing, education and discipline, though I've a different card for that.'

The card she gave Honey was black, shiny and embossed with gold lettering. Expensive. It said she was an actress and entertainer.

The card was added to the profusion of other bits and pieces floating round in Honey's bag.

'Are you really an actress?' she asked.

Zoe Valli's smile could best be described as worldly wise. 'We all are, darling. All the world's a stage and all that . . .'

Just what I said earlier, thought Honey.

Zoe Valli called for a good bottle of Chardonnay and invited Honey to join her. She admitted she was there to meet a client.

'I like to have lunch first. It puts the hotel management at their ease. Like it or not, they benefit from my income. I tip well too.' Pulling back her cuff, she checked the time on what looked like a Bulgari. Real or rip-off, Honey wondered. She suspected the former.

'In case you're wondering, it's real.' Zoe pulled back her cuff so Honey could get a closer look.

'Nice,' Honey murmured.

Zoe had gained confidence. She chatted gaily as though the two of them were merely ladies who had arranged to meet up and take lunch together.

They both leaned back as the waiter placed a silver-plated tray on the table. He opened the bottle and offered it for tasting.

Zoe waved an elegant hand. 'Just pour it, darling. I'm sure it will be fine.'

Honey sipped and sipped again. It was good.

She felt Zoe scrutinising her over the rim of her glass.

'Are you sure you wouldn't fancy earning yourself a bit of extra cash? It doesn't have to be hard work. Sometimes it's just baring your breasts and listening.'

Now it was Honey's turn to raise her eyebrows. 'Literally?'

Zoe nodded. 'Money can't buy youth, and Viagra causes heart failure in the elderly. I've banned the damned things. Can't have a bloke dying on the job, can I?'

With thoughts of her mother's experience zinging into focus, Honey had to agree with her. What was there not to agree with? Zoe Valli was pleasant company.

The waiter brought salmon sandwiches on granary bread accompanied by sweet cherry tomatoes, black olives and an expertly quartered lemon.

This lunchtime had turned out pleasant. Here she was swigging back white wine and listening to a fascinating woman. She almost forgot about Doherty, but managed to avoid looking in his direction. She also almost forgot about why she was here.

'By the way, do you know a guy called Brett Coleridge?'

At mention of Coleridge, Zoe's mood changed.

'I don't discuss clients.'

Honey tried to read the look in her eyes. What she saw there troubled her. Zoe was *afraid* to talk about him.

Honey asked a difficult question. 'Is he a pimp?'

Hollywood usually portrayed pimps as flashy, vicious criminals lording it over downtown slums. But that was in films where the characters were as two-dimensional as the plot.

Money can buy almost everything, and to some sex was a commodity like everything else and sold at the top of the scale as well as at the bottom. Only a man who moved in the upper circles could best provide for clientele from that circle. Was that what Zoe was saying with those baby-blue eyes of hers?

Honey decided not to press the point. Besides, she could see Doherty out of the corner of her eye. He was pointing at his watch.

‘Call me,’ Honey said as she took her leave. ‘And thanks for the wine.’ She swigged back the last from her glass. ‘Lovely.’ A sudden thought occurred to her. ‘Look, I think I should give you something towards the price of this . . .’

A palm-sized laptop appeared from one of the bags. Zoe tapped in some figures. ‘It was expensive, but don’t worry, I’ll charge it to the client’s account. He’ll expect to be screwed — and in more ways than one!’

CHAPTER TWENTY

'I'm starving,' said Doherty, eyeing the heavy traffic surrounding their black London taxi. 'Can we stop somewhere before we go to see Brett Coleridge?'

'I've eaten,' said Honey.

'A policeman marches forward on his stomach.'

'I thought it was only armies that did that.'

'A pot of tea and a few fingers of shortbread aren't enough to sustain a growing man.'

Steve won her over easily, and they stopped at a café. Over coffee and chocolate muffins, Honey related her conversation with Zoe Valli.

'Zoe Valli's her professional name,' she told him, matter-of-factly. 'Exotic names attract the punters.'

'Is that so?'

'Hmmm. Yes. Zoe thought the name Honey Driver could go places if I ever decided to make a career change.'

The look of alarm on Doherty's face surprised her. 'You didn't give her your card, did you?'

Honey's mouth was open, ready to take a bite. She looked at Doherty. What was he suggesting?

'I only gave her my card, for Chrissake! Where's the harm in that?'

'Beware. You could get some very funny phone calls at some odd hours.'

Honey felt her stomach churn over like a concrete mixer. She decided he was joking and chuckled. 'You're kidding me. Right?'

Steve held a deadpan expression for a moment, then broke into a smile.

'Yeah. Just kidding.' He bit into a muffin. 'But if anyone does phone, just tell them you're only the maid and Miss Whiplash is out on a call.'

'Stephen!'

He grinned. 'Sorry. Couldn't resist. So come on. Tell me about how you gained her trust and how you reckon she's got a heart of gold.'

Honey sipped her coffee, took another chocolatey bite, chewed and thought some more. She didn't look at Doherty as she was doing this. She wanted him to stew a bit, to make him think that she possessed some pretty juicy info. In a way she did. The look in Zoe's eyes when she'd mentioned Brett Coleridge spelled out what he was in plain language. But Doherty wouldn't see it that way. Hard evidence counted. Female intuition did not. Still, he had to know, so she told him. His reaction was exactly what she thought it would be.

'A pimp? Come on, Honey. Get real. The guy's loaded.'

'Ah,' said Honey, already primed with a thought-provoking response. 'But is he bored? Rich men get bored and do stupid things to keep themselves amused. They take a walk on the wild side, so to speak.'

Doherty looked off into the distance as he considered the probability. At last he stopped chewing, stopped gazing and brushed the crumbs from his chin. 'Let's get going.'

'You don't agree with me?'

Doherty pulled on his coat and settled with the cashier for the coffee and muffins. 'Let's just say I'll keep an open mind.'

* * *

'Boris, come here.'

Penelope was sitting before the mirror in her spanking-new trailer wearing nothing but a straw bonnet and a pair of white stockings held up with blue garters.

The director's jaw dropped before he swiftly closed the door behind him.

The trailer was bigger than Martyna's; Penelope had insisted. 'I don't want her trailer. She died in it. And while you're about it, get me one at least five feet longer than hers. I deserve it.'

Somehow Boris had persuaded the financial people to put up the extra to ensure the new star's satisfaction. He was about to get his just reward and was salivating at the prospect of it.

His hands slid down her shoulders and cupped her small breasts. He liked small breasts, especially if the nipples were large. Penelope's were perfect.

He rolled her breasts in his palms. His mouth and tongue savoured her neck, her jawline and her lips. His hands slid lower, smoothing her belly and diving between her legs.

'I'm going to make you a star,' he murmured against her ear.

'And I will make you my own special stud,' she murmured back, her voice sultrier than in any part she'd ever played. 'You deserve it for getting rid of Martyna Manderley. You really do.'

'I'd do anything for you, darling,' he said thickly, his breath catching in his throat. 'You know I'd do anything for you.'

'Yes, darling,' she said, her catlike eyes glowing like coals. 'Of course you would.'

CHAPTER TWENTY-ONE

The concierge at the building in which Coleridge had a penthouse was Eastern European, judging by his accent. He was also built like a brick wall and standing squarely in front of them, reluctant to let them in.

'You must have appointment. You not have appointment.'

'I don't need one.' Doherty produced his warrant card. 'Now, how about your papers?' he asked, his voice thick with authority. 'This might be a good time to check them.'

The brick wall crumbled, and they were let in.

Honey was still huffing and puffing from their brisk walk from the Underground. Not wishing to get stuck in traffic again, they'd opted for the Tube the rest of the way.

'You're unfit,' Doherty remarked.

'Untrue! I wish I'd only eaten one muffin, though. I need to burn this off. Can we take the stairs?'

Doherty looked at her as though she were mad.

'You ate three,' she reminded him.

He looked thoughtful for a moment. 'There are better ways to burn off the calories, but I take your point. However, we're talking penthouse and the fifth floor. That's ten flights of stairs.' He held his head to one side and raised an eyebrow. 'I'm up for it if you are.'

They headed for the elevator.

Gleaming doors of brushed steel hushed open, and they stepped in. Doherty pressed the button marked 'Penthouse — Private'. Whoosh! Up they went, the movement almost imperceptibly smooth.

The stainless-steel doors hushed open again in a glass-covered atrium at roof level.

'We've arrived,' whispered Honey. 'He's got bodyguards.'

Two sides of beef in tuxedos padded across the extra-thick carpet.

'I think you may have come to the wrong floor,' said beefy number one. Beefy number two stood two paces behind his colleague and four sideways. They were each sporting spindly earpieces like secret service agents. They looked like the rough end of the service, the sort that get the more physical stuff like breaking people's legs or having them fitted for cement jackets.

Doherty pulled out his warrant card for the second time since arriving here. Honey lingered behind. Bravery wasn't something that came spontaneously. She preferred a lengthy build-up.

The guards scrutinised his identification. Honey could tell by their faces that they harboured an aversion to policemen. Not that Steve Doherty gave a stuff.

'Mr Coleridge has guests.'

The guy sounded as though he was speaking from inside a hollow drum. Honey assumed he'd received a blow to the larynx at some time.

'That's what we are. Guests,' said Doherty.

The big goon frowned at a piece of paper in his hand. 'All the guests are here. There's no one else to check off the list.'

Doherty didn't budge. 'We're the floor show.'

'You must go.' Beefy number two shook his head and took a few small paces forward, trying to force his unwelcome guests back into the elevator.

'I'm sorry. But Mr Coleridge is indisposed at the moment. Perhaps you could call again?'

'You cannot refuse to let me see him.'

'Do you have a warrant?'

'I don't need one. I just want to talk to him.'

'No.'

Doherty took a step forward and stood with his legs slightly apart. Honey had noticed that men did that kind of thing when they were being confrontational — as though they kept some kind of weapon in their trousers.

Beefy number one gave the halt sign with his hand, his palm held inches from Doherty's face.

The air hung heavy with testosterone. Honey snuggled in behind Doherty. 'Shouldn't we summon reinforcements?' she hissed.

Doherty ignored her jelly-tot voice and squared up to the big guy. 'You licensed to do that?'

In the split second the guy had to think about it, Doherty had grabbed his fingers, bending them backwards until his knees buckled. While one guy grimaced with pain, Doherty addressed his companion.

'Stop this pissing about or your pal will be picking his nose left-handed from now on. Tell Mr Coleridge I want to see him. *Right now!*'

Honey held her breath. At the same time she pictured the general layout of where they were just in case they needed to make a swift exit. The stairs, she decided, were the best bet. Smash open the door and run like hell!

As it worked out, there was no need. Beefy number two reluctantly stepped through the copper-coated doors of the penthouse.

Beefy number one was still on his knees, his face screwed up in pain.

His companion re-emerged, followed by Brett Coleridge looking like James Bond — smart suit, smooth hair and strong jaw. He didn't smile. Didn't bid them welcome. His jaw was clenched tight enough to burst his fillings.

A smirk appeared on his face. 'Ah yes! The policeman and his sidekick. Sorry, I don't remember your rank — or name for that matter.' He checked the gleaming Rolex on his wrist. 'I can give you three minutes. What's this about?'

Doherty's expression was impassive, but Honey knew that underneath the cool veneer he was aching to give Coleridge a mouthful of broken teeth.

'It's regarding your statement. We've checked on your whereabouts at the time in question, and it appears you were staying at a London hotel, not one in New York. Do you have trouble telling the difference, sir?'

For a moment Brett Coleridge's face looked as though it had been fashioned from marble. He stood dead still. Given his good looks and perfect grooming, he could have been taken for a tailor's dummy.

He managed one word. 'So?'

'We know you've been lying about your whereabouts. Now's your chance to explain—'

'Look, it would tarnish my image if the news ever got out about what I was really up to when Martyna was murdered. You know what the tabloids are like.'

Honey was a great gal for judging on first impressions. Her first impression of Coleridge was of a man who thought too much of himself. Her opinion had changed little, except that she disliked him even more. Her mother might like him. He had the right trappings for her. But not for Honey. She jumped in with a question to throw him off guard.

'Do you know a young woman named Perdita Moody?'

She sensed a loosening at the point where his jaw met his ears.

'Can't say I do.'

He said it slowly as though he were wracking his memory banks. Honey flashed him the photograph.

'Her,' she said, stabbing at the enigmatic young woman.

He made a dismissive gesture with his right hand. 'I see quite a few girls nowadays. It goes with the job.'

'Excuse me?' said Honey.

Doherty took the photograph from her. 'Members of staff at the hotel are willing to testify that this woman had an appointment with you. She was positively identified.'

Coleridge frowned. 'What does this have to do with the death of my fiancée?'

'Perhaps you were set to benefit from her will.'

Coleridge's manly complexion turned puce. 'That's ridiculous. I have my own money!'

Honey pressed on. 'Isn't there a clause whereby the leading lady is indemnified against non-appearance?'

When he turned on Doherty, Coleridge's expression seemed almost sincere in its anger.

'How dare you!'

Doherty bounced right back. 'This woman . . .' He stabbed at the photo. 'Were you having an affair with her?'

Coleridge blanched. 'Certainly not! She was just a . . .'

Honey sensed satisfaction on Doherty's face. Coleridge's disquiet had caused him to blunder into a declaration — a declaration that until now had remained unspoken.

'Just a what, Mr Coleridge?' asked Doherty.

It's the eyes, thought Honey. *I can see from his eyes that he's beaten.*

With a nod over his shoulder, the two sides of beef were dismissed. They lumbered off; their thick shoulders hunched around their stocky necks.

Coleridge wiped at the beads of sweat that had broken out on his brow. He must have seen they'd noticed.

'I have guests. The room is full of hot food and hot air.' He chanced a grin, bemusement at his own joke.

Neither Honey nor Doherty was swallowing this.

Honey said what she was thinking. 'You're very resilient — partying even before your fiancée is buried.'

His look visibly hardened. 'Friends and family. The dinner party was their suggestion. They felt I needed a distraction. That's why it's so early in the evening.'

Honey opened her mouth to suggest that meeting girls in hotel rooms was pretty distracting, and he'd been doing that on the day Martyna was killed.

Doherty interjected sharply. 'So Perdita — and the other girls?'

Good old Steve! Honey harboured an inner glow. They were so alike, him and her. Yet again they'd been singing — or rather thinking — from the same hymn sheet. They'd had the same things in mind.

Coleridge held a steady gaze. 'Girls? What other girls?'

'Your nieces.'

'Oh. Them. I was interviewing. I own a very large nightclub — the Venus Trap — you may have heard of it.'

Both Honey and Doherty shook their heads. 'We're from out of town.'

'I was interviewing girls for the cabaret. There's no law against that, is there?'

'Were you alone?' Doherty enquired. 'I mean, other than your two *nieces*.'

'No. I had two other girls drop in on me. They work at the club too. They're good to have around to give a second opinion.'

Somehow Honey couldn't buy this. The fearful look in Zoe Valli's eyes kept coming back to her and wouldn't go away. What had she feared? Was Coleridge really a pimp?

'Are they dancers?' Honey asked.

Coleridge nodded. 'Yes.'

'With their clothes on?'

Coleridge threw her a condescending grimace. 'Which century are you living in? They're pole dancers. What other sort would you expect in a nightclub?'

'Did you hire Miss Moody?' asked Doherty.

That grin again, as though there was a secret to keep. 'No. I offered her a job, but she didn't accept.'

'Why?'

'She had reservations about taking her clothes off. Told her it wasn't ballet. What the hell did she expect?'

Doherty asked another question. 'Do you know where she went after leaving you?'

His eyebrows rose quizzically. 'Home? Or another interview. She said she had other options.'

'Have you any idea where?'

'Quite frankly, I don't care. I only care about my dead fiancée. So what are you doing about that, Detective Inspector?'

'My best.'

Beneath the cool exterior, Doherty was bristling. Honey felt an overwhelming desire to reach out and touch him, to tell him she knew how he was feeling and if he really couldn't help himself, he should go ahead and punch Coleridge's lights out. She'd tell anyone interested that it was self-defence — or that Coleridge had fallen down the stairs.

The polished-marble look returned to Brett Coleridge's sun-bronzed features. His top lip curled in a blatant snarl.

'You've no idea who killed her, have you? You think it's me, but it isn't.'

Honey couldn't let it go there. She kept seeing Miss Cleveley's elfin face.

'And Perdita?'

He half turned away. 'Missing tarts and minor entertainers turn up like bad pennies. They always do. See yourself out.'

Doherty and Honey were left facing their reflections in the gleaming copper doors. They only opened again to let out the two sides of beef.

'He's right,' said Doherty as they went down in the elevator.

'That Perdita will turn up?'

'No. That we haven't a clue who murdered Martyna Manderley.'

CHAPTER TWENTY-TWO

Honey struggled to keep up with Doherty as he stomped along Kensington High Street. She didn't like him when he was in a mood, and felt herself missing his witty repartee. He clearly wasn't happy at her for getting sidetracked with the missing Perdita Moody.

'Who the hell has a name like that anyway?' he grumbled.

Honey had to admit that she wasn't inclined towards that sort of name. Too pretentious by far for her taste, along with Araminta, Camilla and Ariadne.

'I promised Miss Cleveley that I'd investigate. She was helpful about the hatpin.'

'The hatpin!' Doherty's tone was disparaging. 'We were there to question Coleridge about his exact whereabouts when Martyna was murdered.'

'You're forgetting that Perdita had an appointment with him.'

'Screw Perdita. She's irrelevant to the case.'

'She might be a witness of some sort, and he could have had her bumped off.'

Doherty looked at her as though she'd taken leave of her senses.

'Honey, this is South Kensington, not the Bronx! And Coleridge is a multimillionaire businessman, not a Mafia godfather.'

She shrugged as she sidestepped a crocodile of tourists talking excitedly in a variety of foreign languages. The crocodile neatly segregated the two of them.

'It can happen anywhere,' she called out over their heads.

He shouted back, 'Not on my case!'

The crocodile passed. They came back together.

'May I reiterate that we were there to question him about his exact whereabouts when she was murdered?' said Doherty as they came back together.

Honey smirked. 'We *know* where he was. Interviewing nubile young women, probably in a state of undress.'

'As many have said before me, it's a crap job but somebody has to do it.' He glanced at his watch. 'Time to go home. We should just make the four fifteen from Paddington.'

Honey remained thoughtful. She knew where Doherty was coming from. He had a job to do, and that was to find Martyna Manderley's killer. However, there was something about Miss Cleveley that stayed with her. There was also something about the look she'd glimpsed in Zoe Valli's eyes.

Doherty misconstrued her reason for being silent. 'No good being stroppy with me. You were the one who promised some old dear that you would look for her niece. I let you drag me into it.'

Honey pursed her lips. 'I want Coleridge to be guilty.'

'Just because he's suave, sophisticated and thinks too highly of himself is no reason to charge him with murder. There has to be proof. And so far we've got bugger all!'

He said the last few words with great feeling.

'Do you believe he was sweating because he'd just eaten a hot curry?'

Doherty shrugged. 'No. But what the hell . . .'

'You need to question those girls he was with. Are they reliable alibis?'

He stopped dead and rocked backwards and forwards on his feet. He flung his head back in frustration.

'Yes! Yes! Yes! While you were having that tête-à-tête with the tart with the heart, I checked out the details with the night porter and the concierge. No way did Coleridge leave in time to do the dirty deed. He left at ten in the morning on the dot. The doorman swore he left at ten.'

'You sure?'

'Positive. Normally he might not have noticed, but Coleridge gave him a big fat tip that caught his attention.'

'How big and fat?'

'Fifty pounds.'

Honey gaped. It was a red-letter day at the Green River if someone left a twenty-pound note.

'London prices,' she said, shaking her head.

She didn't see Doherty hail a taxi or see it slide like a black beetle against the kerb.

He got impatient. 'Well, come on. We'll miss the train.'

Honey stayed put, a string of thoughts whirling around her mind like a carousel. Should she stay or should she go? Her thoughts erred towards the former.

'I'm staying on . . . I think . . . I've got this feeling . . .'

The chirping of birdsong sounded from the depths of her handbag.

'Honey? Are you doing a Mary Jane on me?' Doherty was holding open the taxi door.

Honey whipped out her phone. 'Hello?'

'Hi. It's me. Zoe. I've got a fix on your friend. She's got an apartment next to an old pal of mine. Can you come on over? I'll introduce you.'

'Yes. Hang on.'

She told Doherty who it was and why she was phoning.

'Casper won't like it,' he said, whimsically wagging his finger. 'You're not sticking to the job in hand.'

'Stuff Casper.'

Pushing past Doherty, she positively lunged into the back of the taxi. Once seated, she went straight back to the phone. 'Zoe? I'm on my way.'

Doherty barely escaped getting his jacket caught in the slamming car door.

'Hey! That's my taxi.'

Honey pulled Zoe's card out of her bag and gave the driver the address.

'See you in Bath,' she shouted out of the window.

Doherty waved in a desultory manner and looked crestfallen. She guessed he'd been looking forward to the journey home — an hour and a half to themselves, her head probably falling onto his shoulder.

So what was she letting herself in for? Why so set on finding the elusive Perdita? The look in the old woman's eyes, that's what. That look had touched a chord, the same chord it would have touched if someone she loved was missing.

CHAPTER TWENTY-THREE

Brett Coleridge took a trip to the bathroom before re-joining his guests. Standing before the mirror, he wiped the sweat from his brow with a wet flannel. He then washed his hands and applied a touch of lotion from one of the many bottles ranged along the shelf.

By the time he'd finished, he was back in control of himself. Placing a hand against his chest he checked his heart rate against the gold Rolex gleaming on his wrist. He was fastidious about his health and had a full check every month. Business could kill you. His father's death had shown him that. Well, it wasn't going to kill him. He worked to live, not the other way round.

He checked his reflection, took deep breaths and smoothed a stray hair or two back into place. A face brimming with renewed confidence looked back at him. Hell, he could have been a film star. He had the looks.

The visit from Doherty and the woman had thrown him off balance. Not that he hadn't been warned. That director prat Boris Morris had seen to that. Questions about funding the film and indemnity insurance; that's what he'd thought they'd come about. Who stood to win from Martyna's death? The answer was simple: a lot of people.

That didn't mean that he wasn't upset about her death. Of course he was. They'd been made for each other. Like him, Martyna was the centre of her own world and expected everyone else to orbit around her and her needs. She never, ever went out of her way to suit other people. He was the same and viewed it a sign of strength rather than selfishness.

So what that he'd been playing around with a couple of whores from the Venus Trap? It didn't make him a murderer. Neither did it point the way to any irregularities in the film's accounting process.

Hearing Perdita Moody's name had shaken him. She was just one of many girls wanting a break in the world of showbiz. Shame she'd been so bloody prudish. He'd put her straight as to what he was looking for. Hell, we're talking lap dancers! They wear sequins, not muslin!

Not that it mattered much that one solitary woman had rejected his offer. Her sort were like taxis; there would be a whole string of them along in a minute. Still, there had been something about her, something that spoke to the secrets lurking in his soul.

Satisfied that everything was cool, he re-entered the boardroom.

'Problem?'

The man who spoke was named Hans Hoffner, Coleridge's only guest this evening. He had *not* come for dinner.

Coleridge flashed a brilliant smile that shone in stark contrast to his year-round tan.

'Nothing I couldn't handle — and nothing to do with the job in hand,' he added with a lilt.

Hoffner's expression did not alter one iota. His eyes were a chill blue, like icy water reflected in the sky. They were presently fixed on the man who'd encouraged him to invest in the film.

Coleridge hid his discomfort by aiming for the drinks cabinet.

He poured Hoffner a Scotch; foreigners drank more Scotch than the whole of the British Isles. Coleridge poured himself a single gin, then changed his mind and added an extra measure. He'd need it.

Hoffner's eyes were like lasers, bright but bereft of warmth.

'I know you appreciate a single malt,' Coleridge said with forced bonhomie.

'You know me well,' said Hoffman, thawing slightly. 'I like Scotch. I drink nothing else. Even with dinner. My wife scolds me about this. She says it is not correct dinner etiquette.'

The two men laughed, toasted and drank.

Hoffner's expression turned serious. He had white hair, white eyebrows and a thick moustache. He reminded Coleridge of the German Kaiser as depicted on an old First World War poster, except that Hoffner's moustache was white.

The gin went down well. One sip followed another.

Hans Hoffner raised one snowy-white eyebrow. His white hair made him look distinguished rather than old.

Coleridge immediately felt more uncomfortable than he had before. Everything depended on keeping Hoffner on board. He was the main backer for the Jane Austen film. Martyna, bless her heart, had never quite got her head around a German financier being keen on Jane Austen. 'He's not a fan,' Brett had explained. 'But Jane Austen is a worldwide phenomenon. He smells money. That's what makes him tick.'

He hadn't added that Hans also bankrolled his own portion — a payback for helping him out with a business venture that had gone bad.

Brett's father, Malcolm Coleridge, had been a hard-working northerner who knew how to 'make brass', as they said up there. Brett had not inherited his natural business sense. He liked the kudos but didn't have the skill in making money. However, he was outstandingly good at spending it.

Hans leaned on the table, his whisky left for the moment, his hands clasped before him.

'Explain to me again how the death of our leading lady might ultimately lead to greater profits.'

Brett's smile was one of relief. He'd judged Hans to be a man bereft of emotion. Seemed he was right.

Brett sat more easily in his chair, gulped back some more gin and composed himself. *Humour the guy; he knows less about film-making than you do.*

'Surely you've heard the saying that there's no such thing as bad publicity?'

Hans fixed him with those cool, discerning eyes.

Brett Coleridge felt them burning into him and knew he'd misjudged the man.

'I have taken on a considerable amount of your company's debt, Mr Coleridge. I decided to back this film because others of its kind have continued to spawn profits long after their initial release. So please, do not try to hoodwink me. If this film fails, you too will fail. I shall call in all your debts to my bank, so make it profitable by any means possible. Otherwise I will ruin you.'

CHAPTER TWENTY-FOUR

The taxi dropped Honey off at an address in Chelsea. Zoe was waiting for her outside a solid red-brick building that shouted 'I'm posh' from pantiled roof to white-marble steps.

Zoe waved. Honey waved back.

She couldn't help noticing that Zoe looked different from earlier in the day. She was wearing a scarlet coat with a matching pillbox hat. Her stockings were black. *Definitely not tights.* Her boots were an eye-catching red, trimmed with black piping, possibly Jimmy Choo.

Honey decided a compliment was in order, after all she had been very helpful. 'You're looking good.'

'Darling!' Zoe air-kissed super-celeb style. 'So glad you approve. I took your advice.'

'So I see. I'm flattered.'

'Our friend is on the third floor. She's calling herself Candy.'

A chauffeur-driven limousine glided up to the kerb. With a little wave, Zoe bobbed into the back seat and was gone.

Candy Laurel was dressed in pink hot pants matched with a pink-and-white polka-dot bustier. Her legs were long and brown and she wore skintight white boots. She had a china doll type of face: her skin silky-smooth, her lips a tiny rosebud of redness, her eyes big and luminous, and her hair bottle blonde.

The biggest surprise of all was when she stood to shake hands. Candy was at least six feet tall and had a Barbie doll figure — too slim and androgynous to be human.

Her manner was cute and courteous, her voice as sweet as a sugar mouse.

'Zoe's told me all about you. Please sit down. Make yourself at home.' Her voice had a bit of a squeak to it — something between a child's and a rubber toy.

Home was a top-notch apartment, all sleek and shiny with a white carpet, white furniture and pink accessories. The accessories jarred with the minimalist décor and recessed lighting. Pink gingham cushions and pink, fluffy rabbits were littered along the sofa and on the chairs. White table lamps with pink gingham shades sat on glass-topped tables. It was like an adult's idea of a nursery, very odd but very expensive. Honey wondered how much the place was worth and whether Candy owned it or only rented it.

Candy pushed forward a large box of expensive confectionery that was sitting on the glass-topped coffee table.

'Help yourself.'

Before Honey had chance to indulge, Candy picked one out with sugar-pink fingernails and popped it into her mouth.

Seeing her slender figure and no trace of guilt in the beautifully made-up face, Honey figured they couldn't be that high in calories. What was one small piece of candy between a slender waist and a pair of love handles? Anyway, she needed the energy.

She outlined briefly why she was here. 'I understand you might have a handle on Perdita Moody.'

Candy nodded and popped another selection from the half-depleted box into her mouth.

'If you mean did I know her, then the answer's yes. She was on her uppers for a while. I let her doss down here.'

Candy's terminology — and her accent — was not exactly top drawer, but somehow it didn't seem to matter. Honey could see why she appealed to men. She looked like an oversized Barbie doll and acted like one. But there was more to her than that. Her kindness shone through. To Candy it came as second nature to put people at ease. Besides that, she was as pretty as the proverbial picture, and like a cute little rosebud, ripe for plucking. Bearing in mind her friend Zoe's profession and her own assumptions, Candy was one who got plucked quite a lot.

'I've been told she was looking for a job.'

A square of pink and pistachio-green confection found its way between Candy's Cupid's bow lips.

Relentlessly chewing, Candy nodded. 'She asked me if there were any vacancies in my line of work. She thought I was an actress.' Candy squealed with laughter. 'I suppose I am. In a way.' She tossed her head back, her laughter deeper now and gurgling in her throat. 'She changed her mind once I explained what I did. The sort of acting she had in mind was more serious and didn't require you to take your clothes off.'

Honey frowned. She'd presumed Candy followed a similar line of work to Zoe. Had she got it that wrong? Perhaps Candy was the type of actress whose films were way beyond the nine o'clock watershed — or not fit for mainstream viewing at all. But she couldn't ask outright.

'So,' she said slowly. 'Are you and Zoe in the same line of work?'

'Not quite,' said Candy in a high-pitched voice. 'I did try it for a time, but I didn't like it. I didn't feel loved. And it was all so businesslike — not much socialising, you know? And I do like to be part of the in-scene.'

Honey nodded as though she understood, when in fact she hadn't been part of it for years.

Candy plucked another pink-and-white candy from the box and popped it into her mouth.'

'So I decided to diversify,' she said breathily, her little head perkily swapping from one side to another on her alabaster neck.

Honey tried to get a handle on where this was going. Was she on the game or wasn't she?

There was nothing for it but to ask her outright. 'So what exactly . . . How did you diversify?'

Candy's pretty pout widened into a smile. 'I'm a gossip girl! That's the name for it. I get seen in all the right places and with all the right people. And all for money. Lots of money. Eventually.'

Honey felt her jaw dropping further and further as Candy explained what she did. Basically she was one of a bunch of girls hired to trap the rich and famous. Honeytraps. Tabloid tarts.

Candy seemed to read her mind. 'It's all business and it leads to other things. For instance, I've done a few glamour shots for some top newspapers. We're like . . .' She paused as her eyes rolled in the act of thinking. 'We're playmates. We're not tarts.'

'Of course you're not,' said Honey, not really sure they could be anything else, but swayed by Candy's niceness. 'Does it pay well?'

'Excellent. We "bump into" the object of our assignment by accident, though of course it isn't an accident at all. It's all arranged beforehand, though the man involved doesn't know that. Rich and powerful men are very arrogant. They think they can have everything they see, and they go all out to get it.'

Candy's cynicism made Honey feel quite uncomfortable. There was more than a passing resemblance to the colourful candy she was eating. The wrappers looked pretty and innocent enough. The calories on the inside were downright dangerous.

'So what else besides money do you get from this?' She was thinking jewellery, property and perhaps a nice little sports car. The latter appealed. She'd like one herself.

Jaw still working hard, Candy more or less repeated what she'd already said. 'We further our careers in the process. We become overnight celebrities and once everyone knows your name then the sky's the limit. People want to make you an even bigger star than what you are.'

Candy offered Honey another sweetie. Honey declined.

'I'm on a diet.'

'I'm not,' said Candy with childish charm. 'I'm never on a diet. I couldn't do it. I just *love* sweets! That's why I'm called Candy. See?'

Too right. She was living up to her name. She was also kidding herself. How long would the bimbo body last, Honey wondered. Candy could be heading for a career change if she didn't slow down. Barbie dolls were as meaty as scraped-clean chicken bones. Candy could end up as round and full of suet as roly-poly pudding.

Pink, green and lemon candies winked provocatively from the open box. Irresistible!

'Go on. Have another.'

Candy wafted the box beneath Honey's nose.

Her fingers disobeyed her brain and she took one.

'So what's the score? How does it work?'

Pink lips pouted. The blue eyes rolled and flecks of black fluttered from caked mascara as Candy considered the question.

'I get a phone call from the agency. Date, time and place. I make contact. Mr North does the rest.'

'Any time?'

'Depends on the event.'

'What sort of places?'

The blue eyes rolled around her head again. No doubt in search of profound thoughts.

'Well . . . you know,' she said in her Tweety Pie voice, 'something to do with their professions or hobbies. I have to do a bit of homework beforehand, of course. Take golf. Mr North paid for the very best professional golf instructor he could find. He said I took to golf like a fish takes to water. Isn't that something?'

'Wonderful.'

'I've got quite a good golf swing, so I've been told. Wanna see it?'

'I'll take a rain check on that. So what happens then?'

'Well!' Candy swung her fingers over the remaining array of handmade luxury chocolates and candies. 'I get them in the right room at the right time and usually without their clothes on — or at least in a very compromising position. Mr North does the rest. His photographer pretends to be room service, and there you have it. Photographs and an exposé from yours truly. Sex sells, so they say.'

Honey couldn't argue with that. As Candy talked a thought crossed her mind. *Would I have the guts to do something like that? Nah!* A bit late now to be bimbo material. Still — different men, different tastes. Some guys liked older women. There was one fly in the ointment she couldn't quite get out of her mind. Her mother would kill her. So what about Candy's mother?

'Does your family know what you do?'

Throwing back her head and exposing her long white neck, Candy expelled a deep and throaty laugh.

'My mother thinks it's the best job I've ever had. I'm one of the new wave of celebrities — a nobody who was gutsy enough to become a somebody. I get asked to do all sorts. I've been invited onto a reality TV show. That should help my career some. My mum thinks I don't need to worry about being famous. She's convinced that I'll end up marrying a millionaire. I suppose it's likely. I don't mind if it doesn't last, as long as I get a good divorce settlement.'

'Yes. I guess you would.'

In her mind, Honey was comparing Candy with Lindsey. They had to be around the same age. How would she feel if her daughter was a professional 'honeypot', a lure to the rich and famous?

'Did it take much getting used to — after all, you had a pretty ordinary background, and a job in a chemist shop, I understand.'

Acting like pincers, long fingernails of passion pink studded with sparkly bits neatly lifted another candy — almond-topped this time.

'Yes, I did have a pretty ordinary life before all this happened, and it was strange to start with. First, you kind of miss being boracic lint — purse empty, credit cards up to the limit. Then wham! You've got money in the bank.' She smiled sweetly. 'But I manage.'

'Going back to Perdita Moody; she stayed here for a while?'

'Three days. She went out every day to the agencies. She brought back copies of *The Stage* and other news rags advertising small bit parts and chorus lines.' She shrugged. 'I don't do that anymore myself. They pay peanuts. Play my cards right and I get coconuts.'

'Did she find a job?'

Candy's brow developed more creases. Honey surmised that deep thinking was in progress.

'She says she found a job in the paper, and then she had a phone call. She wrote down the directions and the name of who she had to meet.'

'No idea who it was with and where she was going?'

There was a rattle of paper as Candy lifted the empty top layer from the candy box. The first candy from the second layer disappeared between Candy's Betty Boop lips.

The pink-and-white girl with the extra-long legs pondered as she chewed, or at least that was how Honey interpreted the vacant look.

'Nope,' she said, shaking her head. 'Can't remember.' Suddenly her complexion lit up like a hundred-watt bulb. 'Tell you what. I've still got the newspaper. She circled the more interesting ads with a pen. It's in the rubbish bag. Out in the kitchen.'

She pointed.

Honey sat. So did Candy. Neither of them moved.

'You'll find it in the rubbish bag,' Candy repeated. Her eyes and her fingers were fixed on the ever-decreasing candy layer. 'In the kitchen.'

Honey got the message. There was no way that those finely honed fingernails were delving around in cold pizza, limp lettuce and wet newsprint.

'Thanks,' murmured Honey.

There was no cold pizza, limp lettuce or much of anything else in Candy's rubbish bag. Her kitchen was as modern and shiny as the rest of her apartment. The black-granite worktops and glossy-white units reflected Honey and her surroundings. There were no telltale food smells, no containers marked tea, coffee and sugar — no electrical appliances of any sort. If they did exist, they were behind closed doors. This, Honey decided, was far from being a working kitchen. This was a model kitchen, something to grace the pages of *Hello!* or *OK!* — one of them would do an 'at home' feature of Candy at some time in the future.

She smiled. Smudger would laugh at the fact that the cooker hob had never been switched on. He'd term it a kitchen to be photographed, not to be used. One hour in a decent kitchen and he'd have everything turned on, pots and pans on and off the hob with lightning speed.

There was no sign of a trash can. Honey proceeded to open and close the doors of the shiny, unused units. There was crockery, glassware and cutlery, but no food. Eventually she found the bin neatly hidden behind a false set of drawers. Thankfully, all it contained were newspapers. She guessed they'd all belonged to Perdita. Candy might appear in newspapers, but she wasn't the sort to read one. She wasn't the sort to read anything.

It felt deliciously wicked to spread the grubby news sheets out on the virgin surfaces of Candy's pristine kitchen. She flicked swiftly through the pages looking for marked adverts. There were plenty of adverts, but none circled with biro. Not until she got to the very last page, just before the football section, did she find what she was looking for. She read the advertisement.

CALLING ALL DOLLIES
Over six feet tall?
Best in a dress?
You could be exactly what we're looking for.
New dance troupe being formed.
Contact Miss Lampton at . . .

A telephone number followed. Honey fetched out her phone and called the number.

A crisp female voice answered. 'Can I help you?'

Honey explained who she was looking for and why. 'An aunt in Bath is worried because she hasn't been in touch. Can you help?'

'I'll check our files.'

Candy never came out to enquire if she'd found anything. Honey wondered if she'd ever entered the kitchen at all, except perhaps for a glass of water.

The woman on the end of the phone came back.

'She is on our books.'

Honey breathed a sigh of relief. This was good news indeed.

'Can you tell me where she is?'

'I certainly can. She's in Swindon rehearsing with a newly formed dance troupe. They'll be specialising in nightclub work.'

Honey got the instant impression that the woman didn't believe her story about the aunt in Bath. She asked for the address where she could find them.

'The Goat's Cheese Nightclub. They've filled the vacancies,' she said imperiously. 'They won't want anybody else. I must admit to being quite surprised. There's more around of that sort than I gave credit for.'

The phone went dead.

Honey didn't have a clue what she meant. But never mind. Swindon was on the way home. She headed for

Paddington. It might very well be midnight by the time she got back to Bath, but she didn't care. She was solving this case by herself, if you could call it that. Diminutive Miss Cleveley had needed her help and it had turned out that Perdita had met the dead actress's fiancé — who just happened to be a sneaky, two-timing, son of a bitch . . . Let it be! After finding Perdita and checking her out, it was back to finding out who had killed Jane Austen — or more accurately Martyna Manderley. Hopefully it would turn out to be Brett Coleridge. OK, she admitted to herself, she might be biased.

CHAPTER TWENTY-FIVE

The train from Paddington Station to Bristol, calling in at Reading, Swindon and Bath Spa, was packed. Honey was squashed like a sardine among work-weary people with big bodies and questionable hygiene.

The crowd thinned a bit at Reading, enough for the air to get sweeter, plus it gave her the chance to slump into a spare seat.

The train pulled into Swindon railway station on time. Piles of people fell like a tidal wave onto the platform. Honey piled out with them.

The Goat's Cheese Nightclub was in Swindon Old Town, an area boasting less of its old heritage than its name implied. Swindon had been a railway town where huge workshops had once employed thousands of people. Steam had given way to diesel, and the railway had been superseded by roads, tailbacks and articulated trucks. The once-proud Victorian buildings had been turned into designer outlets, a museum and trendy offices. And, of course, a nightclub!

Honey considered the name. Goat's Cheese? Someone must have been totally paralytic when they'd chosen that one. Hey ho! There was no accounting for taste when under the influence.

Strapped for time, she took a taxi.

The nightclub took up two floors of the old warehouse-style building. It was too early to be open. The door was solid oak and had no knocker, but it did have a doorbell and an intercom panel.

She pressed the button. After she repeated the action, a woman answered.

'I've come to see Perdita Moody on behalf of her aunt.'

The female voice on the other end asked her to wait. After a few minutes' wait, she was back.

'She's not sure she believes you. Can you give me her aunt's name?'

'Miss Cleveley, but sometimes Jane Austen.'

'Hold it.'

Silence fell for a few more minutes before one side of the double doors clicked open and a moon-faced woman peered out.

Thick black eyelashes fluttered suspiciously as the woman gave her the once-over.

'I'm here in peace,' Honey said. 'Honestly.'

Humour was lost on the woman. Or perhaps it was just that she always had a hangdog expression — the corners of her mouth pulled down by heavy jowls. Her cheeks were rouged a less than fetching ox-tongue pink.

She opened the door a bit wider; obviously her invitation to come in.

In turn, Honey gave her the once-over. She was wearing a teal-coloured suit. The collar of a purple-satin blouse put paid to the high-powered look she might have had. So did the pearl choker and heavily made-up face.

'I'm Clara Beaumont, the Dollies' manager,' she said in a deep, husky voice. 'The troupe's rehearsing, so you'll have to wait till they've finished. You can watch from the wings if you like.'

Honey said that she would.

'God, but this thing is itchy. Excuse me.'

Clara whipped off a long wig, exposing soft woolly hair crimped close to the skull.

'I'm Clive without my wig, but still prefer to be called by my professional name.'

'Fine by me,' Honey retorted.

Clara led her along a crimson-carpeted, dimly lit corridor. Clara was a man, but what a handsome one, gliding rather than walking ahead of her.

She eventually found herself in the wings with an excellent view of the stage.

'You can wait here,' said Clara. 'I won't be long.'

'Should I . . . ?'

She'd been about to ask her host whether she should make herself known to Perdita right away or wait until the routine was over, but Clara had already marched off.

Honey's attention snapped back to the stage. A troupe of about ten very tall women was just reaching the end of a number from *Chess*, the musical. Something about a night in Bangkok. Very suggestive.

A tall, slender man she perceived to be the choreographer was snapping his fingers.

'One more time, girls. Take your positions.'

He was wearing a pink chiffon scarf around his neck teamed with a pale-grey sweater and matching pants.

The performers were all wearing sparkly, spangly outfits in varying shades of violet, purple and indigo.

In her youth she'd toyed with the idea of going on the stage, singing her heart out and kicking up her legs. Unfortunately her singing voice wasn't up to much and her legs were a bit on the short side. On top of that, the wages and prospects hadn't appealed. Performing was a precarious career unless you had luck on your side, or a private income — or no other option!

She recognised Perdita from the photos. The dress was something else. It clung to her slender frame and was slit to the thigh on the right-hand side. Sequins set into her tights sparkled like stars all up her leg and onto her hip, terminating at waist height.

The choreographer checked Perdita's pose using his own to show her what he wanted.

The music restarted. Honey tapped her foot in time to the beat. She began to mutter the few words she remembered.

Flash! There it was. Everything coming together.

'Shit!'

Honey's eyes were open. Yes, they were moving elegantly and sexily in their glamorous gowns. To the uninformed onlooker, they were just gloriously tall, athletically built girls. But if you looked more carefully . . .

She recalled the photographs. How stupid that she hadn't seen it earlier. Perdita keeping her hands and feet off camera. She was clearly sensitive about her unfeminine features.

Once the routine was over, the chorus line came towards her in a flash of spangles and sequins.

'Perdita?'

Perdita stopped, expression wary. The rest of the girls swept on by.

Honey studied the handsome face. It was just as it was in the photograph.

'Your aunt sent me to look for you. She was worried. Can we talk here?'

Perdita nodded, produced a handkerchief and began wiping away her lipstick. The wary look persisted. 'Are you something to do with the police?'

'Not in this instance. Your aunt is worried about you. But there is something else I need to ask. It's to do with a man named Brett Coleridge. I understand you went to see him at the Regency Garden Hotel. Can you confirm that?'

Perdita's heavily made-up face stiffened.

'I'm sorry. I don't mean to alarm you. It's just that there's been a murder . . .'

Perdita gasped. Her hands made a slapping sound as she clasped them over her chest. Her moony eyes were fear-filled.

'Who? Who's been murdered?'

She sounded as though she were about to faint.

'Martyna Manderley.'

Her attitude changed. 'That bitch!'

'I see. So you didn't think she was a great star devoted to her work?'

'Devoted to herself, more like. Mind you, she was very fair in one respect. She treated everyone the same. Including the man she was supposed to be marrying.'

The face, plastered in stage make-up, froze as the obvious thought came to her. 'You don't think he did it, do you?'

'You tell me. What makes you say she treated her boyfriend badly? Did you hear them arguing?'

Perdita smiled. 'She carried a mobile phone in her knickers when she was on set. If it rang everything stopped. Anyone else would have been given short shrift or thrown off the set. But there, she was the star. Anyway, he phoned her. I was standing right behind her . . .'

'Hiding a lamp post?' Honey immediately regretted saying something so trite. 'Sorry. It's just that you're so tall.'

Perdita laughed. 'Something like that. Anyway, as I was saying, she said his name so I knew it was him. She then went on to call him every name under the sun. Something bad had happened that she didn't approve of, but I couldn't work out what it was. She called him a pervert; I do know that.'

'Why was that?'

Perdita shrugged. 'How should I know?'

Honey knew it was rude to stare, but it was hard not to. In her eyes, there was something flawed but fascinating about Perdita. It wasn't so much the sequinned gown or the marcasite earrings dangling from her ears; neither was it the make-up. It was the mannerisms, as if she was looking at herself, though far more elegant.

'You went to see him at his hotel. How did you know he'd be there?'

A deep flush suffused Perdita's cheeks.

'A job. I went to ask about a job. I'd heard he was looking for tall girls. I didn't know what for until I got there.'

'You weren't interested?'

'No. Not my kind of thing.'

'You'd been dropped from the production. Didn't that make you angry?'

Perdita glowered. 'If you mean did it make me angry enough to kill her, no. Not literally, anyway. Only in my dreams.'

One particular question niggled. 'What sort of job did Coleridge offer?'

Perdita pursed her lips and shrugged.

She pressed a bit further. 'Nude stuff?'

Perdita shrugged again. 'Stuff.'

It was obvious she wasn't going to be drawn any more on that count. Honey switched.

'How long were you there?'

'Shouldn't you be asking what time I arrived?'

'Oh! Sure. Do forgive me. I haven't been doing this very long. Sorry.'

'That's OK. I arrived about three o'clock, the receptionist announced I was here, I went up in the lift, into the penthouse and back down again . . . let me see . . . an hour? Yes. One hour in total.'

Honey gave Perdita her mobile phone number. She also promised to set Miss Cleveley's mind at rest. 'But why don't you phone her yourself?'

'Number one, she fusses so, and I've got such a lot of rehearsing to do before we go on tour. Number two, Aunt Jane doesn't have a phone.'

'Because Jane Austen didn't have one.'

'That's correct. I usually phone a neighbour. Just tell her not to worry. Tell her I'll be seeing her before very long.'

Honey promised. There was just one very trivial question that was bothering her.

'Do you mind if I ask you . . . ?'

'Look,' she said, pre-empting her question. 'It's different for some of the Dollies, but I'm a woman and my name is Perdita.'

'Your aunt speaks of you as though you've never been anything else but a woman. She doesn't condemn you for it. That must make things a bit easier.'

Perdita jerked her firm jaw. 'It helps. We all need to be loved. Do you have a family?'

The question brought warm visions to mind — of Lindsey, first and foremost.

'I have a daughter. She's eighteen, though sometimes she seems older than me. She's so clever.'

Lindsey would curl up with embarrassment if she'd heard her. But she didn't care. She was proud of her daughter.

'You were supposed to report to the Jane Austen film set but didn't turn up. Was there any reason for that?'

Another deep throaty laugh. 'Because I didn't want to be part of my aunt's stage set. Thanks to her I became as obsessed with Jane Austen as she is; she loved dressing me up in that stuff and to be quite honest, I enjoyed wearing it. I've read all the books. *Pride and Prejudice* is my favourite of course. Everyone's favourite don't you think?'

Honey agreed with her. A vision of Colin Firth on a BBC production, wet and wearing very tight britches came to mind.

'But I'd had enough. Come on, look at this gorgeous dress.' The sequins sparkled and danced as Perdita twirled on high heeled shoes. Her false eyelashes fluttered like bat's wings as she leaned close into Honey's face. 'I'm going to be a drag artist. I was made for it. No more muslins and bonnets. Jeans and jumper like anyone else when I'm not Perdita — when I'm Peter. Though, I will miss my Austen name. I chose it myself. But now . . .' She spread her arms. 'I'll be like Danny La Rue, smooth and cool off duty, and the glamorous Perdita when I'm performing. Life couldn't be sweeter.'

'It sounds amazing. Coleridge didn't have any openings for you?'

Perdita, Honey couldn't think of her as anything else, pulled a face.

'I went along there looking as I would if I was on stage. He took it the wrong way. Was completely sucked in. I ran.'

'I don't blame you.'

'Tell my aunt that I'm OK. That I'm happy. Also tell her that I'll be in touch and that Jane is forever in my heart.'

'I will.'

'Do you have a doting aunt?'

'No. But I do have an interfering mother. She lives in Bath.'

'Does she live with you?'

'Oh, no,' Honey replied with more vehemence than she should have used. 'She's a very active lady with her own apartment and a small business venture dealing in second-hand designer clothes. It's called Secondhand Rose.'

'I know it,' Perdita shrieked. 'Wonderful items! I've bought quite a few things in there that will suit my new career down to the ground. They cater very well for taller girls; and they sometimes get quite long day dresses and wide-fitting shoes.'

'I'll tell her that you are a very satisfied customer.'

'You do that. Brilliant shop.'

The train journey home was uneventful, except for a call to check in with Doherty.

'I'm thinking of my mother's reaction,' she told him, a smile fixed on her lips, 'if I told her of the glowing praise I received about her shop.'

'Surely that's a good thing.'

'My mother sometimes boasts of catering to the rich and famous. Truth is, her most ardent customer is neither of those things. Not yet anyway.'

CHAPTER TWENTY-SIX

Miss Cleveley had to be informed immediately the following morning, Honey decided. Ordinarily she would have phoned to say she was coming, but Miss Cleveley lived in the past. She didn't believe in phones because the blessed Jane had managed quite well without one and so could she. She only hoped there was a flushing loo just in case she had the need. Jane Austen wouldn't have had one of those either.

The small Georgian cottage was halfway up a narrow street leading to Camden, an area of Bath that was uphill all the way from the city centre.

By the time she found the right address, she needed to rest, bent almost double, hands on knees, breathing hard.

A few minutes later she felt slightly less like she needed an oxygen mask. Pulling another gallon of air into her lungs, she finally managed to reach up and give the door knocker a good hammering.

She was almost back to normal by the time Miss Cleveley came to the door.

Her blue eyes lit up her small, heart-shaped face.

'Oh, my dear Mistress Driver, how nice of you to call on me. I see you have been sorely taxed by the steepness of this street. Pray come inside. A small sniff of smelling salts and I dare say you will be quite remarkable again.'

Honey didn't fancy the smelling salts. She'd had them shoved beneath her nose once when travelling on a National Express bus going from Bath to London. The mixed aroma of full lavatory, smelly socks and cheeseburger had been too much to bear.

She suggested a cup of hot chocolate instead.

'Indeed. I will prepare a tray immediately.'

Miss Cleveley showed Honey into a pretty little room. The wallpaper was scattered with tiny blue rosebuds on a grey background. The doors, skirting and other paintwork were pale-blue eggshell. The furniture looked as though it might have been pinched from Jane Austen's house down in Hampshire or her lodgings when she resided in Bath. There were no curtains at the windows, only shutters painted in the same blue as the doors and window frames.

Honey accepted Miss Cleveley's invitation to sit down. She chose an antique balloon-back chair.

As crockery clattered around in the kitchen, Honey eyed a painting above the fireplace. The subject was a youngish man in army uniform. He had a handsome, open face and one side of his mouth was upturned in a smile. It looked fairly modern. She wondered how Miss Cleveley could allow such a modern painting to adorn her house. There again, she supposed the fact it was a painting rather than a photograph went some way to living in the past.

Miss Cleveley came in carrying a tray. The cups and saucers looked like Crown Derby. Honey took a steaming cup, noting that the cups had no handles — just like those back in the eighteenth century.

OK, she thought. Just smile and take a sip. It'll oil your vocal cords. In all honesty it wasn't her vocal cords she was worried about. They worked OK. It was what she needed to say that worried her.

'I take it you've seen Perdita and she's all right,' said Miss Cleveley.

Honey was taken off guard. 'Yes. How did you guess?' She rubbed her fingers against her thigh. Cups without handles were tricky when the tea was piping hot.

Miss Cleveley settled herself in a button-backed chair and looked at Honey with a twinkle in her eyes.

'I know you have. You've seen her and know her little secret. The truth of the matter is there on your face for all to see.'

Hot chocolate and outright surprise that Miss Cleveley was so broad-minded were difficult to deal with at the same time. Before she dropped it, Honey quickly returned the likely very valuable cup to the tray.

'She can live whichever way she wants to,' Honey said.

Miss Cleveley nodded her head primly.

'I am very glad to hear you say that, my dear Mistress Driver. Pray, my dear lady, do not look so surprised that I speak of Perdita with such tolerance. Perdita informed her mother of the way things were when she was but thirteen. My sister, God rest her dear departed soul, and I shared everything, including our darkest secrets. She informed me of the shift in circumstances.'

Honey was taken aback as a coquettish look came to Miss Cleveley's face.

She eventually found her voice. 'You and your sister must have been extremely close.'

'Indeed we were, God bless her. We had no secrets from each other and shared everything we had. We have even shared our men.' She nodded at the painting of the dashing officer. 'That very presentable gentleman is Victor, my sister Emily's husband — deceased now, but a broad-minded and energetic man in his time. He took care of both of us very well. Do you not think him handsome?'

Honey almost choked on her hot chocolate. *Victor was taking care of both of them? Is she saying what I think she's saying?*

She checked Miss Cleveley's twinkling eyes and almost blushed. There was no mistaking that kind of twinkle. Reading her eyes was like reading an open book — something like *Fanny Hill* or the *Kama Sutra.*

Miss Cleveley went on. 'I am so glad that your good services resulted in such a positive outcome.'

Honey raised her teacup. 'Here's to the Dollies' success.'

'Indeed,' said Miss Cleveley, repeating the gesture. 'Perdita is much more suited to dance and light entertainment than films. I told her that before she got the part in the Jane Austen film.'

'I thought she was merely an extra,' Honey said.

'Not at first. She had a small part. Thanks to Martyna Manderley it got cut. I could have killed her for that. So could Perdita. Being an extra is such a downgrade.'

Honey felt a distinct chill, and her chocolate suddenly didn't seem quite so hot. She'd been convinced that Perdita and her aunt had nothing to do with the murder. Now she wasn't so sure. Once again Miss Cleveley read her expression.

'Pray do not let your suspicions run away with you. You have met Perdita. You know she is a kind-hearted soul. As for me . . . well . . .' She laughed a light, ladylike laugh. 'I am just an old and fragile woman . . .'

Elizabeth the First had said something like that just before she'd led the English to give the Spanish a right hammering.

'So she left Bath straight after?'

Miss Cleveley nodded. 'She was quite distraught about being dropped. And then, of course, she went for that interview with that terrible Brett Coleridge. If that make-up girl had not put such ideas into Perdita's head, she might not have gone to London in the first place.'

'Which make-up girl was that?'

'The one that Manderley woman was overly friendly with, if you take my meaning.'

Honey took a sharp breath. Martyna Manderley didn't just have a fiancé in her life, she also had a lover.

CHAPTER TWENTY-SEVEN

Gloria Cross, Honey's mother, chanced poking her head around the kitchen door. She should have known better, of course. Smudger the chef was king in the kitchen.

'Hannah, I need to speak to you.'

Honey sighed. Her mother was the only person in the whole world who called her by her given name. That is, with the exception of her bank manager. She had the distinct impression that he didn't want to get too familiar in case she asked him for a bigger overdraft.

'I'm a bit busy,' she said.

Her mother was adamant. Smudger hated uninvited people coming into his kitchen, but Gloria ignored his glower.

'You've been called,' she said to her daughter.

'Called what?' asked Honey, her attention fixed on the planning of a wedding menu. She and Smudger were bent over it. The bride had requested bread-and-butter pudding as a dessert choice. One of her childhood favourites, she'd said.

Smudger's dark glower got steadily darker. He wore dark glowers as frequently as he wore his chefs' whites.

'What do you think?' Honey asked.

Unable to keep his feelings in, he snarled his considered opinion.

'Bread-and-butter pudding looks a wee bit bland alongside brandy chocolate rococo with sugar orange tracery.'

Honey's mother Gloria was nothing if not persistent.

'Did you hear what I said? You've been called as a walk-on.'

Honey looked up. Ordinary film extras were part of crowd scenes, passers-by and background material. Being a walk-on meant having some kind of exchange with the main characters.

'I suppose I'm a maid coming in with a tray. Or a pickpocket, perhaps. Hollywood will wait with bated breath, or perhaps not. Unfortunately I'm needed here. Dumpy Doris phoned in to say she slipped in the supermarket and dented something . . .'

'Possibly the supermarket floor,' muttered Gloria.

'Now, now, Mother. Don't be cruel.'

Dumpy Doris was big, but you couldn't hold that against her. She would come in and cook or clean or waitress at a moment's notice. Having her around was like having three separate people all rolled into one. She was that kind of size and had those kinds of skills.

'You wanted to get away from this place and now you're turning a good offer down,' her mother pointed out.

Honey began ticking off Smudger's suggested alternatives to bread-and-butter pudding. To her mother, she said, 'Call them and tell them I can't make it today.'

'It's not for today. Call time is six thirty tomorrow morning. Dick Richards has promised to make waffles for breakfast. He reckons they're the best in the world. He specifically told me to let you know.' Her mother frowned and wore a suspicious look. 'Has he got a crush on you?'

'No. He's a guy that relishes my praise. But I don't care. I need something more exciting than that to tempt me.'

Sighing, Honey ran her hands through her hair. The day after returning from London she'd trotted along to an early appointment at the hairdressers. The stylist had created a centre-parting affair in some straggly arrangement resembling an old-time bob. The straggly bits kept falling forward around her face and were becoming irritating. For the twentieth time, she tucked her wayward hair back behind her ears.

Lindsey joined them. 'Is this a secret discussion or can anyone join in?' She squeezed herself between Smudger and her mother.

'The more the merrier,' said Honey laconically.

Lindsey lowered her voice. 'I hear we've all been summoned to be shot at dawn — with a camera, I mean. Not with a gun.'

When Honey turned her head, she found herself nose to nose with her daughter. They stayed eyeball to eyeball.

'I feel you've got something to say to me,' said Honey.

Lindsey nodded. 'I have. Doherty asked if he can meet you at the Zodiac tonight. But there's more. John Rees called. Do you remember him?'

'Hmm,' said Honey. This was an unexpected pleasure. Of course she remembered him. He was American, good-looking and bookish. The only time she'd seen him of late was on passing his shop, which was squeezed in between a home-made fudge seller and the Rifleman, the smallest pub in Bath.

'What did he want? John Rees, I mean.'

'He's going along as an extra tomorrow and heard from one of the film crew that you were going too. He suggested you could both catch up on things.'

'Lovely!' Honey exclaimed. Feeling a pair of eyes boring into her back, she looked over her shoulder. Her mother was wearing a tight expression and standing with her arms folded.

'I heard every word,' she said in the kind of voice James Cagney used to use when he was playing a gangster and itching to blow someone's head off. 'You don't want to get mixed up with a guy who spends his time with dusty old books.'

Honey swallowed a hasty retort about favouring men with dusty digits over accountants and dentists. OK, some did have big bank balances, but she couldn't get enthused about them in the same way she did about Doherty, John Rees or sirloin steak with all the trimmings.

'So I don't turn up tomorrow.'

'But you've got a walk-on part,' Gloria protested.

Honey made a clicking sound and smiled with her eyes. 'Straw bonnets at dawn!'

Sensing that Smudger was becoming exasperated, Honey hustled her mother and daughter out of the kitchen. She kept her arms around their shoulders.

'Six thirty, you say? I dare say I can manage that. I wonder what part I'll be playing,' she mused. In all honesty being dressed up Jane Austen–style took a back seat to seeing John Rees again.

'A flirt,' said Lindsey with a knowing grin.

'A tart,' said her mother, without her earlier enthusiasm. 'This early-morning appearance of yours is nothing to do with suffering for your art, I take it?'

'Of course not, though I'm not going there to see John Rees either. We still haven't solved the murder of Martyna Manderley and there really are more questions to ask. I'll get the low-down from Doherty tonight and base my questions on whatever information he gives me.'

Her mother winced, frowned and pouted all at the same time. 'Don't try and teach your mother how to suck eggs!'

'I'm sorry?' Honey feigned innocence. She was rubbish at it, but it was worth a try.

Her mother's expression went unchanged. 'You're off out with one man tonight and meeting another one tomorrow.'

* * *

The smell of grilled steaks and garlic lamb wafted into Honey's face as she entered the Zodiac. Bare bricks formed the barrel-vaulted ceiling, one complete arched curve from one wall to the other. The bricks were scarred with wear and tear and smeared with grease. Environmental Health might get uppity about it, but the punters didn't mind. Being situated beneath North Parade, it didn't matter how many extractor fans they had in their kitchen, the smell of sizzling meat stayed trapped against the vaulted ceiling.

Doherty was already sitting at the bar with three empty glasses in front of him. She guessed they were all his and that another was on its way. He wasn't one to get unnecessarily thirsty.

He saw her at the same time as the barman brought his drink.

'A vodka and slimline, ice and lemon for the lady.' He turned from the bar to her and raised his glass. 'Brett Coleridge is innocent. Innocent of murder anyway,' he added, closing one eye and squinting through his whisky. He shook his head dolefully. 'I was so looking forward to reading him his rights.'

'Is that so?'

'It would have wrapped things up. We could have celebrated.'

'Back to the grindstone, Detective Inspector.'

He narrowed one eye and studied her. 'You're not my boss. Stop telling me what to do.' He cocked his head to one side. 'You're looking smug. Something good happened?'

She took a sip of vodka. 'I'm back on set tomorrow. I have a walk-on part. I think I'm playing a tart.'

She said it laughingly, thinking it would cheer him up. It didn't. Unusual for him. A bit of flirting usually did wonders for his spirits.

'You're becoming star-struck.'

Oh, well. She'd done her best. She downed her drink. 'I did find out something from Miss Cleveley.'

Doherty looked puzzled until she reminded him of who the old lady was. He nodded. 'Ah, yes. The old bird.'

The bar stool was high, but her feet were aching — a hazard of the catering profession. She perched herself comfortably.

'You remember she was on the set as a historical advisor, though nobody paid her much attention. But she noticed them and their behaviour. In particular she noticed that

Martyna Manderley and the senior make-up artist were more than friends — a lot more than friends.'

Doherty looked at her, bleary-eyed, eyeballs rolling slightly, as he fought to focus his pupils. 'You mean they were lesbians?'

'I don't think it's that simple, Steve, but Miss Cleveley assures me they were very affectionate with each other.'

'How liberal of you.' He downed his drink.

'And there's something else. I don't think things were exactly rosy between the engaged couple. Perdita overheard Martyna calling her intended a pervert.'

'In fun or seriously?'

'I'm presuming seriously.'

'Hmm.' He downed his drink and ordered another.

'That's four you've had.' The comment was out before she could stop it. Oh dear. Now that was seriously blotting her copybook.

He looked at her in amazement. 'Are you nagging me?'

This was all too much.

She pushed his shoulders with both hands so he was forced to sit on the stool behind him.

'So I'm a star-struck, mothering, liberal nag.'

Seeing a clutch of empty glasses, the barman hotfooted it to their end of the bar.

'No more, thank you.'

One snap of her jaw and he got the message.

Doherty was indignant.

'I wanted another.'

'No, you didn't.'

At least he was arguing and not miserable. That was something. But he was getting louder.

'You are not my mother!'

'Did your mother used to tuck you into bed?'

He looked pensive as opposed to grumpy.

'Yes . . .'

'And kiss you goodnight?'

'I can't remem—'

It was wild, it was a whim, and it shut him up. She kissed him full on the lips. Not a short, sharp smacker, but a deep, lingering kiss.

'There,' she said as they parted. 'Are we Mr Grouch of Grumble Bend, or are we Detective Inspector Steve Doherty, top-flight police officer in this fair city?'

He stared momentarily, the tip of his tongue protruding from the corner of his mouth.

Suddenly he was back to being his old self.

'You'd better keep your eyes peeled tomorrow.'

Her response was nothing more than a murmur. Tomorrow she'd be seeing John Rees again — though she wouldn't mention that!

'I saw Casper earlier,' said Doherty. 'He's on set too, though he didn't seem too keen on it. He reckons he's going to ask them for a different part. From that I take it he failed to get a starring role.'

Honey grinned. 'He's togged up as a crossing sweeper.'

'What the hell's that when it's at home?'

'The poorest of the poor. They were employed to sweep the horse poo from the streets. Then it was sold on and used as fertiliser on city gardens.'

Doherty threw back his head and laughed.

Honey tried to shush him. 'People are looking.'

A silence descended after that. This happened regularly between them. Sometimes it was merely a comfortable stillness between friends. At this moment in time it felt like he was waiting for her to tell him something. Honey guessed he wanted to know what she'd found out about Perdita Moody.

She let him stew. Give him a few more minutes and he'd have to ask.

'You're smirking,' he said finally. 'Are you going to tell me?'

And so she did.

'A drag artist? You're fucking kidding me?'

Doherty didn't make a habit of swearing. For a man with a stressful job he was pretty cool on bad language. But this had just struck him out.

'I am not!' She couldn't help the amused look.

'Go on!'

'I'm telling you. I saw her at the theatre in Swindon and Miss Cleveley confirmed it.'

Doherty covered his mouth to stop himself from laughing too loud.

People drinking and talking close by stopped to see what all the fuss was about. Obviously they didn't think Doherty was that interesting and they looked away again.

Having them look over was no big deal; everyone looked round at the prospect of a row between lovers or a jealous husband confronting an unfaithful wife. Not exactly pistols at dawn, more like cracking heads before the police were called.

That's all it would have been, just people seen through a meaty haze, but one face was familiar. Honey looked over, her lips slightly parted as though a bit of extra oxygen might help her think better. It worked. It definitely worked.

Doherty was talking to her so she tuned back in. 'Do you want to hear something really funny?'

'Shoot!'

'I thought you were going to say that he—'

'She. Perdita is a she on stage but otherwise she's a bloke.'

She glowered at him when he ordered more drinks.

'Our last,' she said with grit.

'One for the road,' he said, already tipping his glass.

'How's your liver?'

'How's yours?'

'It's your funeral.'

She waved a hand dismissively and carried on talking about her visit.

'She was very nice, I found her and set Miss Cleveley's mind at rest. Let's get back to basics. I take it you'll be on set tomorrow asking questions?'

'If you mean of the make-up artist, you bet I will.'

'Sure you don't want to question her tonight?'

'Nah! She's probably tucked up in bed at her hotel. Wouldn't want to disturb her beauty sleep.'

'She's not tucked up in bed.'

Doherty upended his glass of Jack Daniel's. 'How do you know that?'

Honey pointed. 'She's over there.'

Doherty looked. Scheherazade Parker-Henson was sitting with a few of the crew, some of whom were staying at the Green River. She looked to be knocking back the drinks as fast as they were. Her face was flushed a deep fuchsia, which contrasted badly with the pea-green sweater she was wearing.

Doherty did his best to focus and take in the details. Being sober, Honey found it easier. The smoky haze thrown up by the charcoal grill cleared a little. The faces became clearer. Her eyes landed on a sweetheart face surrounded by bouncy blonde flicks. The mouth was sugar-pink.

Candy!

Honey had a tight feeling in her chest and a funny sweet taste in her mouth.

'What's she doing here?' Her voice was only a slim rung above a whisper.

Doherty raised an eyebrow and did his best to focus.

'Let me guess. Pink and white with fluffy blonde hair?'

'Candy! It's the first time I've seen her without something in her mouth. Candy in name and nature. As pink and white as the confectionery she eats. Too many candies and I'd be the size of a house.'

Doherty responded. 'Too many candies and I break out in spots.'

Honey frowned. 'What's she doing here?'

'Is she an actress?' Doherty asked.

Honey laughed drily. Calling Candy an actress was a stretch as far as Honey was concerned.

'Not quite,' she responded while keenly watching the pair.

Candy and Scheherazade had their heads together and appeared to be in deep conversation.

'There's some tie-in between this film set and the night-club Coleridge has a share in. I have a feeling about Perdita Moody!'

Doherty was leaning on his elbow, but having trouble stopping it sliding along the bar.

'That's it,' he said, downing the last of his drink. 'Let's get to grips with it. First off, perhaps you could stop sounding like Mary Jane.'

'I do not!'

Much as she loved Mary Jane, her resident doyenne of all things psychic, she didn't like to feel she was that batty — not yet. She couldn't help retaliating.

'My gut instinct was based on fact. Miss Cleveley is a very observant woman and also very caring. One moment Perdita was there, and then she was gone.'

'Of her own volition,' Doherty pointed out.

'But there's a link. You have to admit that.'

His amusement melted away. 'I suppose so.'

He rubbed at his chin stubble as he thought it through. Honey watched him closely — the flickering eyes, the solid and now sober expression.

By the looks of Doherty's face, he was off on a thought marathon. So far he was being generous about the work she'd put in on the case. She'd got somewhere. He hadn't. This was his case, and although he enjoyed working with her, at the end of the day solving it would do his career the world of good.

'Are you going to question her about her relationship with Martyna?' Honey asked him.

He shook his head. 'Not now. She'll keep until the morning.'

'The morning?' Honey's eyes grew as big as doorknobs when she glared at him. 'You're miffed!'

'No, I'm not.'

'You'll be sorry.'

'Stop sounding like an old witch.'

'Less of the old, thanks.'

She wasn't usually into premonitions and shivers down the spine, but she did feel apprehensive. Two reasons for that, she reckoned. Either she was excited at the prospect of seeing John Rees tomorrow — she hadn't seen her favourite bookseller for a while and planned to do so. Or her mother was going to spring something on her that she wouldn't like. Or maybe it was something else — something much worse.

* * *

Candy Laurel took a cab from the Zodiac to the Francis Hotel on Queen Square. Scheherazade Parker-Henson had not been the pushover she'd been led to believe. Mr North would not be pleased.

After paying the cab driver, she headed into reception to collect her key.

The receptionist was a neat-looking girl with clean nails and a confident face. Her hair was tied back in a ponytail at the nape of her neck. She smiled when Candy asked her for the key card.

'I gave the key card to your husband, though we do have a second one if you need it.'

'My husband?'

Candy's nerves knotted in her stomach. She didn't have a husband. There was only one man it could be. Mr North wanted results quickly and had turned up in person.

The receptionist was all sweetness and light. 'He said to tell you that he's ordered champagne.'

She said it with a conspiratorial smile, as though a romantic night was on the cards. She was totally wrong. This was about business.

Candy collected her key, then went to the ladies' room to fix her face. Her hand shook as she applied lipstick and a lick of mascara. How was she going to play this? So far she'd had no luck in seducing Scheherazade Parker-Henson. She pouted at the mirror, her pink cheeks poised as if to kiss her reflection.

'You look good,' she said, and managed a nervous little smile. It was hard to be brave when Mr North came to town. A sense of panic threatened to engulf her and there was only one way to deal with that.

Stillness became swiftness, her bag torn open. Her long nails scraped the bag's lining. She needed a fix. Her fingers touched a piece of wrapping paper. The last piece of candy had been popped into her mouth. The pretty face took on a desperate look. There were no candies left! But she had to have something. She had to appear cool, calm and collected when she faced Mr North!

In desperation she emptied the contents on the long Corian counter connecting the hand basins. She searched frantically, eventually finding the substance that candy had replaced. The small fold of paper was jammed into a compartment at the bottom of her lipstick.

Hands beginning to shake now, she got out her powder compact and opened it. She sprinkled a little of the white powder onto the compact's mirror. The discarded piece of sweet wrapper was rolled into a thin tube — just big enough to fill a nostril.

She bent, she sniffed and she straightened. Three or four deep breaths and her eyes sparkled. After putting everything back into her bag, she once again checked her reflection.

'Yesss,' she hissed. 'Oh, yes!'

The nerves subsided. Of course she could deal with this.

Taking the stairs to her room was her favourite way. By the time she got up there, she'd be floating on a cloud. A little pink cloud with cherubs either side.

With her heart racing, Candy took the stairs two at a time. All the while she wondered: why the personal appearance from Mr North? The knot in her stomach tightened.

The room had that plasticated smell beloved of all mid-range hotels. A single light burned on a bedside table. One of the windows was open. He was leaning out, his back to her, his broad shoulders shielding the view.

The curtains moved in a strong draught. It had been windy all day — the only thing keeping the rain at bay.

The sound of traffic filtered in along with the damp smell of a city in winter. The cold reached around him like icy fingers.

She regretted shivering. It wouldn't be good to appear nervous. Candy knew this from experience. Best be your normal sweetie-pie self, she decided. Digging deep in the inner well, she put the bounce back into her step and a smile back onto her face.

She glanced at the bottle and two glasses. 'Oooh! Champagne! Lovely.'

'Is it?'

His voice was dark and low, like the grumbling sound the earth makes before a landslide.

'Well,' said Candy, exhibiting an ebullience she didn't feel. 'There must be something to celebrate. Otherwise, why the champagne? Shall I be mother?' she added, her fingers already around the neck of the bottle.

'Come here.'

He still had his back to her. Candy put the bottle down. What was this?

The apprehension she'd been feeling turned to fear. But she did as ordered. She was used to doing as ordered. That's how she came to have the money she did, and money was everything to her.

She placed her hand on the nape of his neck. 'Hi, sweetie.'

'Well?'

Her nervousness showed in her tinkling laughter. 'Win some, lose some.'

He grabbed her by the nape of her neck.

'You failed?'

Candy squirmed and tried to prise his fingers off with her own. 'She didn't want to know me.'

'Why is that? I thought you said she was an out-and-out lesbian.'

'I was told that . . .' Candy confirmed. Her mouth opened and shut like a fish gasping for air. 'I can't breathe!'

'Then your source was wrong.'

'Please . . . sweetie . . .'

The pressure was building on her larynx. Her words were strangulated. Nail extensions split and popped off as she tried in vain to wrestle his fingers from her throat.

'I am not your sweetie!'

If she'd had breath, she would have screamed when he flung her across the room. Her head thudded against the marble-topped coffee table. Champagne flutes tumbled, rolled over the edge and onto the floor.

The bottle fell over and champagne bubbled from the bottle, soaking the sleeve of her dress and wetting her hair.

Blearily, she raised herself up onto one elbow. The room spun in ribbons of dark and light. She heard something snap and saw that he'd crushed a champagne flute beneath his foot. The sight of the splintered glass held her gaze. His other foot moved. She watched fascinated, her heart thudding against her ribs. He held his foot over the other flute and did the same to that.

There was a message in his method. Candy grasped the meaning. It wasn't only champagne flutes that could be crushed underfoot.

CHAPTER TWENTY-EIGHT

Brett Coleridge was worried. He'd been used to the high life. There was nothing he didn't have or couldn't afford to buy. But now his life appeared to be unravelling at a rate of knots.

The eyes of the three men sitting around the boardroom table were full of misgivings. He could almost smell their bloodlust. They were the hunters. He was their prey.

'We are not happy,' said Pollinger, financial director and heavyweight shareholder.

'Do you think I am?' Brett snapped back, his arrogance only just about covering the nervousness he was feeling.

The city and international banking people in general prided themselves on backing winners. For the most part their judgement as regards the company started by Brett's grandfather had proved to be a constant in an ever-changing world. The Coleridge family could be depended on to run a sound operation. This fact had been true in the case of George Shavros Coleridge, Brett's grandfather, and also in the case of Malcolm Isaac Coleridge, Brett's father.

Brett Coleridge had not inherited his antecedents' natural ability to make money and neither had he inherited their integrity.

They were experienced enough to know he was not telling the absolute truth about his dealings. Body language was not a new science. It was something that came with experience and dealing with people. Another name for it was instinct.

Brett adjusted the legs of his trousers before crossing one leg over the other. *Bluff it*, he'd said to himself.

He flicked at an imaginary mark on his trousers. The action was casual and meant to convey that he was unruffled.

He adopted a half smile and turned on his boyish charm. 'Look. Let's be sensible here. Don't call in the loans to the Coleridge Group just yet.'

'The group has invested a lot of money in this picture. We're covered by the insurance anyway,' said Pollinger. He was the eldest of the group. Rumour had it that nowadays he only worked for three days a week. He was seventy-five years old, his eyes were still good and he had a quick mind.

Brett wished he were dead.

'Insurance is taken out in the event of failure,' said Pollinger. 'We are not in business to be failures.'

'That's what I'm saying,' said Brett, still cultivating a winning smile and using Pollinger's comment to get into his stride. 'Wait until the film is finished. It's a dead cert at the box office. Jane Austen is a worldwide commodity. We'll be selling internationally. There'll be money plus foreign dubbing rights. Then there are digital rights. We might even get it turned into a novel. Don't you like making money, gentlemen?'

He realised he sounded mocking, but one thing he had learned was that you needed to play people at their own game.

OK, the shares in the company set up by his father were doing badly at present, but a new direction and younger blood would do the trick. He assured them of it.

That had been the plan. Today was a different matter.

The three men conferred. Brett made big efforts to control his breathing. It was of vital importance that he maintained the cool, confident facade. Even when the sweat trickled into his eyebrows, he made no move to swipe at it. Stay cool. He had to stay cool in order to beat this.

Still wearing that faint, confident smile, he kept his eyes fixed on the three wise men as though he deeply respected them.

They were conferring, speaking in low whispers — raising an eyebrow here, pursing slack lips there. Not once did they refer to him either by eye contact or comment.

Respect? Ha! Three wise monkeys more like. He couldn't ignore them; they controlled the global corporation left to him by his father.

At one time he'd been the majority shareholder, but the playboy lifestyle had intervened. He'd also thought he could play the stock market, betting against shares rising or falling. The streetwise kids from red-brick universities had outdone him on that score. Quicker than he could possibly have imagined, the shares and other finances had diminished. Bad judgement and pure extravagance were to blame, but, hell, he was entitled. His father had left it to him to do with as he pleased.

After some deliberation, the three men turned to face him.

'We're doing some much-needed reorganising within the group. Luckily for you it's likely to take us some time. We'll wait, but be warned, we want success. We are not inclined to wait for ever.'

* * *

Once he was back in his own office, he ordered a crate of Krug to be sent to his personal table at the Venus Trap. Tonight he would celebrate.

His secretary, Samantha, made the arrangements.

'By the way, a woman phoned. She said it was urgent and she'd try to call back.'

No time for trivial diversions, Brett Coleridge was walking on air. 'She'll have to wait,' he said. His arm encircled Samantha's ample waist and whirled her around the floor.

'Tonight, I celebrate!'

Samantha giggled like a love-struck teenager. He'd inherited her from his father and had sometimes considered replacing her with a younger model. He'd changed his mind. Samantha was loyal and discreet — and he didn't find her remotely attractive; in other words, the ideal secretary, and well suited to the job.

He finally twirled her behind her desk and into her chair.

'The woman who phoned said she'd send you an email if she couldn't get to a phone.'

'She can wait,' he said dismissively. Probably an old flame or one of the 'tabloid tarts' as he called them — the girls he used to pursue a business that was his very own.

That night, after a bath, a line of coke and a bowl — a whole bowl — of champagne, he checked his emails. He found the one from Samantha's mysterious woman.

The elation he'd been feeling since leaving the directors' meeting vanished. His face clouded over.

'Bitch! *Bitch!*'

CHAPTER TWENTY-NINE

Out of bed by five thirty! Get on set at six thirty. An ungodly hour to get up for some people, but Honey was used to it.

Her mother had phoned the night before to remind her to set her alarm.

'I'll see you on set,' she'd added. 'You remember they're filming at Henrietta Gardens tomorrow?'

Honey had answered that she did. One of the houses there was supposed to be representing the place Jane had lived during her years in Bath. She'd lived in both Sydney Place and Gay Street. Gay Street was out of the question. Even the most skilled of sound technicians couldn't hold back the sound wave created in the wake of a tour bus.

Sydney Place was better, but still not quite right. In desperation they'd decided to use Henrietta Gardens as a backdrop. The road could be closed off when filming. Better still, their trucks and buses could be parked along the back of Henrietta Park and even in the park itself. Mindful of protecting the grass, the city council had laid vast sheets of tarpaulin — all at the production company's expense, of course.

It was pure devilment to phone Steve Doherty and enquire what time he'd be there.

She tapped in his number. His groggy voice answered. 'Who the hell is this?'

'Your early-morning call,' said Honey, squeezing her nose to make herself sound different.

'Get lost.'

'I thought you were coming along to ask Scheherazade some questions.'

'I am.'

'And Candy?'

He suddenly became distracted. 'I'll have to call you back. There's a call coming through on my other phone.'

Just as they were about to take their leave, a figure in pink flannelette pyjamas came lolloping down the stairs. Mary Jane's slippers were the same colour as her pyjamas and had goggle eyes and floppy ears — a pink rabbit get-up. Just the thing for any non-fashion-conscious woman of seventy plus!

'I just thought I'd better warn you,' said Mary Jane in a hushed voice. 'Sir Cedric suggests you take a bacon sandwich and a chocolate croissant with you.'

'Right.' Honey realised she sounded like an automaton, but it was par for the course. Early mornings were not her favourite time of day and everyone in the hotel trade sounded the same this early in the morning. Yes, she was used to getting up early, but that didn't mean to say that her attention span long enough for a full chat.

'Just thought I'd tell you,' Mary Jane said before flip-flopping back up the stairs to bed.

Honey and her daughter exchanged a look: *What the hell was that all about?*

Lindsey shrugged. 'Beats me.'

* * *

They marched through the city in the early-morning chill. Marching kept them warm.

'Quite bracing,' said Lindsey.

Honey wound her muffler that bit higher. Her nose was turning bright red. She could see the tip of it changing colour before her eyes.

'Did Rudolph the Red-Nosed Reindeer ever get a mention in Jane Austen?'

'No. Christmas was non-commercial back then. Did Grandma mention that she doesn't approve of you getting involved with a bookseller?'

'Doherty's going to be there.'

'Ditto her views on him too. She doesn't reckon either of them is good enough for you.'

'In a professional capacity.'

'Grandma pointed out that he's not rich.'

'Onassis isn't available.'

'He's dead.'

'Good enough.'

The trees in Henrietta Park were indistinct, shrouded as they were in early-morning mist. The film crew were moving like wraiths, grey figures hunched in padded jackets, clipboards tightly clasped in mitten-clad hands. Unlike the Jane Austen characters who wore dainty lace mittens, theirs seemed to be knitted from rainbow remnants and likely acquired from a few choice charity shops.

Gloria Cross, true to her word, was on hand to impart the wisdom of her years.

'Hannah! A word before we are called to act.'

Acting was hardly how Honey would describe standing around like bits of scenery, but she let it go. Her mother sidled up close and spoke out of the corner of her mouth.

'I'll be close at hand, Hannah. You'll need someone to keep you focused on the script.'

Luckily Dick Richards was waving at her. She waved heartily back.

'Excuse me, Mother. I think I'm being offered an extra-large bacon sandwich.'

She found herself at the head of the queue. John Rees was right behind her.

'Great to see you.'

His smile was as warm as ever and his eyes twinkled. He sparkled brightly for a guy who spent hours with dusty books.

She didn't have any chance to gush over him. A plate banged down in front of her.

'My speciality,' said Dick Richards, his face already moist and pink. The omelette was colourful — bright yellow with bits of white, black and purple.

'Black pudding omelette. With beetroot,' he said proudly. 'Here's your knife and fork.'

'Amazing!'

It was all she could say. She certainly didn't dare tell him that she hated black pudding, a treat she reckoned should be confined to Yorkshire. The people up north obviously had stronger stomachs than she did.

'It's a bit chilly, so I'll take it over to the bus,' she said breezily. She was already plotting how to get rid of it.

'Wait!'

She did as ordered. What now?

'Here's a nice cappuccino. I've used mint chocolate pieces on the top of the cream — full cream, of course. In fact, Cornish cream.'

She hated mint. And a Cornish cream cappuccino? On top of black pudding?

This called for equal measures of tact and sincerity.

'Well, that'll warm me up, Richard. And so totally unique. Thank you very much.'

She stepped down from the wooden platform set before the counter, where those wishing for breakfast were expected to queue.

The smell of the bacon was so enticing that she half considered turning back and demanding he take what he'd given her back and hand her a bacon sandwich pronto. With ketchup! Or brown sauce!

The exchange between Dick Richards and John Rees put her off.

John Rees was telling him what he wanted. 'Bacon, sausage, potato fritters and fried bread. No egg.'

'No egg? No poached? No omelette? No scrambled?' Dick Richards sounded as though he were the Pope and John Rees had just uttered the ultimate blasphemy.

John Rees explained. 'I hate eggs. I throw up if I eat eggs. Or cream. Can't stand it. Oh, and if you could only lightly fry the bread.'

'I've got toast.'

'I don't want toast.'

'Well, I don't do fried bread. It's common.'

'Fine. Skip the fried bread.'

Dick Richards was plainly reluctant to fill the order. 'Some people have no taste! Especially Americans! If it wasn't for McDonald's, they'd starve!'

'You've upset him,' murmured Honey.

John was looking at his plate. 'He's given me scrambled egg. I specifically said that I hated it.'

'I should have warned you,' said Honey as they made their way to the double-decker bus being used as a dining hall. 'Dick Richards considers himself the master chef of outside catering for films. He's not very good at taking criticism.'

The bus was almost empty. Because it was early and not too many extras were required, there was room downstairs.

They eyed each other's plates with glum distaste.

'We'll share,' said John.

'Good idea.'

Dick Richards had given her a torpedo roll and butter. They cut it open and stuffed it with sausage and bacon. Honey divided it into a third for her and two thirds for John.

'I'll eat the scrambled,' she told him when he was about to protest. 'And if you could spare a mouthful or two of coffee?'

Division of food agreed, they caught up on things.

John Rees had landed himself a part. 'Guess what? I'm playing a bookseller.'

'I'm doing a walk-on. I think I'm a lady's maid. All I have to do is follow along behind. Can't see it's that much more than being an extra, but there you go. Do you know extras are used to hide parking meters and lamp posts?'

'Must be cheaper than using a computer to edit stuff out,' he said, between mouthfuls of bread and bacon.

Honey felt privileged. She'd been told to report to the large trailer, which was divided into two departments — administration and make-up. Only walk-ons, bit players and the stars themselves, of course, got to be pampered in make-up.

John popped the last of his food into his mouth and wiped his fingers on a paper napkin. 'How about we trade food again at lunchtime?'

Honey was agreeable. It was nice to see John again. 'At least it won't be eggs, and please can I ask you to fetch me a coffee?'

He said that he would. They scraped their leftovers into a bin and piled the plates on a table.

'Dawn,' said John, his face turned to the east.

'Are you going to be wearing britches?' Honey asked him.

He grinned. 'I suppose so.'

'They're very tight.'

His grin widened. 'Is that so?'

'I'll look for you. By the way, do you know that Regency ladies never wore underwear?'

'And the point is . . . ?'

'I'm keeping my tights on and a pair of leggings. Do you think anyone will notice?'

Today was no warmer than yesterday. The sun was fighting a losing battle, trying to bust through the mist.

The director's second assistant came to fetch her.

'Let me see your face,' she demanded.

Honey allowed her to stare into her face.

'You're not wearing any make-up?'

'No. You told me not to.'

'Good. You're playing an apple woman. We wanted someone pudding-faced with a bad complexion, ruddy cheeks and all that. You'll do just fine.'

'How sweet,' said Honey in a sarcastic tone. 'Are you always this tactful?'

The girl looked at her blankly. 'Sorry?'

Honey shook her head. 'No worries. Just don't ever get a job counselling the clinically depressed!'

It was bad enough getting up early in the morning, though the chill air was refreshing. Being referred to as pudding-faced and having a bad complexion sent her spirits crashing.

The interior of the trailer was warm and welcoming. Honey settled herself comfortably in a chair in front of a mirrored wall. A footrest also ran the full length, ending in a large locker at one end. The end of the bar forming the footrest was embedded in the locker — a neat trick to keep it level and stable.

'Could you be a bit careful with your feet,' said Courtney, the pink-faced make-up girl. 'That locker's a bit wobbly.'

Glad to put her feet up, Honey wasn't too careful. The locker wobbled.

'Where's Ms Parker-Henson?' Honey asked.

'I don't know.' Courtney's hands were shaking. 'But I wish she were here. I can't do all this by myself.'

'Was she out partying last night?'

Honey already knew the answer but wondered if the girl did.

'She said she was going out with the crew. I didn't go.' The pinkness in Courtney's cheeks intensified. 'I had a date.'

'Your eyes are sparkling. It looks as though you enjoyed it.'

Her blush deepened. 'I did. We're getting engaged.'

'Lovely. I bet you're dying to tell your colleague. I wonder where she's got to?'

Courtney shrugged.

Moving only her eyes, Honey glanced at her watch. Doherty was due to arrive to question Scheherazade Parker-Henson. Had she noticed them last night and panicked? If so, that would mean that she had something to hide.

Honey decided to press on.

'Was she meeting anyone special besides the crew?'

The little girl dabbing at her face was under pressure. The joy that had registered on her face at the mention of getting engaged vanished.

'Not as far as I know, but then she doesn't tell me anything, really. We work together, but we aren't friends as such.'

'She had other women friends closer to her own age?'

Courtney's face turned from strawberry pink to crimson. 'I suppose so,' she mumbled.

It didn't take a genius to realise that Courtney *knew* that the senior make-up technician was keen on Martyna. She could see it in Courtney's face.

'Was she very close to Martyna Manderley?'

Courtney couldn't have turned any redder, but didn't answer what was being asked. She merely nodded. Yes, Martyna Manderley and Scheherazade Parker-Henson had been friends. Obviously more than friends, thought Honey.

The cold morning air came rushing in along with a guy called Deke, yet another assistant to Boris Morris.

In his mid-twenties, he'd at some point demanded a number-one cut from the hairdresser. Unfortunately for him, he had strong hair. It was growing back now and was standing up like the bristles on a scrubbing brush. His eyes were black, and a thin moustache adorned his upper lip. It occurred to Honey that this excuse for a moustache had been adopted to compensate for his close-cropped cut. Perhaps it was drawn on. She wouldn't be surprised. Perhaps Courtney had drawn it on for him.

'Courtney, darling, is the apple woman ready yet?'

No, I'm not, Honey wanted to say.

Under pressure, with only one pair of hands and a queue of crossing sweepers, street vendors and handsome couples in silks, Courtney was on the point of imploding.

'There's only me here,' she blurted in a wafer-thin voice. She sounded close to tears. 'I'm doing my best, but I can't manage it all by myself!'

Honey noticed her hands start to shake.

Deke the Dirtbag, as Honey had just christened him, rolled his eyes.

'Speed up, sweetie. A bit of whitewash won't show. They're hardly centre stage.'

His flippancy only served to make the poor girl tremble even more. Honey felt sorry for her. OK, the guy had a job to do, but interpersonal skills didn't rate too high on his résumé.

'Of course I knew it would happen,' Deke said. 'The time had to come when bloody Scheherazade Parker-Henson fell by the wayside. Too full of her own self-importance, that one. Do you have any idea where she is, sweetie?'

'I don't know,' said Courtney. Her brushes quivered like porcupine bristles in her hand. A thick rouge, the colour of brickyard clay, spilt from a box in her other hand.

Honey kept her eyes wide open and fixed on her reflection. If things went wrong, she could end up looking like a pantomime dame with a bad case of measles. The wart glued to the end of her nose was particularly fetching, more Wicked Witch of the West than apple woman. In the meantime, this guy Deke was pissing her off and Courtney needed reassurance.

'Look,' she said, addressing Deke at the same time as swiftly grabbing Courtney's shaking mitt. 'This girl is trying to achieve the impossible. Don't you think it would be a good idea if someone went to look for the senior make-up artist? Perhaps her alarm didn't go off.'

Deke stared at her as though she'd just beamed down through the trailer's overhead hatch. Even to the lowest of production administration, the extras were persona non grata. Like kids of yore, they were supposed to be seen and not heard.

'I don't need a common little extra telling me what to do!'

'I'm not an extra. I'm a walk-on.'

He jabbed her shoulder. 'You are nothing on this set, lady. Just a fraction up from a big nothing!'

Anger welled up inside her. The apple woman had become Lara Croft. Perhaps it was the make-up. Perhaps not.

'Look here, you little snot . . .'

Unfortunately, she was less than graceful and far too speedy getting up from the chair. The bar she'd been resting her feet on became dislodged. The locker into which the end slotted tilted, toppled and went crashing to the floor.

Deke drew himself up to his full five foot six and three quarters, fists resting on his hips. 'There!' he said with an angry snort. 'Now look what you've done. Well *I'm* not picking it up!'

Honey couldn't speak. She was vaguely aware of Courtney staring at the same thing she was staring at. Deke hadn't noticed. Not the brightest star in the galaxy, Honey decided.

A puddle of dark red liquid was seeping out from beneath the locker.

She reminded herself that she was on a film set. It might not be what she thought it was. 'I take it that's not where you keep the tomato sauce or whatever it is you use.'

'It's blood,' whispered Courtney.

Her eyes fixed on the slowly spreading puddle, Honey slowly removed the make-up bib from around her neck.

'That's what I thought.'

Then Courtney began to scream, the make-up brushes scattering all over the floor.

CHAPTER THIRTY

Filming came to a standstill and no one was allowed to leave.

Doherty was standing outside the trailer giving instructions for protecting the murder scene and taking statements.

'Who discovered the body?'

'There were three of us,' said Honey. 'Myself, this young lady and that man there.'

She pointed out the other two.

'I'll need your names.'

Doherty's movements went into overdrive when attending a murder scene. He spun on his heel, and was about to go off and bark orders to more of his team, when he stopped dead.

There was disbelief in his eyes when he turned round.

'Good God! Is that you, Honey?'

'It is.'

He took cautious steps towards her.

'You're going to say something predictable,' she said to him, her fists fixed on her hips, daring him, double-dog daring him to go on. 'Go on. Say it. I would have recognised you anywhere.'

For a split second he seemed to think about it, but declined.

'Have you ever wondered what you'd look like in twenty or thirty years' time?'

'Neat make-up,' said John Rees, who had appeared from somewhere behind her. 'Didn't have chance to take it off, huh?'

She took hold of his arm and laid her head on his shoulder.

'I'm so happy someone appreciates me.'

She saw the look on Doherty's face. He tried to hide it, but it was there. He was jealous.

She smiled sweetly. One up to me.

They left the trailer and stood out front while Scheherazade's body was examined and finally brought out.

'She's dead,' said the medical examiner.

'So I noticed,' said Doherty.

It was a well-known fact that even if only a part of a body was found — even a finger — the medical examiner had to declare it dead. As if it could be anything else.

Their attention was diverted.

'This is ridiculous.' Penelope Petrie strode past wearing blue silk shoes, her face like thunder.

Deke, he of the lofty nose and unsympathetic disposition, was almost crawling along at her side. His latest job was keeping the hem of her long costume from trailing along the ground. In order to keep it bunched in his arms, he had no option but to crouch and keep pace with her, his head at bum level.

A pair of woollen culottes flapped around the actress's knees and a pair of leg warmers sat like thick sausage skins around her ankles.

'I see *Lady* Penelope came dressed for the weather,' said an imperious, downright sarcastic voice. Casper was on set again and not happy with the casting director and therefore the film as a whole.

Casper St John Gervais, chair of Bath Hotels Association and owner of La Reine Rouge, one of the most luxurious and aesthetically inclined hostelries in Bath, was known as a man of impeccable taste.

'You're here again,' said Honey, somewhat surprised. 'I thought you weren't coming back.'

'I would not wish to let anyone down, though I had hoped to play a different part.'

Unfortunately, the casting director didn't give a hoot which extra played which part as long as the clothes fitted.

Casper was of average size all over, a godsend for the harassed wardrobe department.

Today they had kitted him out in a dirty jacket with torn sleeves, patched trousers and a top hat with a broken brim.

'The things I do for my hometown,' he said, seeing Honey's expression.

'Rather rakish,' said Honey, who was doing her best to pick the wart off her nose. It was not going well.

'Have they finished with us for now?'

He nodded to where the police had added an incident tent in the park, next to the ones already erected by the production company. Blue tape fluttered around both the tent and what had been the make-up trailer. Scene of Crime and Forensics could be there for a while, and the medical examiner had been and gone.

'Fancy a coffee?' asked Honey.

'Is that what he calls it?' Casper said glumly. Boasting that Harrison Ford loved your cottage pie would cut no ice with Casper. He had fastidious tastes, and cottage pie wasn't one of them.

'Stop right there.'

'What did I say?'

'You were criticising the coffee.'

'Do you have a problem with that?'

'No, but our friendly caterer does. He doesn't take criticism well.'

Casper's eyebrows knotted into a disbelieving frown. 'Can you give me a good reason why I shouldn't tell him it's not to my taste?'

'This guy sees and hears everything worthwhile on this set. I need to keep him on board if this case is going to get solved,' said Honey.

'I suppose I could indulge in a bottle of Coca-Cola.' He brightened up suddenly. 'Do you suppose it likely yon caterer might have some freshly squeezed orange juice?'

Honey let him down gently. 'I heard from one of the other extras that he brings his own brand of fruit juice. I'm not sure exactly what's in it, but he does have peculiar ideas about what constitutes top-notch cuisine. He also does the packet-style orange juice you can buy in any supermarket.'

'I don't shop in *any* supermarket.'

'He reckons he's catered for the brightest stars in Hollywood.'

'Then Hollywood standards have dropped considerably,' Casper muttered.

Honey agreed that Hollywood wasn't much of a yardstick to go by nowadays. It had certainly seen better days the last time she'd been there.

A few pink-faced extras in bonnets and top hats were still gathered around Dick Richards's chuck wagon. Most of them had collected hot drinks and food and were heading post-haste back to the double-decker bus. Few had yet managed to go home, though most had had their names and addresses taken in case of need.

Casper stood glumly while Honey ordered for him.

'Coffee for me, and . . .' She glanced warily at Casper. He was standing with his hands clasped behind his back and not looking at her or Dick Richards.

'Coffee for you, sir?' asked Dick.

Honey got a sinking feeling when Casper narrowed his eyes, fixing Dick with a studious stare.

'I would rather drink my bath water!'

This was not helpful. Casper was well known for being outspoken. So far as she knew, he'd never got biffed on the nose for offering his opinion. But there was always a first time. She just prayed that this wasn't it.

Honey froze. For a brief moment, so did Dick Richards. Then his face reddened. His eyes, brown as conkers, looked set to shoot out on stalks.

'It's been a difficult morning,' she blurted. 'What with there being another murder. And I can't seem to get this wart off my nose. Do you have Coca-Cola?'

She offered up what she hoped was a reassuring smile. The only thing she mustn't admit to was that the Coca-Cola was to remove the pretend wart, should it prove stubborn.

Dick Richards dragged his angry glare away from Casper and back to Honey. Once he'd blinked a few times, the anger seemed to recede — thank God!

She thanked him. He began doing some stretching exercises and rolling his shoulders. Bones cracked into place.

'That's better. Sean Bean told me how to roll my shoulders properly to get rid of tension. Works every time.'

Another fierce look flew like a dagger towards Casper — not that he noticed. He was pouring his drink into the paper cup provided. Honey hoped and prayed that he wouldn't pass comment on the cup.

Offer a compliment. That was the way to engross Dick Richards.

'Lovely smell!' she exclaimed.

'Steak and onions with pepper sauce,' he proclaimed in a manner befitting a maitre d' at a top hotel. 'There's a skill to cooking a steak so that the juices still run. None of this bashing with a hammer before cooking. Let it hang, let it mature and let it rest before you lay it on the griddle. No one can cook a steak like me. No one at all! I'm a master at it. A true master!'

'I'm sure you're the best,' she said with a parting smile. 'I look forward to lunch.'

He called after her. 'I'll cook you something special. You just see if I don't.'

'I was afraid of that,' she muttered.

'My goodness! He's cooking you something special? Have you seen the dross he dishes up to the rest of us?' asked Casper.

'Don't excite yourself. You're not missing anything. This morning his special recipe was black pudding and beetroot omelette.'

Casper looked aghast. 'Did you eat it?'

'Do I look like a trash can?'

'I don't want you poisoned while on the case. You're looking rather flushed and you're coming out in warts. I think I'll have a word with him.'

'No! No need.'

Taking a firm hold of Casper's arm, she led him towards the incident tent. 'I think Doherty wants us.'

It was an outright lie, but anything was better than dealing with Casper after he had been covered in fried onions. Neither could she have trusted herself not to argue about who cooked a mean steak. The party concerned could argue for himself. She made a mental note to never, ever, *ever* let her chef Smudger within ten feet of Dick Richards. Wars had been fought for less.

Doherty saw them coming. He stayed on his side of the incident tape. Honey and Casper lingered on their side, sipping their drinks.

Doherty swung his leg over the tape. 'You didn't see anything, did you, Casper?'

'Nothing at all, my dear boy.'

'In that case you're free to go.'

Adopting a sullen and rather perplexed expression, Casper lingered. 'Detective Inspector Doherty, I know this terrible occurrence has only just taken place, but can you give me any idea how long it will be before you apprehend the perpetrator?'

Doherty's expression gave nothing away. 'No idea whatsoever.'

His tone was good, as though he were making a far-reaching announcement. It meant diddly doodah. He was less than pleased at being asked this early in the proceedings. He looked sour, thought Honey. No, he looked hurt. That and the fact that he couldn't seem to tear his gaze away from the mighty wart that refused to leave her nose.

'I will bid you adieu,' said Casper, taking the broken hat from his head. He grimaced as he took the corner of his jacket between finger and thumb. 'These clothes have a life of their own. I believe they are making me itch.'

He strode off, as imposing as ever despite wearing rags.

'So what happens now?' Honey asked Doherty once Casper had disappeared into the wardrobe tent.

'Round up the usual suspects.'

'Do you have any?'

Doherty grinned — a little too sadly to be joking. 'I wish it were that easy.'

Honey waited for him to answer the question which was lurking in her mind.

Doherty caught the look in her eyes. 'She was stabbed.'

'With a hatpin?'

'No. With a comb.'

She frowned at him. Was this a joke? 'A comb?'

'A steel comb with a tail end. Don't you girls use it to tease your hair to stand up or separate or something?'

'More or less.' She shook her head. 'I'll never look at a hatpin or a steel comb ever again without shivering.'

She noticed that Doherty was regarding her with a puzzled expression, his head held to one side like an inquisitive sparrow.

'What's on your mind?' she said.

'I was just thinking that whoever did it exerted a great deal of force. They had to be strong. Fairly strong and very angry, I'm guessing.'

Honey looked back at him in the same manner as he'd looked at her.

'But why? Why was she murdered?'

He shrugged. 'I haven't a clue. Unless . . .' His deep-blue eyes narrowed in thought again. 'Didn't Miss Cleveley say that Scheherazade was having an affair with Martyna Manderley? Discounting our old friend Brett Coleridge, is it possible that there was a third party involved?'

'You may be on to something,' said Honey. She noticed Doherty had that tired look he always got when a caseload was building up. 'I take it you're going to be asking our sweet little Candy a few questions.'

'She's been warned to expect me. She's staying at the Francis Hotel.'

'I'll come with you.'

'That might be useful, though there is a proviso. Get rid of the wart. I'm fussy who I get seen with.'

'It's not permanent. It's make-up. I'm supposed to be an apple woman — a street vendor flogging apples to rich folk. They had to have their five a day, even back then.'

'If I didn't know you pretty well,' Doherty said, 'I wouldn't have recognised you.'

The repartee was no longer getting through to her. Suddenly she felt a jolt in her system.

'The victim was a whizz with make-up!' she exclaimed. 'The best, so I hear. I wonder if someone used her services but didn't want her to tell.'

Doherty was all attention. 'You mean one of those folk who ventured into Martyna's trailer that day . . .'

'Who wasn't the person our Mr Richard Richards thought it was, just by the addition of a bit of make-up.'

'Who? That is the question, Tonto.'

'To which we need an answer, *kemo sabe*, and the catering truck is a good place to start. Richard Richards. Master of the Meat Pie. Lord of the Rhubarb Crumble!'

It was logical to return to Dick Richards's chuck wagon, but when they got there, he was gone.

'We want the owner,' said Honey.

A tall, ginger-haired guy with pale eyes and a freckled face grinned down at her. 'I am the owner.'

'I meant Richard Richards.'

'I am Richard Richards.'

'Then who was . . .'

CHAPTER THIRTY-ONE

The atmosphere at the Green River Hotel felt calm after the shock of the day before, even though Mary Jane was sitting on the floor in front of the main entrance droning some ancient Tibetan incantation. She reckoned it was to ward off blue-painted demons with red, blood-covered tongues.

A good day would be had by all. The staff had reported for duty on time and sober, and it was too early for her mother to put in an appearance. She was doing the important stuff.

Gloria Cross had a scrupulous beauty regime, starting with a variety of facial and body scrubs, a bath in moisturising milk, and followed by more after-bath moisturiser. Finally she would decide what to wear and apply co-ordinating make-up.

Honey was sitting in her office behind reception, musing over rather than dealing with suppliers' statements. John Rees had promised to phone. Doherty had made comments about bloody American booksellers. Whether it was the American bit or the bookselling bit that stuck in his craw, she couldn't make out. But it was nice to be in demand.

Lindsey brought her coffee.

'You've got a visitor.'

Startled out of her reverie, Honey took in her daughter's fresh face and plum-coloured hair.

'Was that your hair colour last month?'

'Similar. Just a shade different.'

'And next month?'

'Who knows,' said Lindsey with a deep sigh. 'It depends.'

On what? thought Honey, but didn't ask. It seemed Lindsey had been changing her hair each month, or maybe it was just that time was passing more quickly.

She ceased wondering about her daughter's hair colour as she remembered the visitor, and her heart leap hurdles. It had to be John Rees.

'He's early.' Even to her own ears, her voice sounded breathless. *Like a silly teenager.*

'It's not a he. It's a she.'

Euphoria and her gushing, rushing heartbeat went walkabouts.

'Oh!'

Lindsey lifted a quizzical eyebrow and hinted at a smile. She turned to leave, then stalled. Purposefully, Honey thought.

'John Rees phoned and said he can't make it for morning coffee as promised. He'll catch up with you again.'

What was it with this man? They were like a couple in a country dance — skip smartly towards each other, then skip to my Lou.

Honey shuffled papers and pretended to clear her throat.

'Never mind. I've got a lot of work to do. Who wants to see me?' she asked, preferring to change the subject rather than deflect questions she didn't want to answer.

That knowing look stayed on Lindsey's face. Honey did her best to ignore it.

'It's that strange little woman who talks funny. I think she must dine on *Pride and Prejudice* for breakfast, *Northanger Abbey* for lunch and *Sense and Sensibility* for dinner.'

Honey stayed sitting at her desk, waiting for Miss Cleveley to appear. A few minutes went by and still her door remained closed. She checked her watch. Best see what was going on. The old dear might have got lost or changed her mind or gone to the bathroom. It wouldn't hurt to check.

She opened the door on an argument. On the other side of the reception desk two elderly women were head-to-head, going at it hammer and tongs.

Mary Jane towered over Miss Cleveley, but, reminiscent of a yappy Jack Russell terrier, Miss Cleveley was holding her own.

Mary Jane was presently holding sway.

'Hell, woman! You're talking like a bull's rear end. Bring the book to the big screen, that's what I say. OK, so the guys in Hollywood take a little dramatic licence . . .'

'Dramatic licence? Dramatic drivel! Dear Jane would turn in her grave if she knew what indelicate . . .'

Honey groaned. Obviously the two had met, got better acquainted, then found they didn't see eye to eye when it came to movie treatments of Regency classics.

For all her eccentricity, Mary Jane was an out-and-out film buff. She loved Hollywood period pieces like *Braveheart* and *Gladiator*. So what if directors dismissed fact and replaced it with fiction? It was the story that counted. In that regard, Mary Jane was a sucker for sheer entertainment value. Whereas Miss Cleveley, it seemed, was a stickler for detail.

Lindsey kept darting in between the pair using suitably placating sentences.

The two elderly women ignored her. Lindsey might just as well have been a fly.

'You deal with them,' Lindsey said, recognising intervention as a useless task. 'I'm off to the bathroom. I'll be in there a while.'

Honey knew she meant it. Lindsey put in her headphones. Tunes on the toilet helped relieve stress, or so she'd heard.

Honey took a deep breath and waded into the fray. 'Miss Cleveley!'

She'd said it at the right time. There was something of a lull in the argument.

'My dear Mrs Driver,' said Miss Cleveley. Tossing her head, she left Mary Jane standing there with a dark scowl on her face. Anyone who hated Hollywood was an instant enemy.

Honey addressed Anna, who was manning reception this morning.

'Can you order us some tea? Hot chocolate for Miss Cleveley.'

Gripping Miss Cleveley's elbow, she guided her into the office, surprised at how firmly muscled she was despite the frail appearance.

Once they were both sitting comfortably, Honey got right to it.

'Now,' she said. 'What can I do for you?'

The little lady fussed her curls back beneath her bonnet. It was made from straw, and a cluster of violets was pinned to its crown.

'I came to give you this,' said Miss Cleveley. She began delving into the crocheted reticule she carried. Like her outfit, it was pale lilac.

She handed Honey a small book with a brown vellum cover. Old, thought Honey. Very old.

'It is a prayer book,' Miss Cleveley explained. 'I wish to bequeath this to you in grateful thanks for finding Perdita and putting my mind at rest.'

Honey opened the stiff covers. Knowing of Miss Cleveley's obsession, she wondered if this had once belonged to Jane Austen. Her heart leaped at how much it might be worth. She turned to the fly page. Her surprise was complete.

'Oh. Emily Bronte.'

'Yes.'

Honey detected a fleeting look that convinced her that Miss Cleveley was far more instinctive than she let on.

'I am assured that the signature is genuine. You look surprised, my dear. You didn't expect I was giving you a book that may have belonged to Jane Austen, did you?'

She said Jane Austen as though it were a prayer all by itself.

Honey considered whether to lie. There was no point, she decided. Instead, she smiled and shook her head in disbelief. She'd been analysed and found out.

'Considering your close affiliation with Ms Austen, I presumed you had no interest in other literary greats.'

Miss Cleveley got up. Her smile was mischievous, even cheeky.

'I would never part with any items pertaining to the greatest romantic writer in the English language — nay, in *any* language. But a lesser one I could part with.'

Honey imagined that comment could cause a riot in the Bronte Society.

'Funny little woman,' said Lindsey, once she'd left the bathroom and had helped the old dear out of the front door.

'Perdita's aunt,' explained Honey.

* * *

Doherty had arranged for them to meet Candy Laurel in the residents' lounge at the Francis Hotel.

'You'll have to be quick,' she told him. 'I've got a train to catch.'

'It's either there or the station.'

She crumbled like stale biscuits.

'All right.'

She was sitting at the end of one of the comfortable settees furnishing the lounge, resting her elbow on the arm.

The brim of a cream suede hat was pulled down over one side of her face. She was wearing matching trousers, dark pink boots and a pale-pink jumper with pistachio-green trim.

Her hair seemed to be tucked up into the crown of her hat.

'I don't know why you want to interview me,' she said, somewhat defensively.

'You know that Scheherazade Parker-Henson was murdered yesterday?'

'So I heard. As I said, what's that got to do with me?'

Honey fancied her bottom lip trembled a little. There was no box of opened candies on the table. Somehow she'd expected there to be. Candy needed her sweet fix. Unless she'd moved on to other things, of course. She marvelled at Candy's skin — it looked almost airbrushed. Amazing, considering her sugar intake.

Despite the fact that Candy's breasts were playing peek-a-boo over her low neckline, Doherty was focused. 'Did you know her?'

'Of course not.'

'Why are you lying?'

Candy's pale cheeks flushed baby pink. 'I don't know what you mean.'

It wasn't for Honey to ask questions. Doherty was the professional. But her natural exuberance would not be held in check.

'Had you met her?' Honey asked.

Candy's honesty would be made or broken on the answer to this. Honey found herself holding her breath. She liked Candy. OK, she looked like an oversized Barbie doll, but you couldn't hold that against her. Neither could she condemn her indulgence. She had much the same problem with almond paste. Smudger had never yet managed to complete a Christmas cake without her having previously nibbled bits of almond paste from around the edge.

Candy stared at her hands and sucked in her lips before answering.

'I never knew her. I only met her last night.'

'You met her last night.' Doherty was harbouring dark looks.

She nodded.

'Why?'

She took a deep breath. 'I was down here for the weekend . . .'

'Just visiting?' urged Doherty.

She was lying. Honey was sure of it.

'Are you sure you weren't down here to do a little job — you know — centre-page tabloid stuff?'

Candy's eyes were big and luminous when she brought her gaze up to meet that of Honey's.

'I just made her acquaintance. That's all.'

'You were meant to seduce her. Get her into a compromising position. That's right, isn't it?'

Candy couldn't cope. She screwed up her eyes.

'Don't keep on at me!' she wailed.

Honey found herself feeling sorry for the girl. 'Look, Candy. Someone had it in for Scheherazade, and we know she liked girls. Who put you up to it? This Mr North you mentioned earlier?'

She sat bolt upright at the name. 'Did I?'

'That's a nice hat,' Honey said suddenly. 'I didn't know you liked hats.'

'I don't . . .'

Doherty reached out. She didn't protest when he removed the hat from her head and her platinum hair tumbled around her shoulders. She just sat there like a rabbit sitting in the middle of the road, hypnotised by a car's headlights.

'You could do with having a stitch put in that.' Honey had half expected it — there was a deep gash from the corner of Candy's eye all the way up to her hairline, and it was still seeping blood.

Doherty got out his mobile phone.

'Hey there!'

Honey looked up to see Mary Jane coming in their direction. She spent most of her waking hours wandering around the city, absorbing the atmosphere. By midday she was thinking about lunch. It seemed that today she'd decided to dine at the Francis Hotel. On seeing them, her face lit up.

'My favourite people. What a coincidence to bump into—' Noticing their serious expressions and perhaps sensing the strained atmosphere, she stopped.

'Am I interrupting something?'

'Just a murder investigation,' Honey replied.

'Hey!' Mary Jane said, spotting the gash on Candy's face. 'Who did that?'

She looked pointedly at Doherty, who held his hands up.

'Nothing to do with me, sheriff!'

'It needs stitching,' Honey said. 'We're going to get her taxi to the hospital.'

'No need! I'll take her. My car's outside.'

Doherty raised his eyebrows. 'Parked on double yellow lines?'

'Only just over there on the square. I bought my parking permits.'

'My luggage,' said Candy.

Honey assured her that she'd deal with it. 'There's a storeroom for guests' luggage.'

Doherty opted to ride shotgun to the hospital. 'I'll let you know what transpires,' he confided to Honey.

Honey couldn't stop the Cheshire cat grin. 'You're a brave man, Detective Inspector.'

'I know,' returned Doherty. 'I've seen Mary Jane's driving.'

CHAPTER THIRTY-TWO

Honey returned home to find that, of all the hotel bars in all of Bath, Boris Morris had walked into the Green River! Was it a coincidence or was he there to meet up with one of his production crew? Or was it something more pertinent to the case at hand? Was he Mr North? Honey was aching to find out. Someone was indulging in a sideline aimed at trapping the rich and famous into compromising situations. He wasn't top of the list of possibilities, but he was also far from being at the bottom.

The pony-tailed film director was well into his cups — half a bottle of Jameson's in half an hour, according to Lindsey.

'He's feeling pretty sorry for himself,' Lindsey added.

Honey beamed at her. 'Hey, never look a gift horse in the mouth — or a murder suspect drowning himself in Irish whiskey. He certainly can't be here for a production meeting with the crew. He'd need a clear head for that — unless I really do know nothing about film-making.'

Lindsey tugged at the trio of earrings hanging from her right ear. She didn't usually play an active part in her mother's detective work, but she was interested. 'Is he the prime suspect?'

'As prime as the rest on Steve Doherty's list,' returned her mother. 'He's got about eight on the list, I think, though it could be more. But Boris Morris is as good a place to start as any. Is he still standing and coherent?'

'Absolutely. I think he's a veteran in the barfly stakes. He seems to be mopping it up like a sponge while bemoaning his lot in life.'

Honey closed her eyes and thanked the fates that had brought his footsteps to her bar.

'Right! If he wants someone to bemoan to, I'm all ears.'

Boris would think he was receiving sympathy, when in fact he was being grilled like a fillet steak.

She arrived in the bar to see the pale-faced film director tipping a full measure of Irish down his throat. He was wearing full denim: denim jeans, denim shirt, denim jacket. OK in spring, but chilly in February.

He ordered another whiskey.

Honey gave her barman the nod. 'I'll serve this gentleman,' she said quietly so that Boris couldn't hear.

The barman moved gratefully aside. He'd been listening to Boris's moaning for long enough.

'Single or double?' Honey asked the well-oiled film director.

He raised his eyes from his drink and squinted at her.

'You're a woman.'

'You must be a genius.'

Her sarcasm was wasted on him. He was peering into his glass as though trying to see the bottom of a very deep well.

'It's this Irish stuff. Gives you the heebie-jeebies at times.'

'Is that so?'

After taking a sip, he took another squint at her. 'Do I know you? Didn't you have a part in a Stallone movie once?'

'Sure. I was playing a fire hydrant.'

'Is that so? Were you naked?'

What did he think she'd said?

'As naked as a fire hydrant ever gets,' said Honey. This wasn't going to be easy. She poured herself a vodka and tonic. 'Not even a walk-on. More of a stand-alone kind of thing.'

He nodded as though she'd made sense. Though it was as if his neck was strung on wires and there was a puppet master someway above him.

'Would you like to be in my movie?' he slurred.

'Sure, why not?' she said, knocking back half of her drink. 'Can you make me into a big star?'

'Sure, sure,' he said, spilling whiskey from the tightly clutched glass. 'Anybody can be a star if they play their cards right. Even the ugliest old battle-axe around. Even the prettiest airheads and the biggest dunderheads in the world of men . . .'

Honey was wise enough not to enquire which of these categories she fitted into — hopefully, none of them.

'You'd have to give me the low-down on what to expect,' she said. 'I'm not au fait with the movie scene at all.'

It wasn't entirely true. After all, she'd had a whole crew of cameramen and sound engineers staying at the hotel for two weeks now. And before that there were old friends — some who'd made good in the industry, but none who'd made big.

'You've got the look,' he said, and patted her hand. 'Shame you're so buxom.'

Honey gritted her teeth. 'How kind.'

'My pleasure.'

'Has anyone ever told you look a right prat wearing your hair like that?'

'What . . . ?' He slurred, his eyes bleary and unfocused.

'I said your hair is really long and shiny. What do you use on it? Margarine or axle grease?'

The subject of his hair — or rather the lack of it — seemed to touch a chord.

'I hate this,' he slurred, running his hand over his bare head.

'Cut the ponytail.'

'Do you think I should cut off my ponytail? Penelope thinks so.'

'Good idea. It is said that grass doesn't grow on a busy street.'

'I don't think I will,' he said, shaking his head.

'How many people wanted to murder Martyna Manderley?'

He laughed and ordered another drink. 'Everybody!'

'What about Scheherazade Parker-Henson?'

He leaned closer, his voice dropping to a whisper. 'She was a dyke.'

'As in Offa's Dyke or a great Dutch dyke?'

The joke was lost on him.

Shut up, Honey, and keep to the point, she said to herself.

'Funny that. She was well-liked. Kept Martyna in her place.'

So he didn't have it in for Scheherazade. That didn't mean he had nothing to do with the murder of Martyna Manderley, she advised herself. Scheherazade's murder could have been an entirely separate matter — not that she thought it was. The probability that she knew something about Martyna's murder had to be considered. Big bucks were involved where Martyna was concerned. It was likely Boris knew more than he let on. There was only one way to find out. Ask questions until she was blue in the face — or Boris passed out.

'What's the film industry really like?' It was the million-dollar question. She could tell that Boris was going to just *love* answering it.

He began spouting about rights, insurance, stars and directors.

'Bloodsuckers! All bloodsuckers!'

'Gee,' said Honey, all sweetness and light. 'How come you say that?'

Out of the corner of her eye, she could see Lindsey at the end of the bar. She was standing with Alex the barman. Alex looked perplexed. Lindsey was pulling a face and rolling her eyes.

Honey returned the look. OK, she sounded like a girl on prom night. But she didn't care. As long as it worked.

Boris began listing all the bloodsuckers he'd known, and Count Dracula wasn't amongst them. Too much of a softie in comparison to the real vampires behind the big flicks.

Honey nodded in the right places and eventually managed to interrupt.

'What about this film you've been doing in Bath? Was that so bad? I mean, were the people running the show out to get their pound of flesh?'

Boris sneered before gulping back another drink.

'Worst ever. Everything Brett Coleridge wants, Brett Coleridge gets. This was his film through and through; he owned everything in it. The star, the script — you name it, he called the shots.'

Honey rested her elbow on the bar and cupped her chin in her hand. She looked into the pale eyes swimming in an alcoholic haze above puffy pouches. Boris's body was as out of sorts as his mind.

The fact that a film could be insured against termination of production was uppermost in her mind. *Go with it*, she advised herself.

'So what about finance?'

Boris made a snorting sound. He also ordered another shot, after which Alex the barman disappeared into the cellar to get a fresh bottle.

Buoyed up on a sea of Irish whiskey, Boris was rambling on. 'Brett had other sources — that's what I heard. He couldn't do it all alone, so a company was formed.'

'Anyone famous?'

'Besides his fiancée, you mean?' He shook his head. 'Not famous. Not in this country.'

'Foreigners?'

He nodded. The effort of nodding seemed to have an effect on his neck. His head began to lower like a bucket on the end of a bulldozer. His legs were folding beneath him.

'For want of a nail . . .' he muttered.

Boris's mind was wandering; it deserved time off after all that whiskey.

Lindsey and Alex caught him before he hit the floor.

A group of tourists from Poland smiled at the supine man, then at each other, as Boris was dragged out of the bar.

Honey followed. 'Take him into number one.'

Number one was a ground-floor room used by staff when they had some reason for not being able to get home. Working late was one reason. In the case of Smudger the chef, it was usually because he'd had one B-52 too many. Naming a cocktail after a Second World War bomber was fairly apt; it tasted more like aviation fuel than anything else.

Boris grumbled all the way to the bed, his legs dragging behind him.

Between the three of them, they stacked him out. Honey took charge of his legs. Taking a firm grip of his ankles, she heaved both up on the bed.

She regarded him quizzically. What did he know? Did he know anything at all?

One thing was for sure. He was well and truly oiled.

'I reckon he'd been drinking before he got here,' said Lindsey. 'Drowning his sorrows big time.'

Whether he'd heard them or not, Honey didn't know, but suddenly his eyes flicked open.

'It was mine! All mine,' he murmured.

Falteringly, his eyes had opened, but they snapped shut again like a camera lens.

'What did he mean by that?' asked Lindsey.

Honey shrugged. 'Search me.'

Even if it was something important, there was no chance of getting an answer tonight. Boris Morris had sunk into an alcoholic stupor and would have one hell of a headache in the morning.

CHAPTER THIRTY-THREE

The filming of Jane Austen's life had come to an end. The bank had pulled the plug.

Honey wasn't sorry, and Doherty was otherwise engaged nursing a sore head and making other arrangements in the furtherance of the case.

Candy had slipped out of the hospital without Doherty noticing. He was dead pissed about that and blamed Mary Jane. He'd noticed that one of her tyres was a bit soft. She'd thanked him for noticing and directed him to 'the trunk', where she kept the spare.

Having sorted out the problem, he returned to the trunk to put things away.

Mary Jane hadn't told him that one of the hinges holding the lid up was a bit faulty. It came down on his head.

'Wasn't it lucky that he was already in casualty,' she'd said to Honey.

It was lucky — in a way. He got attended to pretty quickly. That was when Candy had done a runner. She went straight back to the hotel, collected her stuff and was gone.

Doherty assumed she'd headed back to London. 'I'll get the Metropolitan Police to check her out.'

Honey decided to keep a low profile. Somehow she couldn't see Candy as a murderer. Of course there was the Mr North thing. Tabloid newspapers thrived on seedy gossip.

She reminded herself that there had been no sign of a fight in the trailer. There was only the atomiser on its side belching perfume and the fan heater belching cold air. There was something odd about the two items working in unison, but so far she hadn't figured out what.

Casper had been absent as regards the case so far. Appearing in front of the cameras had proved irresistible. Now it was over, he was back on the case for the City of Bath.

'We really have to get this finalised,' Casper told Honey. 'How dreadful that a reputable star can come here and get murdered.'

There were many people who thought Martyna had got her just deserts, but Honey didn't comment.

Over a light lunch at the Francis Hotel, Honey enlightened Casper with the report she'd had from Doherty.

'In all probability the murderer was in disguise, which is why this Ted Ryker in the mobile canteen . . .'

Perplexed was the best way to describe how Casper was looking — as though someone had flattened his face with a frying pan.

'I thought his name was Richard. *Richard Richards.* That's the name I saw.'

Casper spat the name out as though being unfortunate enough to have matching first and second names was totally out of order. She had to admit it was pretty daft.

'Apparently he was only filling in. The real Richard Richards was catering at Chepstow Racecourse and then had a whole bunch of other engagements to fit in. He tried not to use Ted Ryker because he's a compulsive liar and because he can't stand anyone criticising his cooking. You may have noticed him reel off a whole A-list of stars who'd made complimentary comments about his pies and whatever.'

'An obvious fiction,' said Casper with undisguised contempt. 'Disgustingly ordinary.'

Honey didn't comment that the ordinary folk didn't have smoked salmon for breakfast every day as Casper did. She wanted to get this over and meet up with Steve Doherty. A bigger mystery was evolving, and she wanted to be part of it.

Brett Coleridge was nowhere to be found. His secretary could only say that he was out of the country, but she didn't know where.

This was another thing for Doherty to be miffed about. He'd told Coleridge not to leave the country. He didn't like being played for an idiot.

Casper ran his eyes over the lunchtime bunch. This was far from being his favourite venue. On the plus side, neither was it a great favourite with friends and acquaintances. That fact alone suited him fine. For some time before the filming he'd crowed about having secured a small part — he didn't say extra or walk-on. 'A dandy of ill repute,' he'd related, when asked what part he'd been enrolled to play.

Once word had got round that he'd landed the part of a crossing sweeper, Casper wanted to keep his head down until the period of ridicule had passed.

Honey began telling him about how things were going, when she saw his expression change. 'I have to go,' he said suddenly. 'I'll leave it with you.'

Fast for his height, he swept up from the chair. The Francis bar was long and narrow, and had two entrances — one from reception and one direct from the outside. They were nearest the one leading directly onto Queen Square.

Casper was gone in a flash, leaving nothing but a draught of cold air.

The two men who'd come in bought drinks at the bar, ordered sandwiches, then sat down in a far corner near the reception entrance.

The waiter brought two salmon salads to Honey's table. 'For you, madam?'

'For me,' she said. Well, the portions weren't big and they were only accompanied with lettuce, tomatoes and a few other bits and pieces. She would manage both.

She was just in the process of scraping one plateful onto the other, when she was interrupted.

'Need a hand with that?'

Doherty was looking down at her with an amused expression. She felt as if she'd shrunk to two inches in height.

'They weren't really both for me, only Casper had to leave.'

He smiled. 'I'll believe you. Millions wouldn't.'

He'd come to know her weaknesses — or rather her biggest weakness. Food. Good food, mind you — none of this processed stuff out of a packet or a tin.

She found herself in a quandary as to whether to share, but Doherty forced her hand. 'Her with the long name didn't die from the stab wound, and if you want to hear more you'll let me have one of those. I'm starving.'

She set the plate down in front of him, her appetite for details temporarily outweighing her appetite for food.

Steve swooped on the smoked salmon. 'I could eat this stuff every day.'

'Casper does.'

'He can afford to.' His tone was guarded but had undercurrents.

There was no animosity between Doherty and Casper. They were men from either end of the spectrum of sexuality, but respectful and tolerant of each other. Doherty was wary. Casper was aloof.

Between mouthfuls of salmon, Doherty reeled off the pathology details of Scheherazade Parker-Henson's demise.

'It seems it could have been an accident. She may have been pushed, or fell, and hit her head. Whoever was responsible panicked and decided to blur the evidence by stabbing her in the neck with the steel tail comb. First the hatpin, and now this. How many sharp instruments does that wardrobe department have, for Chrissake?'

'Like I told you, they shouldn't have had any hatpins,' said Honey, recalling most vividly what Miss Cleveley had told her. 'Back then they wore bonnets with strings. Hatpins weren't really necessary until the late nineteenth century, when women began wearing those elaborate concoctions of ostrich feathers and garlands of flowers.'

He raised his eyebrows. 'Is that so?'

'Nor corsets. Nor underwear. Did I mention that before?'

She waited for this parcel of info to sink in. Once it did, he looked at her, his eyes opened wide.

'You may have done. Still, it takes a while to sink in. No knickers, you say?'

'None.'

* * *

The sponsors backing the film had given orders to up sticks and call a halt to everything. Doherty refused to let them go until Forensics were finished.

For the most part, Honey shadowed his movements, writing things down and working things through in her mind.

Not being part of the scene was quite relaxing. She didn't have to dress up or be made-up. She wandered around as she pleased.

That was the great thing about film sets and the people who worked on them. Stars, production staff and crew alike were so embroiled in their own world or busy watching their backs that they failed to see what was under their noses.

Even now, as everything was being packed up, nobody really noticed that there was a big banner across the front of the catering truck: 'Ted Ryker — Caterer to the Stars.'

Honey had got into the habit of looking up at him.

'So what happened to Dick Richards?'

'He had other contracts he wanted to concentrate on. I made him an offer. He accepted. Anyway, they couldn't do without me. I'm more original than Dick and getting all the praise. He was getting jealous. It was only a matter of time. I've just baked some Cornish pasties from what I had left. They're a bit different from usual. I've used everything I had left: bacon, leeks, onions, mince, mushrooms, carrots, eggs . . .'

'Sounds great!'

In all honesty it did, but what would it taste like?

'Here.'

He passed her a warm pasty wrapped in two paper napkins.

'I guarantee that you've never tasted anything like them before.'

This was exactly what Honey was afraid of. She only hoped that he knew the difference between edible mushrooms and a death's head. If not, she was as done in as a squashed hedgehog.

Honey bit into the pasty. The crust was golden brown. It looked good, but that didn't mean anything in Ted Ryker's world.

The taste surprised her. It *was* good.

'Lovely,' she said, nodding her head and spraying breadcrumbs.

'I'm a dab hand with the rolling pin.'

She swallowed. 'So you're not really Dick Richards? Why didn't you say?'

'Why should I? Anyway, it's all mine now.'

He looked up at the banner and beamed.

After polishing off the pasty, she found Doherty. He was studying a notepad on which he'd listed the chain of events since the film crew had come to town. He glanced up at her.

'I've got something to tell you.'

'That I've got crumbs around my mouth?'

'I've got no problem with that. It was the wart I couldn't cope with.'

'So?'

'I have custard slices. Fancy a stroll in the park?' Doherty was carrying a small, white pastry box that he'd picked up from the bakers on the way there.

'Let me check my diary.' She pretended to think about it. 'Seems good to me.'

They strolled back across the road. Although it was cold in the park, the absence of tourists and lunchtime escapees from the office meant they'd have it mostly to themselves. It would give them time and space to evaluate what they knew.

Honey eyed Ted Ryker, who was locking down the stainless-steel fitments of the canteen, prior to it being towed away. Honey repeated what Ted Ryker had told her about buying out Dick Richards.

'Strange that he didn't admit it from the outset. You'd almost think that Ted Ryker *wanted* to be Dick Richards.'

'A lot of people want to be somebody else.'

'That's what acting is all about, I suppose.'

'So did somebody go into Martyna's trailer in disguise?'

Doherty shrugged. 'If they did, we don't know who. That's the thing about disguises. If they're any good, they work.' He spotted Ryker. 'A last word, Mr Ryker.'

Hearing him, Ryker straightened. He was tall and powerfully built.

'Can you clarify exactly how many people you saw enter Martyna's trailer before she was found murdered?'

'No problem with me,' said Ted Ryker. 'Anyone who knows me will tell you I'm a stickler for perfection. Keep going over things and you perfect them. Have you tried one of my coconut pyramids?'

Doherty said he had not. He also added that he was on a diet and also on duty. The custard slices didn't count. He hadn't eaten them yet.

'Point taken,' said Ryker forcibly.

He struck Honey as the sort of guy who liked things his own way. The lantern jaw didn't help. Neither did the bulging biceps. Overall, Ryker looked as though he'd been cast in an iron foundry.

He turned to her. 'How about the young lady?'

'On duty. Sorry.'

'Your bad luck,' said Ryker. His smile had grown thinner and stiffer. 'They're freshly made. Can you smell them?'

Closing his eyes, he turned his nose skyward, sniffing the air like a hungry dog.

Unfair, screamed Honey, though not out loud. She put a brave face on it, but her taste buds began salivating in treachery. Coconut pyramids! She hadn't sampled a jammy, coconut-covered, pyramid-shaped sponge since, since . . . She couldn't remember when, but she could remember the taste. Hence, her taste buds were following their own slice of memory.

'Your Cornish pasty was wonderful,' she trilled. It sounded like a consolation prize. And it was. She didn't want to let Doherty down and go for the coconut pyramids.

It was obvious that Doherty was in serious mode. He wanted answers.

'Can you tell me who you thought you saw go in there prior to Ms Manderley's death?' he asked.

'Sure.' He began counting on his fingers. They were meaty fingers. 'First, there was Boris.'

'The director.'

'He was very present on set,' Honey pointed out. 'I doubt whether he had the time for either murder.'

'A very busy man.' Ryker wore a self-satisfied smirk. 'We're pals. He said, "Ted, on account of your delicious meatballs, call me Boris." He don't invite just anybody to call him by his first name.'

'Great buddies,' Honey murmured under her breath.

Doherty continued. 'You said he came and went a few times.'

'Three or four.'

'Who else?' asked Doherty.

'There were the usual — make-up girls, wardrobe, second director's assistant . . . Any of them could have done it, of course.'

Honey considered. Surely only the last person — or second to last if you discounted the one who'd discovered the body — could have done it. 'Who was the last?'

'Couldn't say. I was busy, you know. Everyone was busy going in and out. People just went in and left things if she was having some shut-eye. She got a nice trailer, you see. It's got a bed in there, so if she felt tired she could just get her head down. I bet she had her head down on them lace-trimmed pillows up front. Lovely! How the other half live, eh?'

They already knew that Martyna Manderley was sleeping while a variety of people popped in and out. She'd been awake when Courtney, the make-up girl, was touching up her face, and also when Scheherazade had arrived. Scheherazade was the last to see her, but had been adamant she was still alive when she'd left her. Now she was dead, but even in death she was still a suspect — perhaps a convenient suspect for the real murderer.

Doherty was of the same mind. Once this interview was over, he was off to speak to the director again.

'Think carefully,' urged Doherty. 'Was there anyone else at all after the make-up girls and before the director?'

Ryker looked skywards, puffing out his cheeks as he thought about it.

'I was busy but got the chance to glance up now and again. Let me rewind the old memory banks . . . I know. The bird in the bonnet. I forgot about her. But, yes. She went in. Definitely.'

Doherty frowned. This was something he hadn't heard before. A mysterious someone. Perhaps the same someone Honey had seen running away?

'Who was it?'

Ryker shrugged and shook his head. 'One of the cast, I suppose. She was bundled up in a bonnet and shawl. Could have been that batty old bird that used to hang around.'

His description was enough to bring a figure and a name into Honey's mind.

'Miss Cleveley,' she whispered.

Ryker looked at her. 'Don't know her name. A bit batty. Waffled on about historical accuracy and all that.'

Honey felt sick. Miss Cleveley was a little eccentric, but she couldn't believe she'd kill simply because the script favoured fiction above fact.

Doherty thanked Ryker for his help. Neither of them was allowed to leave without having a bag of coconut pyramids foisted on them. Honey planned to eat hers at tea-time — sharing them with whoever was around. One or two wouldn't be too bad for the figure. Then Doherty reminded her of the custard slices.

There was nothing else for it. The diet would have to go on hold until April.

CHAPTER THIRTY-FOUR

Honey had spent more money than she should have on renovating the conservatory at the back of the hotel. It had been a place of broken chairs and stored crockery when she'd first taken over.

The gardener had also stored his lawnmower there, alongside a variety of rusty garden implements and hundreds of seedlings that he told her were tomatoes. Once she decided to renovate, the plants got thrown out with the rest of the rubbish. She left one as a reminder of what had been there. It had since grown to rather generous proportions and produced seedlings of its own. The whole family of plants sat on a wrought-iron plant display in one corner. The rest of the furnishings were also wrought iron and embellished with comfortable cushions. The conservatory was now something to be proud of.

At present, except for an elderly gentleman from Canada, sound asleep on a full-length recliner, only Honey and Casper were out there.

'I'm concerned,' said Casper. He flicked his fingers out across the chair before sitting down.

Honey bit her tongue. Casper was a finicky old fusspot, but in a way he helped pay the bills. Biting her tongue was the way it would have to be.

On this occasion he caught the look in her eyes and, to her surprise, apologised.

'Old habits die hard,' he said. The corners of his mouth seemed to twitch with amusement.

Some old memory, no doubt, thought Honey, but she wouldn't pry.

Following the interruption at the Francis Hotel, he'd called in to check on progress and to book rooms for a party of Dutch tourists. Hardy types, obviously, and used to February weather.

Filling her rooms at this time of the year was by way of repayment for her work as crime liaison officer. Not that she minded being dragged away from the hotel. Liaising with Detective Inspector Steve Doherty was an appealing pastime and, after all, she was assisting the tourist trade. Tourists liked to think that everywhere they visited was as safe as Disneyland.

Casper gave her the details of the booking in writing. 'Neville would have emailed, but I needed a walk. Fresh air in the lungs, blood flowing through the veins.'

Honey understood. Like her, he preferred the written word to computers. Neville, his manager, took care of that, just as her daughter did for her.

Just as he was about to ask her how the case was going, there was a clattering of kitten-heeled boots and her mother barged in.

She was wearing a suede jacket with matching culottes that ended at the knee. Her boots were of tan leather and had brass-tipped toes. She vaguely reminded Honey of an elderly, though more upmarket, Calamity Jane — the Doris Day variety.

'Hannah!' she exclaimed, totally ignoring Casper and looking flushed and terribly put out. 'My play is going to be read and could win a prize. I so wanted you to hear it being read, but you can't. They've run out of tickets! Would you believe it?'

'That's a shame.'

Honey thanked heaven for small mercies. No matter what her mother had said, she was pretty sure that the play readings would send her to sleep and be a waste of two or three useful hours of ironing, or dusting, or anything!

'I think I can assist.'

To Honey's horror, Casper's face lit up and his hand dipped into his inside pocket.

She knew — she just knew — what he was going to say and what he'd be waving in his hand.

'You can have these.'

The nightmare had come true!

She held a sickly smile on her face as he passed her the tickets.

Her mother looked ecstatic. 'What a wonderful man you are!'

Casper received a kiss whether he liked it or not.

'This is wonderful,' said Gloria, 'You are a knight in shining armour.'

He waved her gratitude aside. 'Think nothing of it, dear lady. They were surplus to my requirements. I have another engagement that night.'

'My, my,' said Gloria, turning to her daughter. 'Just you wait until you hear my play. You'll be so glad you were able to get tickets.'

Honey's smile stayed fixed. 'Great.'

Gloria studied her watch — a gold number from Gucci. 'Look at the time. I have to meet the girls for lunch. Do excuse me,' she said to Casper. 'And thank you again. Just wait till I tell the girls that I could win a prize!'

The 'girls' she referred to were all in their seventies. Running their daughters' lives came pretty high on their lunch-time agenda.

Gloria did a little wiggle and winked at Casper on her way out.

Casper raised a querulous eyebrow. Honey was mightily embarrassed, and made a mental note to tell her mother that she was barking up the wrong tree.

'Lucky you,' said Casper, smiling at her from beneath lowered eyebrows. 'I take it you know these are *amateur* playwrights. Their offerings will likely be an insult to the ear, if not the intelligence — the meanderings of would-be playwrights with big egos and small talent.'

Honey wiped a hand across her forehead in a fair imitation of a theatrical tragedienne. 'Angst is us! Casper! How could you do this to me?'

'My profound apologies, but needs must.'

'I'll have a few drinks beforehand.'

'After might be better. Falling asleep and snoring would not be appreciated.'

* * *

Doherty called for her just after lunch. He'd toyed with the idea of calling on Miss Cleveley with a female police officer, but had changed his mind. He didn't want to be responsible for giving the poor old dear a heart attack. He had to question hard to get results, and having Honey there, someone Miss Cleveley knew and trusted, would be an asset.

Two cats greeted them at the door of the little cottage. Miss Cleveley's bright eyes looked up at them quizzically from beneath a lace-edged mop cap.

'My word. It is not my custom to receive visitors after midday. I favour the morning for receiving.'

'This is official business,' said Doherty, flashing his warrant card.

Honey was worried about upsetting the old dear, though like Doherty she was intrigued to know what she'd been doing in Martyna Manderley's trailer.

She kept her voice soft, her expression mild. 'He wants to ask you some questions about the death of Martyna Manderley. I hope you don't mind.'

If Miss Cleveley did mind, she showed no sign of it, perhaps because her mind lived in the past and her body in the present. Besides the mop cap on her head, her body was enclosed in floaty muslin of pale blue, sprinkled with tiny pink rosebuds. She wore flat ballerina shoes, laced up around the ankles.

'Do come in. Please excuse my attire. I was not expecting visitors.'

She led them down the hall and into the drawing room.

'Dig the outfit,' Honey whispered.

Doherty looked at her blankly. 'Why?'

Honey sighed. 'Doherty, you will never be a fashion victim.'

He grimaced. 'Thank God for that.'

Miss Cleveley invited them to take a seat. Doherty seated himself in a winged armchair. Honey perched on a love seat with a curved back and velvet cushions.

'Can I offer you hot chocolate?' the old woman asked.

Doherty declined.

'Not for me,' Honey said. 'Have you heard from Perdita?' Asking about a member of family she hoped would put Miss Cleveley at ease.

Miss Cleveley smiled. 'Yes. She apologised for not writing. Very naughty of her.'

Honey reminded herself that the house had no phone. Perdita either wrote or phoned a neighbour.

Doherty swung into action. He asked Miss Cleveley where she was on the day in question.

'Did you ever go into Martyna Manderley's trailer?'

Miss Cleveley's face darkened. Her brows knitted in a deep V above her nose. 'No,' she said adamantly. 'No. I was not there.' She turned to Honey. 'I told you, they banished me from their presence. I was humiliated. I don't mind telling you that, but I did not go back and do this foul deed! I most certainly did not!'

Doherty nodded sagely as though he were older in years than he really was.

'Can you tell me where you were that morning?'

Miss Cleveley's bright blue eyes blinked a few times. Her jaw moved as though she were chewing the matter over. There was something about the action that made Honey think that she was hiding something; was it something incriminating?

'I was at the beauty clinic.'

She touched her chin in a telling manner. Honey got the drift. Miss Cleveley had been at the clinic having a touch of electrolysis.

Doherty didn't get it. 'We'll get that verified.'

There was nothing more to be said.

After thanking her for her time, they left.

'I thought you said she lived in the past and didn't indulge in modern luxuries? What's a beauty clinic if it isn't a modern luxury?' said Doherty as they made their way back down the cobbled alley to the road.

'She was having her bristles removed from her face. Saves shaving.'

Doherty muttered, 'Oh. Right.' He obviously didn't get it straight away. Then he said, 'Oh' a second time, but louder.

'It'll check out. No beautician is going to forget a bristly chin like hers. Which begs the question, if it wasn't her in the bonnet and shawl, who was it?'

CHAPTER THIRTY-FIVE

A plain black dress worn with a matching three-quarter-length jacket trimmed with beige was just the thing to wear on a night out. The jacket had a swing to it. On inspecting her appearance, Honey decided it was just the thing for a play reading.

Dallying with some paperwork after an evening meal and a good Shiraz would have been preferable, but this was something she couldn't avoid. Damn Casper for having spare tickets.

'You look very nice,' said Alex the barman as he poured her a vodka and slimline tonic.

'Make it a double.'

Being a good barman and half her age, he obeyed immediately. Alex was a boy who had respect for his elders — and his boss.

Lindsey was taking her time getting ready. Honey phoned her while Alex poured her another vodka.

'Are you ready yet?'

'Mother, there's plenty of time.'

Honey glanced at her watch. 'I don't want to be late.'

'You're not worried about being late, Mother. You're just in a hurry to get it over with.'

Lindsey was wise beyond her years. Where did she get that from?

By the time she'd finished the second vodka, her daughter had appeared in blue jeans and a thick, padded jacket.

Honey's opinion of the outfit must have shown in her face.

'I've got a pretty top on underneath, but I have to warn you, that old place they're giving the readings in hasn't changed much since Winston Churchill was a boy.'

'Right! How about one for the road?'

Alex was poised and ready.

Lindsey put an end to it. 'Two's enough.'

'Three would be better,' Honey protested.

'No!' Lindsey shook her head in that schoolmarm style of hers which made Honey feel about fourteen years old. 'Grandma will be livid if we fall asleep. We'd never hear the last of it.'

Lindsey was proved right. The heating at the Old Pavilion was provided by an ancient boiler with a mind of its own. There was no equilibrium in its heating technique. It was either lukewarm or piping hot. Tonight it was the latter.

People were fanning themselves with their programmes. Some began dozing. Within the hour, the first subdued snorts sounded as those drifting off were nudged back into consciousness.

The woman sitting next to Honey had obviously been expecting the venue to be sub-zero. She took a hot-water bottle out from under a thick Welsh wool poncho.

'The warmth won't last. Forewarned is forearmed. I'll put it at my feet,' she said in response to Honey's enquiring glance.

'Good idea.'

The poncho followed, placed over the knees.

Lindsey was looking around.

'I know her,' she said.

Honey couldn't see who she meant, and as things were about to start, wasn't about to pursue the matter.

'Ladies and gentlemen . . .'

Here it was. The master — or rather mistress — of ceremonies had stepped on stage.

The first three or four readings were introduced. Three short one-act plays about inner angst, social inequalities and a student's opinion of how awful the world was and how best to change it.

'As if the ideas had never been touched on before,' murmured Honey.

'Grim,' Lindsey said.

'He'll learn,' Honey responded.

The old boiler was galloping away. The ancient radiators accompanied the readings with a metallic humming and the odd clunk from its piping.

Feeling her eyelids getting heavy, Honey attempted to take her coat off, but there was no room. Like an apple pie in a hot oven, she was destined to bake until her outer covering was at least crisp if not brown.

'Grandma's next,' said Lindsey, as they clapped for the previous reading.

Honey's eyelids blinked wide open. 'Thanks for the nudge. I was beginning to doze off.' She forced herself to sit bolt upright. She mustn't fall asleep, however bad the play might be.

'Our prize winner . . .'

Honey listened. The presenter was going on at lengths about her mother's play, plus two others that were in contention for the top prize — a day at a Robert McKee scriptwriting workshop in London. The suspense was awful.

'I wish he'd spit it out and get it over with,' she said to Lindsey. 'Then we can commiserate and go home.'

'Or celebrate. It might just happen, you know.'

Honey shook her head. 'Doubtful. It'll be a sickly sweet romance. You just see if it won't.' Her mother read Mills and Boon by the bucketload.

Lindsey agreed it was a safe bet.

The mistress of ceremonies stood up again. She was a gangly woman with buck teeth and a five o'clock shadow on her upper lip. She started off by praising the entries and saying how difficult it had been for the judges. Eventually, once she had noticed that the audience were fidgeting and shuffling their feet, she got to the nitty-gritty.

'After great deliberation, the judges came to a unanimous decision. This season's winner is . . .'

Just like on the television talent shows a pause was held before the announcement was made.

'*Jack and Me* by Gloria Swanson-Cross.'

There was a great deal of clapping.

Honey sat dumbfounded.

The clapping subsided. The mistress of ceremonies recommenced her announcement. 'Tonight it gives me great pleasure to hear our winning entry being read.'

Honey and her daughter looked at each other in stunned silence. Gloria *Swanson*-Cross? The name had been swiped from the old-time movie actress. Grandma had no real right to it, except as a dramatic device.

There was something else. Honey and Lindsey stared open-mouthed at the man and woman doing the reading. The woman was not known to them. The man most certainly was. There was only one person they knew with a spider web tattooed on his neck and enough earrings and nose rings to hang a curtain.

'Our readers are Mr Rodney Eastwood and Lady Cynthia Morrison-Poage. Please give them a warm welcome.'

Under the cover of more applause, Honey hissed to her daughter, 'Since when has Clint been into amateur dramatics?'

'Interesting contrast,' Lindsey hissed back.

Honey was of the same mind. Clint was a man with fingers in many pies, and not all of them legal; obviously this was one pie they'd not known about. It was a strangely exotic one for him, seeing as they'd only seen him washing up, running a shop part-time for a friend, and working as a bouncer at the Zodiac.

Lady Cynthia had snow-white, shoulder-length hair, wore a black-velvet Alice band and was at least sixty years of age. Being titled, she was also at the opposite end of the social structure to the likes of Clint.

'Before we begin, I will give you just a brief description of the subject matter,' said the mistress of ceremonies. 'This is a one-act play about President John F. Kennedy and Marilyn Monroe. The premise is that she seduced him and not the other way round, as believed by many. I have to warn you that this work does contain material of a very sexual nature, plus some explicit dialogue.'

Honey and Lindsey sat dumbstruck.

The subject matter drew mumbled comments from the audience around them. Those who had been snoring suddenly awoke, sniffing the air as though the subject of sex had a smell all of its own.

There was a hushed silence. Not one person got up to leave. Even an old gent wearing a hearing aid turned up the volume and leaned forward expectantly.

The play commenced. The readers put on convincing voices. Thankfully, as this was not a visually produced play, they refrained from taking their clothes off and getting into some of the clinches referred to in the dialogue. The audience didn't seem to notice that.

At the end there was stunned silence. It was as though the audience was expecting more. Once it became obvious that the play had finished, there was clapping. Then more clapping. Then an encore, and another encore.

The actors bowed and smiled.

Clint beckoned for Honey's mother to join them on the dais.

Gloria 'Swanson'-Cross beamed as brightly as a Spanish morning as she took her place.

Up until now she'd been sitting, unseen by her family, at the front with other would-be playwrights and members of the society.

As she took the stage, Honey and Lindsey sucked in their breath.

'My God!' said Honey in a loud whisper.

'Move over Danielle Steele!'

Honey could have reminded her daughter that this was a play not a novel, but she knew what she was getting at. Her mother was dressed in a sharp black-and-white outfit, the dress black with white buttons and a wide white collar. The brim of a white Panama shaded one side of her face. A pair of spectacles hung from a chain around her neck. They were totally unnecessary; her mother had had laser treatment two years ago. This, Honey realised, was just a prop, as was the ebony cigarette holder.

'Has Grandma taken up smoking?' asked Lindsey.

Honey shook her head, too stunned to answer. Her mother was good at playing a part. Tonight she was a playwright and had gone all out to look the opposite of the 'starving in attics' bit. The outfit was new. No expense spared.

'Do we wait for her?' Lindsey whispered.

'We have to.'

Her original plan had been to pop in, listen to her mother's work being read, then pop out again. But winning a prize put a different light on things. They could hardly leave without giving her hugs and kisses and saying what a clever cat she was. Woe betide them if they failed to provide due congratulations. She'd also expect supper at the Theatre Royal restaurant accompanied by a bottle of bubbly. Perhaps two bottles of bubbly.

'There's a downside to this,' Honey pointed out.

Lindsey demurred. They were obliged to sit through the runners-up. This was worrying, or to put it more honestly, sitting through more than an hour of recitation could be soul-destroying. The best had been read. What were the rest going to be like?

Honey resigned herself, and Lindsey followed her mother's example. Her body relaxed, slumping as comfortably as possible in the conference-style chairs, the sort designed to stop you from dozing off.

The next play was awful — a dreadful dirge about the futility of war, but full of clichés and a scenario that better writers had used before.

Her mother's play, *Jack and Me*, was still in Honey's mind and stopped her from falling asleep despite the near tropical heat.

She vaguely realised another prize was being given, this time for a play with a historical leaning. She probably wouldn't have given it much attention if she hadn't heard the magic words: *The Life of Jane Austen*. And then something else.

'*The Life of Jane Austen* was written by Perdita Moody. Unfortunately she had other commitments this evening and couldn't be here. She sends her apologies.'

Honey sat bolt upright. Had she heard right? Yes. Of course she had. A few physical bits and pieces were going west into the sunset, but not her hearing.

The scene was between Jane and one of her sisters. The lady with the snow-white hair and the Alice band took Jane's part. A woman in a tie-dyed skirt and dangly earrings took that of the sister.

Honey listened. She'd merely glanced at the script that she'd found covered in blood, but her memory was good. She was pretty certain the words being spoken were the same.

One thing she was definitely sure about was that the script she had found was not accredited to Perdita Moody, but to a Chris Bennett. But who was Chris Bennett? She hadn't come across him, and to her knowledge, neither had Doherty.

'I've got to go,' she whispered to Lindsey.

There was a look of surprise on her daughter's face.

'Where are you going?'

'Swindon.'

'What about Grandma?'

'Take her to supper. Here, take my credit card. You know the pin number.'

CHAPTER THIRTY-SIX

Honey hurried along the road towards North Parade. There was a smell of leaves in the air. There were none on the trees. Perhaps spring was thinking of springing early, tiny buds wanting to burst out.

She waited by the traffic lights. For the first time this month, she was glad of the chilled night air. By the time Doherty arrived, her pink cheeks were pinched not roasted.

The MR2 slid into the kerb. Doherty pushed the door open, and Honey jumped in.

As he pulled out into the traffic, she blurted out the business about the script in more detail.

His eyes studied the cars ahead. At last he said, 'It's not important. Not anymore.'

'How come?'

'We've arrested Brett Coleridge.'

'So what's his motive?'

'We don't know yet.'

Honey shook her head. 'No. I don't believe it. Why would he kill his fiancée? There was no life insurance out on her.'

'But there was an insurance policy on the film. Scrap the film and — hey presto — a massive twenty-million-dollar fallback from the insurance company.'

'There's still the script. Blood on the script. Perdita Moody wrote that script, not Chris Bennett. Have you actually met this Chris Bennett?'

'No. No reason to. He wasn't on set.'

'Or was he?' Honey sat back and thought about it.

'The script was being passed off as being written by this bloke who's never there. OK, I know this kind of thing goes on a lot nowadays — professional writers complete the work, and a big celeb, who can barely write their name, gets the kudos, but this is slightly different. This is plagiarism. So where is this guy?'

'Listen to me, Honey. It doesn't matter. Anyway, I thought you wanted to nail Brett Coleridge. You didn't like him the moment you set eyes on the guy.'

'Arrogant, male chauvinist, rude, snobby . . . yes, all of those . . .'

'That's beside the point. The production company — head of which is you know who — has claimed on the insurance. Everyone has to be paid off, but the insurance is holding off until we've finished our investigations. They smell a rat, and King Rat is Brett Coleridge.'

He turned off and headed out of Bath.

'So when are you interviewing him?'

'Tomorrow. The Met have him in custody.'

'So you're off there tomorrow?'

'Do you want to keep me company?'

She thought about it. 'You're going by train?'

'Yes.'

He pulled into the parking lot at the top of Tog Hill. The view was extraordinary. Behind them were the dark trees and hills that girdled the City of Bath. Ahead of them were the lights of Bristol, spread out like a twinkling counterpane.

'I'll come with you, but only as far as Swindon.'

She felt his eyes on her.

'You look good in this light.'

'You mean darkness? I look better when it's dark? Charm doesn't come naturally to you, Steve Doherty!'

Folding her arms, she glared glumly at the city lights.

'It's not easy to flatter you, Hannah Driver!'

It rankled when he used her real name. Only her mother used it. Everyone, but everyone, called her Honey.

'OK,' he breathed on the back of a sigh. 'So I'm no Casanova. Words are not my thing, so I'll try again. The subtle light up here accentuates your cheekbones. There! Is that any better?'

It was hard to be ratty when he was trying so hard.

'Thanks.'

At first he didn't react.

'You can apologise when you're ready,' he said finally.

'For what?'

'For snapping my head off.'

She turned to face him. He was right about the subtle light — amazing that the distant glow of city lights could reflect this far. Her features were better defined.

'Hmm,' she said. 'You look quite good in the dark too.'

She saw him smile. 'I like flattery. Flattery's number seven in my top ten turn-ons.'

'I know what you're playing at. I'm not going to ask you about the rest.'

'Not even number ten? It's fairly innocent.'

She considered this.

'OK. Tell me.'

She waited. What would it be, she wondered, as a gooey feeling took over her insides. Something that came behind flattery.

One corner of his mouth lifted in a lopsided smile. 'I like having the nape of my neck tickled.'

She looked at him. Having the nape of his neck tickled had not occurred to her.

'Do you mind obliging?' he asked when she failed to move.

Overall, this evening had been full of the unexpected. First her mother's play, replete with sexual content and bad language. Now this. Perhaps if it hadn't been for the play, she might not have played ball. Perhaps her libido had been touched or even tickled by it. Whatever! Her arm rose seemingly of its own volition. If a job's worth doing, it's worth doing well, and she was a girl who was always up to the job.

'You're hairy,' she said.

'Pardon?'

'I said, you're hairy.'

His eyes were closed.

'I thought you said something else.'

Honey knew from experience where this was going. 'And are you?'

'Hairy or horny?'

'Doherty!'

She started to remove her fingers, but didn't get the chance.

Doherty kissed her. Her arm was still resting on his shoulder, her fingers on his neck. There was nothing she could do. Nothing she wanted to do.

'Are you coming with me on the train tomorrow?' he asked between kisses.

'Yes. But I'm getting off at Swindon.'

CHAPTER THIRTY-SEVEN

Doherty got off the train with her at Swindon.

She hadn't dared look him in the eyes so far this morning, but there had to come a time. Why had he decided to get off at Swindon with her?

'Is this because of last night?'

'No. I've had a text message. The Met police have let Coleridge go.'

Perdita was having a break from rehearsals. Someone got them tea and crumpets. The butter was melting a treat, and blackcurrant jam had also been supplied. Railway food on the train coming up had been basic and expensive.

Doherty tucked in. Honey prided herself on resisting temptation — just!

'Are you on a diet?' Perdita asked, noting Honey's hungry eyes and tight lips. 'They're very good. Freshly baked at a small place round the corner.'

Resistance crumbled. 'Diet, schmiet!' Honey exclaimed, and tucked in.

Perdita crossed her extremely long legs and tossed a curtain of dark hair back from her eyes. She did it twice — visible evidence of how nervous she was.

'He paid me one thousand pounds for it and said he would give me more once it had gone into production and he'd sold some rights. I asked for a written contract. He said a handshake was good enough for him and that he was a man of his word.' She swallowed hard. Honey presumed she was about to sob. She was wrong.

'Shyster!'

Honey jumped. Even Doherty stopped layering jam on his crumpet.

The comment was obviously heartfelt.

'I take it we're talking about Brett Coleridge here.'

Perdita gulped again. 'No. Not initially anyway. Boris Morris bought the script from me, then sold it on to the production company. He didn't give me any extra money though.'

Honey frowned. 'So who's Chris Bennett?'

'That's him too. He didn't want Coleridge to know it was his script. He wanted to direct it as well, you see. Brett Coleridge had assumed head of production and wouldn't be keen on Boris wearing two hats. That's what he said.'

The picture was gradually becoming clearer. She felt angry for Perdita's sake. She'd been made promises and they'd been broken.

'So you didn't go to see Brett Coleridge about a job; you went to see him about the script.'

She nodded. 'I threatened to sue. I didn't tell Candy and Zoe that though. I didn't want to muddy the waters — if you know what I mean. So I let them believe that Brett Coleridge had made advances towards me . . .

'I hit him. Wish I'd hit him harder. If I had done you would have noticed. Shame. You would have sorted it out earlier. Scheherazade knew. She was appalled. A fighter against injustice that one. It was her idea to turn the tables on him once I told her about Candy and the other girls. He called them "tabloid tarts".'

'Honeypots by another name.'

'And he was Mr North.'

'Sounds a bit Jekyll and Hyde to me,' Doherty remarked.

Perdita handed him a tea towel. She indicated the butter around his mouth. She continued to speak.

'That's about it. Scheherazade wanted revenge on Coleridge for taking Martyna away from her. She hated him and knew him for what he was. She'd tried to persuade Martyna not to marry him, but she wouldn't listen.'

'And you told Scheherazade that the script was yours and she knew . . .'

Honey stopped. She wasn't sure how to say it.

Perdita finished for her. 'She knew my little secret, not that she cared. Most thespian types don't care much about anything like that, but macho man Coleridge — well, that's a different matter.'

'His ego was too big to cope.'

'Much too big.'

Her expression saddened. Scheherazade was found dead shortly after she'd called Brett Coleridge and mentioned her affair with Martyna. It had all been too much for him to swallow, especially when she'd threatened to tell the press. Just tittle tattle, but the public does love a bit of tittle tattle.'

'Why didn't you tell us about the script earlier?'

'I didn't think it had anything to do with the murder. Anyway, I felt such a fool. Boris had paid me. In law there was nothing left to do. I had to accept things as they were.'

'So the bit that was read out at the play reading?'

'It shouldn't have been. Aunt Jane put it forward and I completely forgot about it. The copyright lies with Boris Morris.'

* * *

Steve Doherty was already phoning the station. 'Get Brett Coleridge back in. There's new evidence. I'm on my way over.'

He turned to Honey. 'Stay with her. Try and find out anything else you can that'll nail Coleridge. He's our prime suspect. I don't want him walking free.'

She nodded. Her eyes sparkled when he kissed her on the cheek. She doubted he noticed, fired up as he was with hopes of bringing things to a swift conclusion. Last night was one thing. Today was another.

Honey sat back down opposite Perdita. The facts of this case were falling into place and Brett Coleridge was about to tumble. She was under no doubt he would have tumbled a lot earlier if Perdita had mentioned the script. There was only one reason for her silence.

'So! You thought your aunt — Miss Cleveley — killed Martyna?'

Perdita looked up, a startled expression on her face. 'He said he saw her going into the trailer.'

Honey frowned. 'Who said?'

'The man on the mobile canteen. He said he definitely saw her enter the trailer.'

Ryker! It had to be Ryker. But all he'd told the police was that he'd seen a woman wearing a shawl and bonnet enter Martyna's trailer. He told Perdita that it was *definitely* Miss Cleveley. Had anyone asked about height? Miss Cleveley was quite short.

Honey felt her own expression clouding. Why would Ryker do that? Anything was possible, of course. The man was a mix of chameleon and liar. He'd pretended to be Dick Richards, for a start. The real Dick's words came back to her: *'I only use him when I'm pushed. He's a bit of a liar and is downright pompous about his cooking.'*

Perdita's continuing description of events interrupted her thoughts.

'He was a good listener — and a good cook,' Perdita added with a smile. 'I told him all about the script and how Boris had bought it off me for a song. He commiserated and said he hated people like that. They deserved their comeuppance.'

A chill ran down Honey's spine as she listened. She thought back to the day Martyna was murdered. She'd inadvertently sat in the chair next to that of the director, though she hadn't noticed at the time. It was all about shifting the blame. He should have picked up the bloodstained script.

* * *

Brett Coleridge closed his eyes and exhaled a deep sigh. Being questioned by one police detective after another had got to him. It was only with the insistence of his lawyer that they had let him go.

What with them and the pressure of dealing with Ross Gordon, his nightclub partner, and the insurance company, the going was heavy.

Ross wound him up no end.

'Silver spoon in yer mouth and gold-trimmed underpants! You don't know nothing! Came from the rough end of town, me. Grew up with crap, made a living from crap!'

Brett could imagine Ross being the school bully, nicking the other kids' pocket money, flogging ciggies in the playground, even drugs at the school gate. Ross had no scruples, though he liked to think otherwise.

As for his bankers, they were on his back, bullying him in a different way, but nonetheless just as overbearing. The insurance money had paid off a lot of debt, but not all of it. The banks were not happy with the group of companies left to him by his father. They'd told him to his face that he wasn't up to the job. Either they bring in outside help or the Coleridge Group would be no more.

He poured himself a double Scotch, tipped back the glass and closed his eyes. It helped, but he needed something else. He needed to forget his problems. Self-indulgence suited him best. Drink, coke and sex — not necessarily in that order, but plenty of it. Two bottles of champagne rather than one — and two girls to match.

He reached for the phone and dialled a familiar number.

'This is for you, old chap,' he said out loud, before she answered and he put in his order.

* * *

Eight hours later he woke up naked in a king-sized bed at a top London hotel. The room was in semi-darkness, lit by the light of a black-and-gold-shaded table lamp.

He attempted to raise his head. It hurt. He groaned. His head ached something rotten.

The girls were gone. He hadn't expected anything else. Girls like them were a regular habit. He tried to remember what they looked like but couldn't. He tried to remember the events of the night before but couldn't — not in any great detail.

OK, he'd taken a little this and that to help things go with a swing. The girls had brought the stuff with them — high-quality cocaine. A fitting accompaniment to two bottles of Krug — or was it three?

Mixing drugs and alcohol didn't usually knock him out, but there was always a first time. Suddenly a thought came to him. Had they given him more than what he'd bargained for? Had they drugged him up and cleaned him out?

It felt as though a guy with a hammer was pacing around his head and taking swings at a cast-iron bell.

Christ, what had they given him?

Pushing himself up on his elbows, he blinked until his eyes focused. His clothes were still folded over a chair. His wallet, mobile phone and gold Faber cufflinks were still on the bedside table along with his Rolex.

'Must have been bad stuff,' he muttered to himself. Closing his eyes, he let his head fall gently back against the pillow. All was well with the world. He'd just had one hell of a night.

* * *

The Zodiac was its usual dark, smoky self. The fact that it was situated beneath North Parade in the old wine vaults meant extractor fans had their work cut out keeping the atmosphere pure and sweet.

Succulent steaks straight from Scotland sizzled on the grill. The bluish smoke kept coming even when the steaks were exchanged for garlic prawns. The smell from both was delicious.

Doherty was late.

Honey lingered over her drink. Tonight was to have been a purely social event. She'd dressed accordingly: a black dress with a cowl neck, long sleeves, and a sleek crossover panel that flattened her stomach and emphasised a pretty neat waistline.

He came in with a grin on his face.

'You're late.'

'You sound like a schoolmarm,' Doherty replied.

Honey narrowed her eyes and fixed him with a penetrating gaze. 'Who's rung your bell?'

His grin blossomed into a fully-fledged smile. Reaching into his pocket, he brought out a photograph and slammed it down onto the bar.

'Bet you don't know who this is.'

Honey held the photo up to an overhead spotlight.

'I know *what* he is. The number underneath is a dead giveaway.'

'Serial number from a mugshot album courtesy of Thames Valley Police. His name's Ross Gordon. Used to be a mover and shaker in the criminal world. He'd like us to think he's changed his spots — a successful businessman nowadays. Wears genuine Gucci suits instead of knock-off jeans and a leather jacket. He also knows our old mate, Brett Coleridge. His business partner in that nightclub of his.'

'So dear old Brett is in league with a gangster . . .'

'Word was he used to be open for contract in times gone by,' said Doherty. The smile had gone from his face.

Honey felt a sense of horror run through her. Had she guessed right? She looked him straight in the eye.

'You think Coleridge paid him to kill the woman he was going to marry.'

'More than likely. Thames Valley are taking him in for questioning. I've got the job of putting the million-dollar question to Coleridge. Did you do it and why?'

'Don't we already know why? The insurance money?'

He made a so-so kind of nodding movement. 'Not necessarily. I'm going to take another look at the stuff that Forensics lifted from Martyna's trailer. It's a long shot, but there could be something we've overlooked.'

CHAPTER THIRTY-EIGHT

Once a month the staff at the Green River Hotel had Monday lunch together.

By the time they actually sat down to eat it, lunchtime — that period between twelve noon and two o'clock — was long gone. It was usually four o'clock by the time they tucked in.

A group of Dutch tourists, checking out that morning, had commented on the crispness of the bedlinen.

'Such a pretty lace trim around the pillowcases.'

Honey had thanked them. Receiving compliments first thing made the day go with a swing.

Lunchtime had been busy, and now they were all sitting down together.

Conversation had flown back and forth. Honey was being asked about the case. They were more interested than usual, simply because it was the movies and a famous actress was involved.

'It all goes back to Martyna Manderley.' She sighed as she pushed the Brussels sprouts to one side, the potatoes to the other. Today she wasn't really interested in food. They'd reached a dead end. Suspects had been questioned and discounted. So what next?

'Phew!'

Smudger collapsed into the chair opposite her, congratulating himself on introducing a carvery the day before. His idea had turned out to be very successful. 'Carveries suit Sunday lunchtimes. Said it would, didn't I?'

Honey nodded. 'True.'

'They can't take their eyes off the food. People eat with their eyes. Didn't I tell you that?'

'True. You did.'

'Course I did. I asked this bloke if he wanted a bit from the breast and the leg. He nearly jumped out of his skin. Thought I was being rude. Another woman asked me for a bit for her pussy.' He grinned. 'Turned out she had a cat and wanted to know if I had any scraps. Anyway, this guy told me that he was so engrossed in what was going on his plate that he forgot that someone was standing behind the carvery serving him. That's how it is when folks are ravenous.'

Honey was about to agree in an offhand kind of way, when the immensity of what he had said clicked into gear.

The chair scraped the floor as she got up. Two casual comments and everything had suddenly fallen into place. First, the Dutch tourist remarking on the bedlinen and how crisp the lacy borders were. No one commented on plain pillowcases but put a bit of lace around them . . . they noticed!

'Right,' said Smudger, seemingly perplexed that his statement had triggered such an abrupt reaction. Struggling with an explanation, he looked up at her. 'What did I say?'

Honey cupped his face and kissed him on both cheeks. *Smack! Smack!*

'You stated the obvious. When people are hungry, they don't really notice who's dishing out the food. Ted Ryker didn't see anything because he wasn't there. The last extras to be served had food heaped on their plates. Ted was usually pretty hot on portion control. Someone else had to have been serving at the time. Nobody really noticed who. After all, who notices a caterer? So where was Ted Ryker during that period? Did he sneak into Martyna's trailer himself?'

She was on a roll. She couldn't stop. All eyes were on her.

'And then there was the atomiser. It was knocked over, yet it didn't look as though there'd been a struggle. Ryker would have smelled of bacon and sausage and greasy things cooking for breakfast. The atomiser helped hide that. So did the fact that the fan heater was blowing cold air. It was a freezing-cold day. The heater should have been blowing hot. But smells don't carry as well on cold air as they do on warm or hot air. Don't you see?'

Smudger sat frowning. This stuff was beyond him, but he liked his boss and wouldn't want her to think he was dumb or uninterested. He asked what he thought was a relevant question.

'So what good reason did he have to murder her?'

'She might have criticised his cooking?'

'Cool. I'll go with that.'

* * *

Doherty was not persuaded. 'You don't know about Coleridge's business partner in the nightclub. He used to make his living as a hitman.'

Honey was sceptical. 'And you think he may have killed Martyna?'

'He might have done.'

'And Scheherazade?'

'Possibly, though he does have an alibi.'

'I bet you Ryker doesn't. I bet you he was the figure I saw running away. Perhaps he thought he dropped something in there. A plastic fork, crumbs from a Cornish pasty . . . or something.'

Doherty went quiet. 'I'll check with Forensics.'

Honey put the phone down. 'Right. I need a man.'

Smudger stopped hammering a veal cutlet and looked at his watch. 'At this time in the morning?'

'I cannot go alone. He's a big man and we've got some uncomfortable questions to ask.'

Smudger leaned on his meat hammer. 'Give me one good reason I should come with you — besides being a gentleman.'

'Because Ted Ryker reckons he's the best chef in all the world and all the rest are rubbish?'

Smudger began discarding his whites. 'Take me to the guy. He's got a lesson to learn.'

* * *

They'd left by the time Doherty phoned. Mary Jane answered the phone.

'They've gone to nab a murderer,' said Mary Jane.

Doherty groaned. 'I was afraid of that.'

'Shall I tell her you called?'

'No.'

After he put down the phone, a woman in Forensics eyed him over her shoulder. 'Was it helpful?'

He looked down at the contents of the forensic bag removed from Martyna Manderley's trailer.

She made a comment that it was only a plastic fork.

Martyna Manderley was used to the best. The plastic fork was the only item removed that did not fit into her lifestyle.

He rang Honey's mobile phone, warning her to let the police deal with Ryker. She cut him off before he had chance to say that he believed her now. He needed to find out where she was going . . .

CHAPTER THIRTY-NINE

She learned from the real Richard Richards that Ryker had bought himself a small hotdog trailer, which he intended to park at the side of a busy road.

'He's had it sign-painted,' said Dick. 'You can't miss it. It's called Begone Ronnie Two Star.'

Honey frowned at the phone. 'That's a bit of a mouthful.'

'Egon Ronay?'

Honey nodded. 'I get the picture. Where can I find him?'

She felt nervous asking. He was bound to say that Ryker had hauled his trailer off somewhere to do business at some highway pit stop. Her car was blocked in at a city car park and Smudger's vehicle was in Jones the Engine's garage following a fracas with a cast-iron bollard. That left Mary Jane and her pale-pink Cadillac coupe, circa 1961. Driving with Mary Jane could send her totally round the bend.

'Last I heard he was off buying equipment in the Kitchen Shop.'

It was music to her ears. The shop was in Quiet Street. Going there with Smudger in tow was a bit risky. Chefs are like kids in a chocolate shop when confronted with brand-new kitchenalia. But needs must.

She spotted Ted Ryker's big frame eyeing up a display of extractor fans. Even from this distance she could smell his greasiness. Extractor fans in static kitchens, such as hotels, were great big things meant to suck up heat and grease. Mobile ones were supposed to do the same, but were not so efficient. The smell of grease lingered on clothes, hair and skin.

And that was why the atomiser and the heater had been so crucial . . . Smell grease and you'd think Ted Ryker.

Overcome with the possibilities, she paused by a display of copper-bottomed saucepans. Her shocked expression was reflected in their shininess.

Doherty was wrong. She was right.

The urge to accuse was too strong.

You did it! That's what she wanted to say, but wouldn't. She had to shout something that would put him off guard, something that would throw him off balance, perhaps draw out his inner violence.

'You're a lousy cook, Ted Ryker! Your gravy's lumpy! Your pies are indigestible. You couldn't even boil an egg properly!'

What was she doing?

Ryker looked round. So did the other customers. They probably thought her a bit mad. But she didn't care. The look on Ryker's face was worth it.

Honey gulped. Surprise would have been a good result, but this was more than that. Ryker's eyes became hard peas in deep wells as his brows knitted and his red face contorted. His bottom lip hung wet and shiny, exposing his gums. This was Doctor Jekyll turning into Mr Hyde, an exceptional horror film makeover.

'What did you say?' His lower lip quivered.

Honey recalled once meeting a bulldog who did that. An unfortunate meeting. She'd been eating a ham sandwich on a park bench. Said bulldog had obviously been hungry. Its lip had drooped just like that prior to snaffling her sandwich. But Ryker wasn't after her sandwich . . .

It could be suicide, but she forced out a few more culinary insults.

'Your rissoles are rotten and your flapjacks are like corn plasters!'

Suddenly she heard a rumbling sound. She realised it was coming from Ryker. His shoulders were hunched, his body stiff. The rumbling resembled the noise a volcano makes just before it blows its top. Common sense told her to run. The other customers, aware that something odd was happening, had thought better about staying to purchase that pie edger or handsome tortoiseshell and chromium wine bottle opener. They'd manage with the old ones, thank you very much.

Heart racing, she stood her ground. By instinct alone, she knew that Smudger was standing behind her, though she couldn't tell where.

If she had been able to turn round, she would have seen him hiding behind a dummy. The dummy was standing on a foot-high plinth. It was attired in a complete set of chef's whites and brandishing a rolling pin in one hand and a large whisk in the other.

'You should *not* say that!' said Ryker. Each word coincided with a shake of his head. 'Take it back!'

Was she hell!

She turned on the turbo control.

'Your food's rubbish! Martyna thought it was rubbish. She told you so, didn't she? She told you your food wasn't fit for pigs! And you weren't having that, were you? So you killed her. You stabbed her with a hatpin because she criticised your food.'

'She had no taste!' Ryker shouted. 'And she was nasty. A stupid, nasty cow. She didn't deserve to . . .'

'Live?'

Honey knew it was the truth then. Martyna Manderley had not deserved to live because she'd insulted Ryker's food.

A member of staff shouted for the police to be called. Another assistant, who seemed a little less in tune with the situation, told them to leave if they weren't going to buy anything.

Ryker didn't seem to hear.

'I made her a special pie. Poussin and orange. She said, what did I think she was? A bleedin' peasant? Laughed at me, she did. Laughed in my face and said my cooking was crap.' A glazed shininess flashed in his eyes as he shuffled menacingly towards her.

Honey swallowed what felt like an iceberg. Her blood temperature was plunging to sub-zero. Fear was cold and hot and well . . . dead, plain frightening!

Ryker's face was grizzly, a face glimpsed in a dozen nightmares. Horror of horrors, this was the face Martyna Manderley had seen before she died. Total, uncontrolled anger! And all because she'd criticised his cooking.

Honey offered up a little prayer to the god of kitchenalia. With a bit of luck, the Kitchen Shop's knife department was somewhere over her side of the shop. If it was closer to him, she was dead meat.

Though penned in by shelves and all manner of cookery utensils, Honey took backward steps until she couldn't take any more. Metal things were prodding her back. Things hanging from overhead tumbled and tinkled around her head. Worst of all, the hem of her skirt caught on a skillet handle. Drat and double drat! That was the trouble with a skirt cut on the bias; it swirled more than a straight skirt or even an A-line. The skillets were displayed on a wrought-iron tower. Tower and kindred skillets toppled over. Cast iron hitting tiled floor drowned out the sound of running feet. Members of staff who had remained to observe were now quitting the building.

Ryker grabbed a jumbo-sized spatula. It made a whooshing sound as he swiped it through the air. Using that same swiping action, he took off the head of a mannequin that was wearing the latest black-and-white harlequin trousers and tailored chef's jacket. His eyes flicked from dummy to Honey; no prizes for who was next to have their head swiped off!

The end was nigh. She had reached the point of no return, backed up against a portable gas barbecue. Her heel caught in the mesh of a particularly handsome grill pan that had fallen to the floor at the same time as the skillets.

She thought about bending down to retrieve one of the fallen items to use as a weapon. If she timed it right, she might be able to bash him over the head. If she didn't then she could use it as body armour. Not that it would do much good. The pan was a bit on the small side and likely to cover only one breast; the rest of her body would be at his mercy.

And where was Smudger?

No time to check. Think positive. Think self-defence.

Did she have time to bend down? Could she reach?

The arm she reached out with seemed inordinately heavy. She looked at her elbow. A muslin bag containing boxed weights for an old-style kitchen scale had hooked itself onto her sleeve.

Damn! Why did so much kitchen stuff get in your way when you weren't even looking for it?

If she swung it . . .

Too low. But then the dummy chef standing on the plinth raised a polycarbonate arm. The rolling pin went up. The rolling pin went down.

Honey heard the sound of hardwood thudding on bone as the rolling pin cracked into the back of Ryker's head. He groaned, staggered, but didn't go down.

Smudger, hiding behind the dummy, tried another strike; Ryker found enough presence of mind to parry the blow with his spatula.

Honey found herself praying that his strength wasn't returning — though it seemed it was.

But Smudger was not finished. Snatching the mega-size egg whisk from his mannequin colleague, he shouted, 'On guard!'

The two men circled each other, one armed with a spatula, the other with the unfair advantage of one rolling pin and an egg whisk.

Ryker swung his arm.

Smudger parried.

His face contorted with violent intent, Ryker grabbed a skillet. A skillet could deliver a hefty whack, but it had its drawbacks. Ryker realised this when the hinged handle caused it to fold in two, trapping his fingers.

Smudger caught Ryker's ear with the egg whisk.

Honey flattened herself as best she could. At the same time she had to ask herself: what was it about Smudger and egg whisks? This wasn't the first time she'd known him use the humble item as an offensive weapon.

Ted Ryker, doyen of the mobile catering unit, blinked his angry eyes. His complexion turned an unhealthy shade of red. His wide mouth curled back from his lips like a rabid dog.

'Who the bloody hell do you think you are?' he growled.

Smudger, the brilliant, courageous and slightly unpredictable chef, had a ready answer.

'A better chef than you, mate. A *much* better bloody chef than you.'

Unbeknown to either Honey or Smudger, what he said was the proverbial straw that broke the proverbial camel's back. Not that they fully realised the implications at the time. Not until half a minute later when Ryker's redness turned a similar shade to a Victoria plum. His lips turned speedwell blue.

The spatula clattered to the floor. The fingers that had held it now clawed at Ted Ryker's broad chest.

'Aaaagh!'

Ted Ryker followed the spatula to the floor, though not nearly so noisily.

Honey's jaw dropped and didn't firm up until she gasped a heartfelt, 'Oh, crikey!'

A few members of staff and even a few customers began to creep back into the store. Someone even asked her if it was possible to purchase a pair of sugar tongs. Honey explained that she was phoning for an ambulance and could they please wait a moment. The customer, a lady of advanced years and a genteel-looking persuasion, looked uncomprehending at first, until she noticed Ted Ryker lying on the floor.

'My goodness. What brought that on?' she said, then nodded as though she'd majored in something complicated

— like brain surgery. 'I know: smoking. Smoking has a lot to do with getting ill. And alcohol, of course. Alcohol is a very big problem, so I hear.'

'He's been hit on the head,' said Honey to the emergency services. 'With a rolling pin . . . no . . . it didn't belong to anyone. It was part of a display. A chef was holding it . . . well, no, not a real one . . .'

The old dear requiring the sugar tongs presumed she was talking to her.

'Really?'

Her eyes opened wide, then blinked at the dummy chef from behind a pert pair of gold-rimmed spectacles. The fact that it was wearing prescribed whites and stood upright obviously threw things out of balance. She wasn't to know that the real chef who had done the dirty deed was kneeling down beside Ryker.

'My, my. These mannequins are terribly clever nowadays. It's robotics, isn't it? That's what I've read anyway. They say it won't be long before they rule the world.'

The paramedics on the end of the line were asking for more details. Honey continued, and the sugar tong customer merely listened and remarked on whatever was being said, still presuming Honey was talking to her.

Smudger was giving Ryker the third degree — and judging by the smirk on his face, he was just loving it!

'Now look here, mate, we all come to a point in life when death stares us in the face. It's like they say, there's two dead certs in life; one is that you die, the other is a nurse. Now, you ain't in no position to take advantage of a nurse and her generous nature, but as for the former . . .' Smudger shook his head forlornly and made disapproving noises. 'Best make your peace mate, or it's fire and brimstone for you. I guarantee you won't like the cooking too much down there. Nothing but burnt cakes and the hot prongs of a toasting fork forever prodding yer jacksy.'

Ryker's eyes rolled frighteningly in his head. His lips went from speedwell to violet. He looked terrified. Honey wasn't too sure whether it was due to his heart attack or Smudger's total lack of sympathy.

'So go on, mate. You can tell me. She thought yer cooking was crap. Is that right?'

Smudger wasn't too hot on tact either!

Ryker gave a weak nod.

Smudger shook his head. 'You can't get like that, old son. Take it from the best chef in the city — yours truly, just in case you didn't know. You've got to take the good with the bad. Everyone's got their own opinions. They ain't necessarily right, but there . . .'

Smudger spread his hands and jerked his head in a matter-of-fact manner.

Honey could have died. What a liar he was! A good chef, but boy . . .

'We're on our way,' said the emergency services. 'Keep him comfortable till we get there. Try to keep him from getting excited.'

Honey leaned into Smudger and whispered into his ear, 'You shouldn't have hit him so hard.'

He smirked. 'Why not? I enjoyed it.'

CHAPTER FORTY

A week or so later a huge bouquet of flowers arrived in reception. They were encompassed by Steve Doherty's arms and festooned with a crisp red bow.

'For you,' he said.

Honey was all ready for lift-off — in other words they were dining out, dressed up and had booked a taxi. No curtailing their pleasure because of having to drive home!

'They're lovely,' she said, burrowing her nose into the mix of winter-warming exotics.

'So are you,' said Steve, his lips plush against her cheek. His blue eyes lapped her up like a hungry dog.

She was wearing a blue silk skirt, a slim sheath of a thing that rasped against her legs like surf against shingle.

The slinky, sexy Victorian corset matched it well. Its tightness emphasised her cup size while holding in her stomach. Two swelling bosoms pulsated against the lace-edged trim.

'Like pigeons on a platter,' said Lindsey.

Judging by the hungry look in Steve Doherty's eyes, she wasn't far wrong.

'Tonight's the night,' said Lindsey as Honey passed her the flowers to put in water.

'You bet,' Honey whispered back.

* * *

The job was done: both Ryker and Coleridge were under arrest. Coleridge had made bail. It helped that he could afford the best lawyers that money could buy. His partner, the hitman, had taken the rap for Scheherazade's death, although he said it was an accident. It seemed she had made the mistake of thinking she could blackmail Coleridge.

Ryker, on the other hand, had been charged with murder. Smudger had been right about the reason he'd murdered Martyna Manderley. Ryker was obsessively protective about his cooking. When faced with criticism, hostility rose like newly baked bread. Like a lot of chefs, he couldn't take criticism, and in his case rejection resulted in a lot more than a dialogue of four-letter words!

Who knows, he too might have got away with a lesser charge if he hadn't done so much to cover his tracks. He had deliberately brought the atomiser fan from the bedroom in order that its perfume would mask the smell of cooking oil. Smelling like a chip pan or a bulb of extra-strong garlic was an occupational hazard.

On top of that, the bloodstained script was meant to place blame elsewhere: at Scheherazade. At some point Ms Parker-Henson had eaten one of Ryker's concoctions, which happened to include cheese. He hadn't known she was lactose intolerant, and she'd brought the lot up in front of everyone — then accused Ryker of trying to poison her. The bloodied script had been left on the chair for her in revenge. He hadn't expected Honey to arrive early and pick it up, not noticing that the make-up artiste's name was pinned to the back of the chair. No wonder extras were frowned on; they just didn't know correct form.

* * *

Honey was feeling pleased with herself. She'd beaten Steve Doherty to this one. Her mother had agreed about her victory, though inexplicably she had sent Doherty a bottle of sparkling white wine to enjoy before he collected Honey.

Honey frowned when he told her about it. 'White sparkling wine. Not champagne. Are you sure of that?'

'Of course I am. I'll save it for us. I'm on my way over.'

True to his word he brought it with him.

She frowned at the bottle. Something wasn't quite right here.

'Are you sure my mother gave you that?'

'Of course I am. What's the matter?'

'Number one, it's sparkling wine not champagne. And number two, it's got a screw top. My mother's no lush, but even so, she wouldn't be seen dead with a bottle of fizzy that wasn't champagne. And a sparkling wine in a screw-top bottle? Something is seriously wrong here.'

'She's a pensioner. Perhaps she's being careful,' offered Doherty.

Honey threw him a warning frown. 'Do not ever — under *any* circumstances — ever call my mother a pensioner, and certainly not to her face!'

He laughed. 'Handbags at dawn?'

'You'd never hear the last of it.'

'Here. To your health,' he said, passing her a wine flute.

She took the glass. 'Are you having some?'

'I don't like champagne.'

'Fine. I can manage — even if it is only cheap bubbly.'

She poured him a gin from the office supply. Despite its provenance, the sparkling wine was reaching the right parts. It wasn't so bad and it kept pouring into her glass. Doherty got himself another gin.

'Seems your mother made a good choice.'

'Hmmm,' said Honey, between sips.

'Good.' He was smiling like the cat who got the cream — or at least was about to. 'All relaxed and feeling good now?'

'Very.'

'You look good,' he said, one arm snaking around her, pulling her gently towards him. He set down his glass.

'Do you really want to go out? I mean,' he said, his fingers stroking the nape of her neck, 'we could make ourselves comfortable around your place. Send out for something. Turn the lights down and put something sexy on the stereo.'

Honey giggled. 'The stereo? You mean the jive box.'

'How does that work?' he said, his other arm around her now, his lips placing gentle kisses down the side of her face.

She giggled some more. Those bubbles were going straight to her head. 'I don't know. Lindsey's got one.'

One hand ran down her back. He cupped the back of her neck in the other.

She giggled again. At him?

He held her back a bit. 'Are you OK, Honey Driver?'

Honey smiled and was about to say that everything was fine, when something went ping!

'Ouch!'

Steve looked curious. 'Something wrong?'

Yes. There was.

'Ummm . . .'

It was hard to speak due to the stabbing sensation in her lower ribs. Hunger pangs had nothing to do with it. 'I've been stabbed!'

Doherty's eyebrows rose. 'Not me,' he said, raising his hands.

Honey struggled with the protruding stay that had dug through the silk and into her flesh.

She took deep breaths. There was no way she was going to tell him that she was wearing the sexiest item ever worn by a woman for a man. And this time it was next to her skin, not a voluminous flannelette nightgown. Sod it!

Then there was that groggy feeling. Where had that come from?

She had to have air. She also had to change.

'I won't be a minute.'

She dashed off as best she could. The stay was digging into her, and her legs seemed wobbly. It felt as though she was running on a blancmange. Wobbly or not, she headed out past the kitchens and along the path to the coach house where her bedroom was.

Stumbling and wobbling was bad enough, but something else was happening. There was a mist coming down. No big deal in February, except that this mist was whirling around her head. She was wearing it like a wreath at eye level.

Despite great gulps of fresh air, she couldn't keep her eyes open. Perhaps my eyelids have turned to lead, she thought. You'll feel better once you change and have a sit down. Perhaps a drink of water . . . or something . . .

It occurred to her that if it hadn't been for the whalebone stay, she would have passed out.

No! Think positively.

Who said that? She looked about her, convinced that someone else was telling her to do that — not the common-sense, conscious side of herself.

Once inside, she fumbled with the fastening of her skirt. It didn't give up easily, but after a bit of tugging and a few well-chosen magic words, the skirt fell to the floor.

She kicked it to one side. At the same time she fumbled with the laces that bound the corset tightly to her body. It was the last thing she did before falling onto the settee, an inelegant figure in smoky-grey stockings and a sexy corset. Her head hit a cushion and her legs flaked out in all directions, one foot hanging over the scroll end of the Georgian settee.

That was where Steve found her. At first he was a little angry. He'd been looking forward to this for a very long time. Then he smiled. He had to admit it was funny, and decided to make her more comfortable. First he laid her out a bit straighter, then he loosened her stays. Finally, he covered her with a velvet throw that was usually hanging on the back of the settee.

On his way back through the hotel, Lindsey asked him if everything was all right.

He grinned. 'I gave your grandmother a lift home and left your mother with a whole jug of Singapore Sling. Tasted like the traditional thing, but my cocktails tend to have a bit more kick. By the time I got back she'd drank the lot.'

'Shame,' said Lindsey. 'She had something really sexy to show you.'

Steve lowered his eyelids. 'If you mean the corset, forget it.'

Lindsey frowned. He could see she didn't understand, so went some way to explaining.

'I'm a guy that likes plain cooking without the garnishes. Tell your mother that when she wakes up, will you?'

Lindsey nodded and said that she would. After he'd gone, she went out to the coach house, saw her mother lying flat on her back, and sighed resignedly. It looked as though the corset would wing its way back to her grandmother — or into another auction.

THE END

ALSO BY JEAN G. GOODHIND

HONEY DRIVER MYSTERY SERIES

Book 1: MURDER, BED & BREAKFAST

Book 2: MENU FOR MURDER

Book 3: WALKING WITH MURDER

Book 4: THE JANE AUSTEN MURDERS

Thank you for reading this book.

If you enjoyed it please leave feedback on Amazon or Goodreads, and if there is anything we missed or you have a question about, then please get in touch. We appreciate you choosing our book.

Founded in 2014 in Shoreditch, London, we at Joffe Books pride ourselves on our history of innovative publishing. We were thrilled to be shortlisted for Independent Publisher of the Year at the British Book Awards.

www.joffebooks.com

We're very grateful to eagle-eyed readers who take the time to contact us. Please send any errors you find to corrections@joffebooks.com. We'll get them fixed ASAP.

Printed in Great Britain
by Amazon

16014912R00154